SOUL SEARCH

The First Zackie Novel

Reyna Favis

Dedicated to my mother, Elke Favis,

and to the memory of my father, Reynaldo Favis.

CHARITIES SUPPORTED BY YOUR PURCHASE

Thank you for purchasing this book. Fifty percent of author's profits will be donated to charity, divided equally between two 501(c)(3) organizations:

- Search and Rescue Teams of Warren County
  www.sartwc.com
- Wayward Plotts
  https://www.facebook.com/WaywardPlotts/

If you would like to make additional contributions, please visit their websites.

CHAPTER 1

Every thought was a battle and every breath drawn was an act of will. I no longer thought about winning. At best, I might survive until the next time. The bell on the search dog's harness clanged in the distance. Maybe he would get here before the dead boy found me. This was supposed to be an ordinary search and rescue training exercise. All I had to do was hide in the woods and let the canine handler teams find me, easy peasy. But thanks to earthbound spirits, dead sons of bitches who wanted me to join them, I was psyching myself up for my last fight.

The dead boy came over a crest and back into my line of sight. Choking back a sob, I cursed instead, my gut churning with acid as I pushed sweaty bangs under the bill of the baseball cap and out of my eyes. I bit back fear and schooled my thoughts so I could go down fighting. Craning my neck for a clear view of this spirit, I tried to get a handle on what I was in for. A dirty hat with a wide brim hid his face, but he was small and might have once been around six or seven. Years of fighting taught me not to underestimate him. A young spirit might be easier to fight off, but I was going into this already drained and exhausted. *Focus. Go down fighting.* His clothes were torn and mud spattered, but the suspenders and loose, mid-calf pants placed him squarely in the nineteenth century. My stomach took another shot of hot acid and the sob escaped between gritted teeth. He'd been dead a long time. The longer they're dead, the stronger and more determined they became. *Oh God. Go down fighting.*

The spirit darted from tree to tree through the burgeoning April woods. And then it started. His panic rushed over me in waves and it was all I could do to stay where I was and not start running crazy through the woods like him. Digging my nails into my palms, I fought to control the stress and focused hard on my reality - the rough tree bark etching its pattern on the skin of my back and the sour sweet smell of decaying leaves in the soil around me. But despite knowing that afternoon sun shone through a sparse spring canopy, the quality of the light began to shift. I strained to keep the sun's radiance on my face, but I lost my hold, and a weaker sun penetrated my awareness, filtering through fall foliage. I shivered with the autumn chill.

When K9 Merlin bounded out of the brush, panting and clanging, I let out a whooshing breath of relief as the dead boy's reality receded and spring returned. But my breath caught in my throat as the spirit sought the next tree, running into the dog's path. With canine grace, the Belgian Malinois adjusted and veered slightly, as he continued up the hill to find me. The dead boy kept up his running too, and I chewed on my cuticles as I tracked him and again felt the creeping influence of the spirit over me. Clamping down hard on the raw desire to flee, I fought to stay in my own head. Steve, Merlin's handler, was close and if I was going to get him out of the line of fire, I had to follow his instructions to the letter and finish the exercise.

Merlin approached and gazed at me through the dark mask of his face. I held still with difficulty and ignored the dog, but I was sweating with the effort and still hyper-aware of the dead boy. Merlin turned from me and bounded down the hill to find Steve and after a moment, five short barks echoed through the woods. This was Merlin's trained indication to tell Steve that he had found someone. A flash of high visibility orange worn by search and rescue personnel appeared through the brush and a few seconds later, the dog and a slightly built blond man raced up the hill to reach me. Forcing my voice to sound light and happy despite the urge I felt to scream at them to run, I stuck to the script and gave the dog praise, ruffling his ears and telling him he was a star.

Steve sucked in air after the uphill run. "He's working really good today."

I nodded absently as my eyes kept darting towards the dead boy. "Yeah, he found me pretty fast." The thing was even closer now, crouched behind a scrubby bush. Anxious for us all to go, I stood up, shouldered my pack and started walking down the hill. Any minute now, my will would fail, the dead boy would break through and the real fight would start.

Steve shot me a sheepish look as I tried to leave. "Hold up, Fia. I know you're in a hurry, but this dog needs a real paycheck." He presented Merlin with the tug toy that was the dog's reward. As Merlin pulled mightily on the toy nearly tearing Steve off his feet, he spoke to the dog in a high pitched voice, telling him what a good boy he was. I stood near them, rigid with fear and impatience, mentally urging them to get the hell out of here. The dog danced with the praise, shook Steve even harder and put his rump in the air with his elbows on the ground, ready to play for as long as Steve would allow it.

After a few long minutes of them playing and me shifting from foot to foot like I needed to pee, just as I thought I would vomit, Steve put the toy away and offered Merlin some water. "Ready to go back? Or do you need to hide again for someone else?"

My throat felt thick and I bit off an answer. "You and Merlin are the last ones." I adjusted my pack and then led Steve and Merlin down the hill at double time, my body angled sideways to accommodate the steepness and speed. As I came to the level ground, something cold and clammy grabbed my hand and my face twisted with revulsion. I shook hard to make it let go and walked faster.

Steve missed nothing. "What's wrong with your hand?"

"Ugh… tick!" I blurted out just as it grabbed my hand again. This time I could feel how spongy soft the flesh felt, like it was ready to slough off the fingers. I yanked my hand in front of me and picked up my pace.

Steve was grinning, clearly amused by my discomfort. "You ought to be used to that by now, girl."

The cloying smell of decay became stronger, flooding my nostrils and I clamped my mouth shut to keep from tasting it. I gave the dead boy a mental shove to get him to move away, but he came back more insistent. With my hands out of reach, he now grabbed at my braid and made my baseball cap tip backwards. I shoved him again with my mind, swearing out loud.

"C'mon, Fia, it's only a tick. Suck it up."

With the dead boy now holding the tail of my t-shirt and the rotting smell in my hair, I just glared at Steve. "They're disgusting. I can't help it." At least that thing was not coming after him. I walked rapidly to increase my distance from Steve and Merlin.

"You know what? I'm going to run back and get some cardio in. I'll see you later." I tightened the straps on my pack and took off down the trail with the dead boy following, snatching and grabbing at me every time I slowed my pace. As I approached the parking area where the search teams organized the training runs for the canines, I pulled into a copse of trees and whirled to face the wraith. Seeing red in the corner of my vision, I bared my teeth as my hands clawed at the air between us. The energy focused into my hands and I shoved the spirit back with everything I had. The creature wailed and crumpled to the ground. "Good… good, you deserve that, you son of bitch!"

Fighting back tears, I gasped as my heart stuttered and my legs grew weak. I had to accept the futility of my situation. He would get up eventually and after that last shot, I was running on empty. Sweat beaded on my brow and I took shuddering breaths as I struggled to power up and strike the putrid revenant a second time. *Go down fighting, damn it.* Just as I thought it was over for me, a red hound with a short, glossy coat burst through the trees and began to nuzzle the dead boy. On the heels of the dog, a man in a bright orange shirt exploded into the copse of trees and then stopped short, breathing hard. He was tall with a mop of gray curly hair and the sagging features of late middle age. Like many tall people, he had poor posture and stooped slightly forward, as if trying to negate his height. The look on his face moved rapidly from shock to anger as he stared first at the whimpering dead boy and then at me. In the next second, he smoothed his expression and turned to look only at me, stepping between me and the wraith. "Oh, sorry," he said with a clipped British accent. "Didn't mean to disturb a call of nature. Zackie, come!" The hound came to the man's side, its gaze never leaving the dead boy. "We'll be off, then. Sorry again."

I stood frozen and wide-eyed as the dead thing crawled and then limped after the retreating man and dog. Never in my life have the dead just up and left after finding me. I had been fighting for days to make the things that came out of the woods go away. My heart wasn't beating right anymore and my arms and legs felt weak, trembling and cramping painfully whenever I moved. The dizziness and vomiting would come eventually if I didn't get some rest or something to eat.

Shaking myself out of my stupor, I staggered out after the man, desperate to know how he managed to make that dead thing leave me. A quick look up and down the trail revealed nothing of the man. I bit my lip and my gut cramped as I worried that something bad could happen to him because he had intervened. I should not have let that shade follow him. Even though I had been distracted, this was no excuse for being irresponsible. The fact that the man might be able to see what I see, every bit as well as I could, was an aberration to me. It appeared that the man looked right at the dead thing, not with the vague sense of unease of someone with limited sensing ability, but with a full recognition of what he perceived. However, sensing and purging these entities are not necessarily matching skill sets. I had to find the man quickly.

With no better options, I grabbed a protein bar out of my pack and crammed it into my mouth. Randomly choosing to follow the trail east, I began a quick Hasty Search, designed to rapidly cover areas with the highest probability of finding a missing person. The man was tall and could probably move a fair distance rapidly, but still, he could not have gone far. I limited the distance that I checked and looked carefully for signs of brush disturbance or fresh footprints along and on either side of the trail. Nothing. Frustrated, I turned around and started jogging west. As the trail turned, a deer path appeared, flattening the brush and heading downhill into the deeper woods. Squatting, I saw a partial footprint along the path. The step had crushed some vegetation, which was now in the process of springing back. Encouraged, I decided to take a chance on the deer path. Moving more slowly through the brambles and thicker growth, I sidled down the hill until I reached a more open area.

Fifty yards away near a crop of boulders, the dead boy knelt with his arms around the red dog, sobbing into its fur. The man, crouching behind with a hand on the dead boy's shoulder, spotted me and gave me a hard stare. I could not make sense of what I was seeing and began walking forward over the rocky ground, but the man immediately put his hand up to signal me to stop where I was. Another shot of acid washed into my gut, but ignoring my misgivings, I held my ground at his gesture. The man disregarded me now and gently turned the dead boy around to face him. He got on his knees to be on eye level and said something that I could not catch. The dead boy appeared to nod once. As the wraith turned back to the dog, it grasped the harness and the dog began leading it towards the farthest edge of the clearing. After three steps, my eyes were suddenly blinded by a light so bright that it made me lose my equilibrium on the uneven ground. The weight of the pack pushed me forward and I came down hard on my knees as my hands flew up to shield my eyes.

"What's happened?!" I shouted as I frantically rubbed my eyes. "I can't see anything! Are you all right?" I had no idea a wraith could do this. I was blind and defenseless if this thing came after me now.

My breath caught as I heard footsteps approach me and I sensed someone was near. As I rubbed my tearing eyes, I began seeing shapes, albeit poorly. The man was standing above me, but he did not offer to help me up from the rocky ground. All he said was, "How could you? Are you a psychopath? He was just a child." I then heard him stalk off before I could think of anything to say.

I was in a nightmare, alone in the woods and all but blind. I grabbed the radio out of my pants cargo pocket and tried to call for help. No use. The radio transmission was blocked because I had gone downhill into a bowl. My heart was thudding rapidly and a fear-sweat was starting to pool under my arms. Close to losing all sense of direction, I forced myself to bite back the panic and think. Stumbling blindly through wilderness could get me killed. Either the dead boy would find me or I would take a bad fall and break every bone in my body. Fumbling in the breast pocket of my 5.11 tactical shirt, I found my sunglasses and put them on to ease my eyes. At least I was visible in this shirt. The color was so brightly orange, you could see me from space. With several search and rescue teams training in the area, someone would find me if I could not walk out on my own. The SAR teams would probably be delighted to put their skills to use. But what if that thing came back for me? That would be the greater danger compared to anything the wilderness had to offer. I sat back on my haunches and began rubbing my bruised knees to get the feeling back. The sunglasses were helping and I was able to see a little more of my surroundings. I kept alert for the return of the dead boy.

After a short while, I could see enough of my surroundings that I was confident of finding my way out. As I staggered to my feet, I cursed the man. Why had that bastard left me like this? And what difference did it make if that dead thing was once a child? It only *looked* vaguely like a child now. It was just a freakish imitation of life. I was bone tired of dealing with these things, but it was not like I could just decide to avoid them. God knows I tried to do that by coming here. Feeling trapped, I ground my teeth and forced myself to move.

I struggled up the hill, my pace slowing with every step as I sunk deeper into despair. To distract myself, I thought about the man who I now called The Bastard. Little by little, my thoughts turned towards revenge. I had a fixed blade knife in my pack. I could slash his tires if I could figure out which car belonged to him. Maybe this makes me a bad person, but I justified it as psychological self-defense. If I've learned nothing else, it's better to feel anger than weakness. When I reached the trail, I used all my senses to probe the woods for The Bastard and I realized that the dead thing was really and truly gone. It had not come back for me and it was not waiting in the woods. The Bastard made it follow him and, more importantly, made it disappear. While a part of my brain argued that I was just being a masochist, I allowed myself to feel a sliver of hope. I did not have to face endless days of fighting it off or brace myself for another dangerous bout of fatigue. Maybe, just maybe, The Bastard had a solution. I started running towards the parking lot to find him and nearly collided with Steve.

Steve staggered, but regained his balance. "I was trying to find you. We have a call out! There's a missing autistic boy."

CHAPTER 2

We arrived at the scene in a neighborhood of neat little houses, all built in the same style. The only thing that varied was the colors. The lawns were still blanched from the winter, but areas of green were beginning to show. There was the usual suburban landscaping, but nothing too thick or prickly that would be hard to force my way into. This area was not going to be physically difficult to search, but there were a lot of nooks and crannies where a small boy could hide. I wiped the sweat from my face with a trembling hand and concentrated on mustering my energy for the search ahead.

Police directed us to go to a post office parking lot. It had been selected as the staging area because of the parking capacity and the proximity to the family home. After squeezing our vehicles into the lot, Steve and I went to sign in. While Steve checked the box indicating he handled an air scent dog, I identified myself as a land searcher on the sheet. We returned to wait near our cars for Incident Command to call the searchers for a briefing. Steve took the opportunity to check the weather forecast on his phone and I just sat hunched on my car bumper, trying to conserve my strength. The evening was already cool and with the overcast sky, it was no surprise that the forecast predicted light rain with temperatures dipping into the forties overnight. The kid would be hypothermic if we found him. Forcing myself to get up, I reorganized my pack with shaking hands and put the space blanket in a quick access outer pocket and then dug out my rain gear and chest harness from the pile of equipment in my trunk. As I put the gear on, Steve handed me one of his protein bars and I took it gratefully. Under normal circumstances after a full day of training, I would be low on calories and a little hungry. After dealing with the dead boy and the others before him, I devoured the protein bar like my life depended on it. After a few minutes, the sugar kicked in. My heart still beat a little irregularly, but at least the cramping in my limbs was receding. My bruised knees were starting to swell and sang with discomfort when I walked, but I would have to suck it up. It was going to be a long night.

"Come on over to the trailer for the briefing," a

woman called out. I grabbed my rock helmet, figuring I'd need the attached headlamp as the night deepened. Groaning, I heaved the pack to my shoulder for the umpteenth time that day and headed with Steve towards the trailer. When a crowd of people dressed in high visibility orange crowded forward with us, I did a quick check of the searchers, but saw no sign of The Bastard. We waited for the briefing to begin and I pulled out a small pad and pen from my chest harness, watching as the pile of photocopies made its way to me through the crowd. Grabbing two sheets from the stack, the first page was a map of the neighborhood and the second showed a picture of the missing boy, along with a short description.

A burly older man with gray hair came out of the trailer and quickly assessed the headcount of searchers. "Listen up!" he barked. "My name is Fiske. Our subject is a four-year-old Caucasian male. His name is Denny, and he is autistic and non-verbal. He has brown hair and blue eyes and is wearing a red and white striped shirt, jeans and sneakers."

I looked at the picture of Denny on the photocopy. He was a skinny kid with big blue eyes that slanted upward like a cat. In the picture, he was grinning big time at the camera, showing off his dimples. He looked like a kid who thought fun was priority one.

"Denny was last seen playing in his room around 16:00. The mother thinks he left the house and may be wandering around the neighborhood. He's snuck out before. Police have searched the house and the surrounding neighborhood. A reverse 911 has gone out to the community, so folks here know to check their properties for the boy. Denny loves dogs, so I want all the canine handlers out on task first. Trailing dogs will work the scene and establish direction of travel. Air scent dogs should go on lead with their handlers to the perimeter set up by the police to see if we can draw him out. Make your dogs bark if you can. Any questions?"

Someone asked if the boy was on any medications. Another person asked what he did previously when he went missing from the home. Fiske answered that, according to the mother, Denny was taking Risperdal, and the times when he disappeared previously, he was found hiding in the neighbors' yards. The family and the police had already searched all the usual places, but did not find him.

"If there are no more questions, Kate here will start assigning your tasks." With that, Fiske returned to the trailer and a woman carrying a clipboard came forward and began calling names. Steve and I stayed near the trailer and waited with the rest. Eventually, another man appeared with a clipboard and also began calling names. Teams of three and four were being sent out in rapid fire.

"Cam Ramsay, Bill Fry and Fia Saunders!" At the mention of my name, I grabbed my gear, told Steve that I'd see him later and moved forward to find out about my task. A middle aged man with a balding pate also stepped forward.

"I'm Fia," I told the woman with the clipboard.

"Bill Fry." The balding man identified himself for Kate and then extended his hand to me.

Kate scanned the crowd. "Okay, good. Now, if we can just find Cam." Raising her voice, she called out for him. "Cam! Cam Ramsay! Would you please come to the front?"

A voice responded from the edge of the crowd. "Coming! I'm coming." I turned to look and got a clear view of The Bastard making his way forward. He carried a dog harness, a pack and something that looked like a small toolbox. In tow was the red dog, attached to a long, coiled lead that kept her close to her handler.

"I'm Bill. Glad to meet you," the balding man said as he offered his hand to The Bastard.

"A pleasure. I'm Cam and this is Zackie," he said, indicating the dog. Turning to me, he asked, "And you are?" He raised his hand half way for the handshake and then looked into my face. His lip curled back in a look of disgust and he lowered his hand. "Nevermind. I believe we've met."

Before I could respond in kind, Kate called us to attention. "Thank you all for coming to help. You are Task 7. We need you to go to Denny's house where Cam and Zackie should try to establish direction of travel. Bill and Fia, you need to flank Cam. Officer Reynolds is over there on the sidewalk. He will be the police escort in case you need to enter the yards of any residents."

She handed us the paper with the task assignment and began calling names for the next task. As we approached Officer Reynolds, I spoke in a low voice to Cam. "When this is over, I need you to tell me how you make them go away. You and I need to talk."

His lip curled again and he responded in a voice just

above a whisper. "No, go away."

"Asshole!" I whispered back. "You left me blinded and off-trail in the middle of the woods. The least you could do is provide an explanation!" I tried to look him in the eye, but he was steadfastly looking forward and ignoring me as he walked. "You can get rid of those things," I hissed. "I need to know how you do that!" That stopped him in his tracks, and he turned to look at me. His face was flushed and his eyes were wide with fury.

"Those 'things' are --" he began with a low, shaking voice just as Officer Reynolds spoke up. Clamping his lips into a white line, he held his peace as the officer greeted us.

"Thanks for coming out to help. I'm Officer Reynolds." He shook our hands and we introduced ourselves. "The house is over this way." Taking the lead, he guided us down the block to a small ranch style house with white siding. Cam's mouth was a grim, angry line and he took several deep breaths, struggling to master his anger as we walked. A police cruiser with the emergency lights flashing was parked outside of the house and other officers stood in the front yard.

Taking another deep, calming breath, Cam

approached Officer Reynolds. "I'm afraid I'll need to go into the house to collect a scent article for Zackie." He held up the small toolbox labeled with the words 'Scent Kit' as if in explanation. After placing his pack and the dog harness on the ground, he handed Zackie's lead to Bill, deliberately ignoring me. Officer Reynolds then led him to the house and knocked on the door. A short while later, both men emerged. Cam carried a clear ziplock bag containing something made of blue fabric.

"Here's how this is going to work." Cam looked each of us in the eye and began his instructions. "I'm going to take Zackie to meet everyone standing in front of the house. I want her to take their scent, so she can rule them out. She'll also take a whiff of each of you. I'm then going to walk her in an acclimation circle to let her take in all the scents in the immediate area. She'll then get the bagged t-shirt and the command to take scent. The next command will tell her to get on trail." He paused to give us a chance for questions and then continued. "Zackie will be point. All of you stay behind the dog and to either side. Keep your eyes out for any clues the subject may have dropped or any signs that the subject has been through the area. I will have my entire attention focused on Zackie, so you will need to warn me if a car is coming or if there is a loose dog. Are we ready?"

We all nodded and he began walking Zackie from person to person. The dog quickly passed each person as they offered their hands for the dog to sniff. I stood still with my hands extended as the dog took my scent. Rather than move on to the next person, she paused and stared directly into my face. Her eyes were the color of whiskey and surrounded by dark fur, as if someone had outlined them with kohl to emphasize their distinct color. While I thought her gaze would be gentle like all the other dogs I have encountered, I instead saw a disturbing intelligence that I was not prepared for. Without thinking, I took an immediate step back and away from her. Cold shocked me and I shivered involuntarily. The acid rushed to my anxious stomach and my shoulders rose defensively around my neck. She gave a quick snort and dismissed me, walking on. Taking a shaky breath and trying to relax, I felt a crazy mix of emotions. Most of all, I felt shame. Tears welled up in my eyes and I ducked my head, trying to control myself before anyone noticed.

By the time I looked back up, Cam had thrown down the scent article with harness on top. He caught my eye and looked at me grimly for a moment, but then focused his attention back to Zackie, talking to her in an excited voice. Cam led her in a large circle around the house and allowed the dog to sniff at whatever enticed her. Once back to the harness, he oriented her head towards the front steps of the house and, grasping her hind end between his knees, he quickly slipped the harness over her head. Cam momentarily opened the bag and passed it near the dog's face, all while talking to her. She began squirming and whimpering, eager to be off. I could not reconcile the dog I saw before me now with what I had just experienced. With a final click of the snap buckle, he secured the harness and shifted the anchor of the lead from her choke collar to a ring on the back of the harness. Lifting the bag again, he let her stick her nose into the bag to inspect the T-shirt. "Track," he told her. She lifted her head and pointed her nose behind them. As he loosened his knees from the hold on her flanks, he told her, "Find 'em."

The dog lunged towards the sidewalk, placed her nose to the ground and began walking rapidly away from the house. Bill reported our status by radio to command. "Task 7 has departed, heading east on Locust Avenue,"

I grabbed the GPS from my chest harness and cleared the old tracks as I stepped off. Following the others,

I hung back as far as I could and nursed the extreme discomfort I now had from being near this dog. It's not like I thought she was going to do something as mundane as bite me. She was not a large dog after all, maybe fifty or sixty pounds at best. The team dogs I had worked with were mostly around hundred pounds or more, incredibly strong and really driven. Zackie, by contrast, appeared to have a calm demeanor. I do not know what I feared, but I felt unsafe, as if the earth could suddenly open up and swallow me whole. I frequently feel uneasy in my life, but stark fear is something I left behind in childhood. I hated feeling this weak and defenseless. Had it not been for the missing kid, I would have turned around and put a lot of miles between me and that dog.

While Cam methodically let the long lead play out and then reeled it back in to match the dog's pace as she worked the scent, Bill, Officer Reynolds and I checked bushes and shrubs along the route. Calling Denny's name every few minutes, we strained our ears and eyes for any sign of a little boy. All we heard was the occasional faint bark of the air scent dogs in the distance. Providing occasional words of explanation to concerned homeowners, Officer Reynolds smoothed the way as Zackie weaved in and out of neighborhood yards following the scent. With the ambient light dimming, one by one, each of us turned on either a flashlight or a headlamp. The chill in the air became more pronounced and a light drizzle danced on my face. After about a half mile, my knees were starting to feel a little swollen and stiff and I wished I had taken some ibuprofen before we started the task. Just as I was about to abuse my knees some more by getting down to check yet another clump of bushes in front of yet another house, I saw the dog's head suddenly snap towards the house. Zackie stopped walking and stared intently into the darkness surrounding the house. We all followed suit and studied the house and front yard for any movement. No lights were on either outside or inside. It was unlikely anyone was home. Zackie began moving into the yard at a brisk trot. As if we were all attached to the same lead, we fell into step behind her and began calling Denny's name more urgently. As we entered the backyard of the house, my headlamp shone on a children's playground set. It had swings and one of those slides that had a little fort built around the top of it. Zackie scrambled to the playground set and pounded on the ladder leading up to the fort with her front paws.

Cam looked up at the fort. "He's up there, I'm sure of it." Being the lightest and smallest of the searchers, I immediately started climbing up the ladder, calling Denny's name. Squeezing myself through the opening of the small fort, I could see a little boy in a red and white striped shirt sitting in a corner and shivering. He paid no attention to me as I clambered forward, slipping my pack off to grab the space blanket.

"Denny's here!" I cried. "He looks okay, just really cold." I could hear Bill repeating this information into his radio and Cam praising Zackie. I flipped my headlamp to the red setting, so as not to blind Denny and crept forward. "Hi, Denny. How are you doing, little guy? I'm going to get you out of here, okay?" Wrapping the boy in the space blanket, I tried to gently pull him towards me and the opening. He was cold to the touch and damp from the rain, and as I tried to move him, he began crying and kicking. "C'mon, dude. You'll be warm and dry real soon if you just let me move you." Backing off, I called to the searchers outside. "He is not happy about being moved. You're going to have to give us a minute." As long I didn't try to move Denny towards the opening to the fort, he was all right with me coming closer to him. Eventually, I was able to sit next to him and put my arm around him. There was still no kicking and screaming, so I moved in closer and removed the wet shirt. He was freezing. I opened up my jacket and

26

wrapped my arms around him, trying to give him some of my body heat. We sat that way for a little while and he seemed to settle in, generally ignoring me now. I lifted him and made a move towards the opening while he held this mood.

As we got to the top of the ladder, Officer Reynolds positioned himself below and reached up to take the boy. I handed Denny off, wrapped in the space blanket and then grabbed my pack before descending the ladder myself. I felt almost giddy with relief that we found him, but I was now close to shivering myself.

"Are you sure he's okay? He's not really responsive. Is that the autism?" Bill asked quietly as he took my pack to ease my climb down.

"It might be autism or it might be a side effect from taking the Risperdal." I grimaced, betraying the unease I felt at the mention of the drug. This reaction was not lost on Cam, who now studied me through narrowed eyes as I stood there and shivered. Determined to distract him from my real source of discomfort, I deliberately rubbed my arms. "I'll warm up now that I don't have to sit still." Zipping up my jacket, I began walking in small circles.

"Bring the dog here." Officer Reynolds motioned for the dog as he checked the boy over. "Maybe Denny could use some distraction while we wait for the ambulance." Zackie was now naked of harness with the lead clipped to her choke collar. With a word from Cam, she ambled over to the sitting child. I took a step forward to stop this, but Cam grabbed my arm and shook his head. As I was about to yank my arm back and run to the boy, the dog snuffled Denny's face, causing the boy to erupt in giggles. The men smiled to see Denny's reaction, but I could feel the blood drain from my face and I kept my guard up, still not trusting the situation. In a little while, with another word from Cam, the dog was lying next to the boy, keeping him warm as Denny ruffled her fur. Zackie's face unexpectedly reflected both stoicism and tolerance of the situation. This was definitely not the look of ecstasy that some dogs display when kids pet them. We offered Denny food and water, but he was uninterested in anything but the dog. While everyone else was focused on the dog and boy, I could sense Cam was dissecting me in some way. Just as I thought I would start squirming from this scrutiny, a police car carrying Denny's parents and an ambulance pulled up in front of the house. The EMTs checked Denny over again and then wrapped him in an additional blanket. After reassuring the parents, they then loaded the family into the back of the ambulance for the short trip to the hospital.

"Good job, folks!" Officer Reynolds was all smiles. "Can we give you a lift back to the post office?" It would have been a tight squeeze for all of us and a dog in the back of the police cruiser, so we declined and began the walk back. On the way, Bill ran into some of his teammates as they returned from their assigned tasks. Chatting amiably, the group inched in front of us as they congratulated Bill on helping to make the find. I trudged along next to Cam and Zackie.

Cam caught my eye and then tilted his head toward Zackie. "I don't think my dog much likes you."

I pursed my lips and replied, "I think the feeling is mutual."

"You are not inherently cruel to children." He zipped up his coat as he walked. "You did all right with that young lad just now."

I stopped walking and glared at him. "I've always been kind to children. What in the hell are you talking about? I wouldn't be in SAR if I didn't care about other people."

"Who taught you? I can only conclude that there is either something lacking in your training or something lacking in your morality and ethics. So, which is it?"

"Taught me? I learned from my team and I read a lot of SAR manuals. Is that what you're talking about? And by the way, I don't appreciate you denigrating the work my team put into me. I do okay." I stopped walking, warming to the fight and jabbing my finger into his chest. "As for my morality and ethics, at least I don't have a dangerous dog that could go after someone at any time."

Cam cocked an eyebrow at me. "Has she ever growled at you? Bared her teeth?" As I shook my head no, he continued. "Then what has she done to you to make you feel so unsafe?"

"She--- she looked at me." I was stuttering and instantly realized how lame that sounded. "What I mean is... I don't know what I mean. I can't explain it, but there's something really wrong with that dog."

"More likely, something wrong with you. I think she looked at you and found you wanting. You were judged unfit."

At that, my mouth opened and closed uselessly as I struggled to find a way to defend myself. I finally just asked the obvious question. "Why am I unfit?"

"You were very unkind to that other boy. I was shocked by your behavior. I think if Zackie were going to bite you, it would have happened then. So, back to the paradox. Why did you behave so distastefully to the first boy, yet act the very picture of a saint with the second?"

"What first boy? That thing in the woods? Is that what you're talking about?" I stopped walking and threw my hands up in disgust and frustration. Turning his head, Cam pinched the bridge of his nose and closed his eyes, trying to maintain calm. Eventually, he took a deep breath and looked back at me.

"I really hate that you refer to them as things. He is not a thing, he was a living boy once." Cam looked steadily into my eyes, gauging my comprehension as he went on. "He was frightened and alone…." As I stared back at him with incredulity, Cam dropped his eyes and sighed. Finally, looking up again and he met my eyes. "You were never taught, were you?" He nodded his head as if he finally understood. "Look, I'm starving. After the debrief for the search, we should get something to eat and talk a bit. Things cannot go on as they have."

CHAPTER 3

Cam fed Zackie in the parking lot of the fast food restaurant and then left her to doze in the car while we ate. The restaurant was largely empty at this hour, most customers preferring to satisfy late night cravings using the drive through. We chose a booth at the back and while my stomach was nervous, I was still able to easily devour my food. I am not a picky eater and because of one thing or another in my life interfering with regular meals or draining my energy, I am almost always starving. These conditions in combination create the potential for awkward moments during meals, since lessons in the normal social graces were never a high priority during my childhood. I prefer to eat alone rather than risk displaying what must be appalling table manners. As I caught myself in the mirrors surrounding the booth, I saw a pale young woman with deeply shadowed eyes and dark russet hair messily pulled into what remained of a braid. My cheeks were stuffed with food like a hamster. I looked away and tried to swallow. In deference to what I thought might be British sensibilities, I refrained from speaking with my mouth full, leaving Cam an opening to start the conversation.

"Right then." He concentrated on wiping the grease from his hands with a napkin, avoiding looking at my distended face. "I was taught by my maternal grandmother and she was taught by hers. This has been the way of it in my family for every generation where I have been able to trace back. I was the first male in three hundred years to be provided this education." There was no trace of either pride or shame in this statement. He was merely presenting it as fact. "Was there no one in your family who was willing to teach you?" He looked steadily at my eyes as he asked this.

I was loath to reveal anything about myself, but this felt like a transaction and the only way that I was going to get any information was to provide it. After some hesitation, I responded. "I was adopted." At this, he began nodding again, as if he could possibly understand my situation.

He pointed to his right cheek. "You have a little ketchup." As I scrubbed my face with the napkin, he sat forward and continued. "Do you know anything about your biological parents?"

"Nothing. All I know is that I was adopted as an infant."

"And how did your adoptive family take to your abilities?"

"They sent me to psychiatrists." I shrugged and feigned indifference. "Made me take drugs."

"Risperdal?"

I nodded numbly and slipped in my first lie. "They did everything just short of actually having me committed."

"If they believed you were insane, why didn't they commit you?"

"They were going to. I left before they could do it." By omitting the word 'again' from my answer, I committed my second lie.

"Ahhh..." Sitting back, he continued the inquisition. "And how have you avoided the same fate now that you are a free range human?"

I shrugged again and tried to assume a poker face. "I lie. A lot."

"And are you so certain of your own sanity?"

We stared at each other for a moment and then I finally broke. "Not always. But today's events seem to support my view of reality. You saw it too, after all. More importantly, Zackie saw it."

"Again, not an *it*." He raised his eyebrows and nodded to me to make sure I got it. "In my book, harboring doubts about one's sanity are points in your favor. But, while Zackie and I did see *him*, this proves nothing. Did you know there was a case of a shared psychotic disorder involving a dog? The dog's owner was an elderly woman with psychosis. She most definitely saw things that weren't there and her dog displayed behavioral responses conditioned by her delusional beliefs."

I quirked an eyebrow at Cam. "Shared psychotic disorder involves closely related individuals, like a parent and child, husband and wife, siblings... It's also extremely rare. Since you're a canine handler team, it's possible that you and Zackie might be sharing a delusion." I put the eyebrow down and leaned forward. "But we've never met before and I know for a fact that we both saw something that looked like a boy. I'll bet if we each independently wrote down a description of what we saw, they'd be identical." I sat back and folded my arms across my chest. "I'll also bet that people like us spend a lot of time trying to self-diagnose by reading books on psychiatry."

The corner of his mouth lifted in a wry smile and he spoke softly. "You understand that I need to be careful here. By agreeing with you about what we saw and not trying to convince you to return to your family and take your meds, I could be doing you harm. There are far more people in this world who see things and need the meds than there are people like you and me."

Sighing, I pushed the hair out of my eyes and looked askance. "How can you be sure that we don't both need the meds?"

Cam responded with a grin. "To paraphrase Freud, sometimes a banana is just a banana… and sometimes a ghost is just a ghost." That made me smile and for the first time in a long time, I began to relax a little.

I finally asked him again the question that was burning in my mind since the encounter in the woods. "How do you make them go away?"

"I don't." He jutted his chin towards the parking lot. "That's all Zackie's doing."

"What, is she like a guard dog that protects you from these things?"

He sighed dramatically and slouched down tiredly in the seat. "I can see we have a lot of work ahead of us. You persist in thinking of them as objects. You need to think of them as people if you're to do any good. And no, Zackie does not guard me from them." Cam was back to studying me now. Tilting his head, he said, "You've had some experience with her now. What do you really think Zackie is?"

"She's not a dog." I sat quietly for a moment and examined what my senses told me. "Other than being able to say what she's not, I can't say what she is. Really, all I can say for sure is that she scares the crap out of me."

"You've had a bad start with her, but I think we can remedy that. She's nothing if not patient. You made the mistake of doing harm to one of her charges and this is something you must never, never do again. I can't protect you from her if you decide to be foolish." He gave me a penetrating look to see if his words had any impact. I felt my brow wrinkle with worry and I swallowed reflexively. I did not want to find out what would happen if I did something 'foolish.' Seeing that I was taking his warning seriously, he nodded and asked, "Do you know what a psychopomp is?"

"I – I've never heard the term before." I was stuttering again, unsure of myself and almost hoping that he wouldn't tell me.

"Zackie is a psychopomp." Folding his forearms on the table, he leaned forward to explain. "She conveys the dead to the afterlife. Every culture has sacred stories that speak about these beings. Most relate to animals. In religious texts from around the world, these guides have been described as everything from dolphins, to birds, bees and foxes. The stories from the Aztecs and the Greeks have dogs who serve as the escort. Think Cerberus guarding the gates of Hades, with a singular appetite for living flesh, only allowing the spirits of the dead to freely enter the underworld." I swallowed and nodded for him to go on. "Sometimes, there are human representations, like the Norse Valkyries or the Roman Charon, ferrying the dead across the river Styx. The Grim Reaper with his scythe is all over headstones from the Victorian era. These beings can take on any form they choose."

I sat there in stunned silence. Even after all that I have gone through with the unseen world, I would not have believed him if I had not had firsthand experience with her disapproval.

He looked at me and gave me a second before he continued. "Do you understand the nature of your offense?"

"I interfered with what is rightfully hers."

"More than that. She protects and shepherds these souls. She saw you take out your anger on one of her flock. What did that dead child do to elicit such a response from you?"

"It – he kept grabbing my hands and pulling on my clothing. I was afraid Steve, the guy I was training with, would notice. Things can go downhill fast if that happens. I'd have to move. It's happened to me before." Gritting my teeth to keep my emotions in check, I tried to explain. "The dead see me and they're all over me. If I don't push them away, if I don't punch, kick and scream to get them off of me, I stop seeing my world. What they see and feel takes over and it's always a horror show of their last minutes before dying." I roughly yanked the bangs back and out my eyes and forced myself to keep my voice low. "If someone sees me when any of this is going on, the best thing that happens is that they want to medicate the hell out of me.

My own family tried to put me away, for shit's sake." I took a deep breath to try to regain some calm. "Look, I don't want to have to move again, and I can't risk being sent back to the psychiatrists."

Cam looked steadily at me until I was calm enough to listen. "This child died because he ran into the woods to escape a bear. He was panicked and he lost his way. After days of wandering, he could not find his way back and eventually succumbed to exposure. He died cold and frightened and crying for his mother. He kept grabbing your hands because he was trying to slip his hand into yours. He grabbed your clothing because it was like hanging on to his mother's skirt. He wanted you to take him home."

Cam paused to give me time to process what he was saying and then continued. "If you found a little boy lost in the mall and he tried to take your hand, would you push him to the ground and strike him? This is what Zackie saw."

My gut churned and the meal threatened to come back up. I whispered my question, afraid of the answer. "Will she kill me for what I've done?" I felt deserving of death, but frightened nonetheless.

"No. If she wanted your life, you'd right now be a pile of cooling meat in the woods."

He let me chew on that a bit and I thought back to other encounters, reinterpreting them in light of what I had just been told. I remembered the teenager in the subway, pushing me closer and closer to the edge of the platform as the train came rushing through. Was he trying to show me what happened to him? Did he need me to tell someone that he had been pushed, that it wasn't suicide? I thought about the charred and blackened remains of a young girl that crawled towards me along the floor of my dorm room. I freaked out and my roommate immediately made the request to move to another room. I learned later that someone had died in a dorm fire on that campus. Did she want me to know that she tried to do all the right things to escape the blaze, staying low to avoid the smoke and desperately trying to make it to an exit? Did she just want someone to help her to finally make it out of the burning building?

My face crumpled with remorse and the tears were about to flow. Relaxing his posture, Cam stretched his long legs under the table and kicked me lightly in the shins to get my attention. He looked at me with a faint smile. "You haven't asked the obvious question."

"Huh?" I was startled out of my downward spiral and took a moment to focus on him.

Having my attention now, Cam posed the question. "Is Zackie her real name? Seems a bit informal, don't you think?" I had to agree and nodded my head slightly. He began fiddling with a straw, occasionally glancing at me as he spoke. "It's something of an inside joke between her and me. I had no idea what to call her when she first came into my life. I was traveling in the hills of North Carolina at the time and ran across a backwoods hunter. Most humans are too insensible to understand her power and, sure enough, he offered to buy her from me." Slipping into an Appalachian twang, Cam continued. "Said she was a fine looking Plott hound and would be great to hunt bear with. He'd name her Zackie if I'd sell her to him. He promised me that he would never use Zackie as a coon hound. 'Damned waste of the breed,' he said." In his normal voice, Cam finished the story. "From that day on, she was Zackie to me. I think this proves she has a sense of humor, since I still walk among the living." He winked at me and smiled more openly.

Just then, a restaurant worker came to mop the floor near our feet. "Are you folks about done? We'd like to close up." Stretching tired limbs and marshalling our trash, we left the restaurant and walked into the night.

I stopped Cam before we reached the parked cars. "What's next?"

"What's next, indeed?" Yawning and stretching, he drawled out the instructions for my future. "You will start your apprenticeship tomorrow."

As we exchanged cell phone numbers and discussed where to meet, I glanced uneasily at Cam's truck. "I should say something to her." Nodding, he opened the tailgate. Zackie lounged comfortably on a thick blanket and did not deign to rise as I approached her. Blurting out what I had to say, I was unable to meet her eyes. "I'm sorry." I quickly turned to go to my car.

At home, I peeled off my clothes and immediately hit the shower. As physically and emotionally drained as I felt, I still could not allow ticks to attach and exchange bodily fluids with me. Every week, it seemed that a new incurable tick-borne disease was being heralded by the evening news. I forced myself through the ritual of checking my scalp and all the cracks and crevices in my body for unwanted passengers. As much as I scrubbed, I didn't feel cleansed. I finally admitted the futility of this and stepped out of the shower to towel off. Collapsing into bed, I closed my eyes and tried to let tomorrow worry about itself.

The more I tried to relax, the more Cam's words started to come back to me. I turned on my side, took a deep breath and tried to clear my thoughts. No good. My monkey brain kept churning. Flipping to my other side, I berated myself, thinking that I can't make this right. I worried about what it would take to learn Cam's lessons. Could I trust him, or was he leading me into something really dangerous? Was I prepared to devote myself to the lessons? If I didn't, would I even have a life worth living if things went on like this? No matter how committed he was to teaching me, it was entirely possible that I would never pass muster.

I had a long history of not passing muster. A colicky baby from the start, I was a thorn in the side of my adoptive parents from the get-go. They lost a lot of sleep as I shrieked for hours at a time. I tend to think that the dead were coming to me even then, although I do not have clear memories of this time. As an older child, I lacked the good sense to keep my mouth shut. At first, my parents chalked it up to a vivid imagination, but they were disturbed by the graphic images of death and injury I described. I was taken to many, many child psychiatrists to try to straighten me out. Diagnoses of psychosis resulted and when you hear that kind of thing from many different experts, you tend to believe them.

My parents thought they could keep everything under control and deal with the visions and voices in my head through logical, calm discussion paired with frequent doses of antipsychotics. We started with a daily regimen of 300 milligrams of Clozaril, 100 milligrams of Thorazine, 900 milligrams of Lithium and two antihistamine pills and then moved on to ever increasing doses of Risperdal, Olanzapine and Haloperidol. I spent my days in a drug-induced stupor, listening to my parents parrot the phrases provided by the psychiatrists. *'I want you to know that I'm here for you. How can I help you?'* and my all time favorite, *'Tell me what I can do to support you.'*

We hung on like that for a while until the bruises appeared. This was followed in short order by bites and scratches, broken bones, deep puncture wounds and lacerations and that required stitches. While my parents and the doctors panicked that I was inflicting harm on myself, the truth was that the antipsychotics made me vulnerable to attacks from the dead. I was no longer able to use even my child's abilities to defend myself in a small measure. To everyone concerned, I was a psychotic child with bizarre and morbid auditory and visual hallucinations that I could no longer master. They were out of options. They had me committed to a children's psychiatric hospital, immobilized in five point restraints and force-fed meds every few hours. I was completely incapacitated and defenseless.

If I had a weaker will to live, I probably would have died there. I was eight years old, but even then, I knew what bullshit meant and I wasn't going to put up with anymore of it. I started cheeking my pills and telling everyone who would listen that I was better. I told them that the visions and the words in my head were gone, so this was proof that I was cured and they could let me go home. Meanwhile, I spent my time focusing my abilities to ward off attacks. This was when I first learned how to fight back and I've been honing my abilities to a fine edge ever since.

When they at last believed that I was cured, I went home and perfected my lying. I could keep up the act most of the time, but there were incidents where I was confronted by things beyond my developing skill set. I was so good at the lie that everyone gave allowances when this happened, since I was doing so well otherwise. I did all right up until the advent of adolescence. That's when the visitations became more frequent and more intense. I managed to graduate high school, but I was definitely considered weird and ostracized by every caste of teenage society. College was supposed to be a new beginning and I resolved to control things and fit in better, but … Suffice it to say, I graduated, but upon moving back to my parent's home, I found myself under constant psychiatric observation. Eventually, the day came when my tight control slipped and there was an incident. They were about to commit me again when I gave them the slip and headed for the city.

A few incidents later, I decided it would be in my best interest to get the hell out of the city. Too many people. Too many dead. Serial encounters with spirits left me unable to do the most basic things to keep myself going. I couldn't sleep because the homeless man who died of exposure clawed at my apartment door and snatched at me,

drawing blood whenever I ventured through the door.
When I tried to get to work, the teenager who had been
crushed by the subway train grabbed at my ankles as I
stood on the platform, trying to drag me under speeding
trains. I lost my job because a woman who had been struck
down by a speeding car wailed incessantly as she followed
me, dragging useless limbs and leaving a bloody trail. I was
supposed to deliver documents around the city, but she
would trip me into oncoming traffic. Everywhere I went,
there was a waiting ambush. It wouldn't stop. When I could
no longer sleep, eat or work, I knew I had to leave. I would
try rural life. Maybe go to the empty woods if I could
manage it. What a bust that was....

Sighing, I flipped my body again and spent a long
time waiting for sleep.

CHAPTER 4

I found Cam sitting with Zackie on the stone wall outside of the old Methodist church. Cam held the lead loosely in his hand to stay in compliance with the leash laws. In contrast to my mood, they looked relaxed and comfortable, waiting in the softly filtered light beneath the budding branches of an old oak tree. It was late afternoon and I had timed my arrival in Hope Township to make sure they would get there first. Hospitals, cemeteries and historic buildings are places I avoid. There are too many dead and I can easily be overwhelmed.

Cam looked me over. "Ready?"

"Sure." With no real conviction I threw down the challenge. "Bring it on."

Doing a fair imitation of Fiske from Incident Command, Cam launched into the lesson. "Listen up! Our subject is a Caucasian female. The Point Last Scene was on the steps of that church. She was wearing a bridal gown and was weeping copiously."

I rolled my eyes. "What do you want me to do?"

"Go to the church steps and see if you can draw her to you. When she comes, I want you to hold very still and to resist the urge to push her away or silence her. It's natural to want to avoid the flood of negative emotions that may come, but again, resist the impulse. Look at her closely and allow yourself to take in whatever impressions may come."

Dubious about what I would learn from this, I nevertheless followed the stone wall to the steps leading into the church. The dark red doors sat below an arched transom and made a nice contrast with the white clapboards and gray stone foundation. I thought this would be a great place for wedding pictures. Gazing up, I admired the steeple centered perfectly over the doors and how arched windows to either side provided a graceful symmetry. The overall effect gave the building a sense of strength and dignity. A small plaque affixed to the church's wall indicated that this was Saint John's Methodist Church. Built in 1876 in the Gothic Revival style, the structure had recently been added to the National Registry of Historic Places.

I did as Cam said and I drew a deep breath, relaxing and opening myself up to her presence. This was contrary to every impulse I felt, but I forced myself to be still and to unclench my fists. I was not here for a fight. Cam would back me up if anything happened. I took another deep breath and then I felt it. A light breeze, scented with roses. The bride shimmered slightly as she manifested, carrying a large bouquet of roses. Dressed in a white gown that was loose and unfitted, it had a low waist and a hemline that ended at her knees. She wore a tight fitting Cloche hat and her entire ensemble was covered in beads and sequins that caught the light and glittered. She was the picture of a 1920s flapper bride.

Cam paced slowly along the stone wall. "What are you getting?"

My jaw dropped as I took in the sensations. "Joy. I'm getting joy. She is incredibly happy…" The bride wept, but these were not the tears of despair I expected.

"And there you have your first lesson. They are not always distraught or in torment. This one is reliving a happy moment that led to an even happier life. Let her go now."

I looked at him and frowned. "Aren't we expected to do something for her? Not just leave her like this?"

"No, let her go. She'll move along in her own time." I did as he suggested and let my concentration wander, wishing the bride well as she dissolved into her history. This was certainly a first for me and a true revelation.

As I stood there with a goofy grin plastered on my face, a film crew suddenly burst through the church doors and clambered on to the landing leading up to the entryway. Their cameras were trained on a man dressed in a black long coat and white poet shirt. Large silver buttons decorated the length on either side of the coat, but the suggestion of vintage military styling was spoiled by the addition of jeans and high top sneakers. Heavy eyeliner accented gray eyes and his long blond hair was swept back in a ponytail. I resisted the impulse to laugh at this walking affectation.

"I know you can hear me." The man paused for dramatic effect. "You and I both know that he was right to leave you at the altar. You weren't good enough for him, after all. Or maybe he preferred a younger woman or a prettier woman?"

I hastily moved out of the way. Not my monkeys, not my circus. Joining Cam and Zackie by the wall, I was a safe enough distance from the spectacle. "What the hell is going on?"

Cam's lip curled in distaste. "This particular hell is an idiot trying to provoke a spirit. He's taunting our weeping bride."

I slowly shook my head. "Why would anyone want to do that?" The thought rattled around like a ball in a pachinko machine and I came to the conclusion that Cam was right. The guy was an idiot. I spent a great deal of time trying to avoid notice. It made no sense to me why a person would try to force the attention of the dead by pissing them off.

"He's trying to get something on film for his show. If he succeeds in enraging a spirit, he might get something physically revealing of a presence. Depending on personality, things might be thrown, a person might be shoved or struck... He won't get that kind of reaction from our bride, but I'm sure you've seen this type of behavior in other circumstances."

I nodded my head as we watched the man continue his capering. I was all too familiar with this behavior. "So, I enrage spirits?"

"More like frustrate them. They're expecting a deeper level of understanding from you."

"Really?" I thought back to what Cam told me about the dead boy and realized that none of this information had percolated to my senses. "How do I get to that deeper level?" I looked at him earnestly. "Is it something you can teach me?"

"In time. But at the moment, I'd say that we'll have to abort our lesson plan for the day."

"If this guy is trying to rile things up, shouldn't we stick around? In case we need to do something to calm things down?"

"Do you see the bride anymore? I certainly don't see her. We really have no need to stay here. I say we let the idiot carry on playing the fool and let nothing happen for the cameras."

I looked at Cam and narrowed my eyes. "Oh ye of little faith! He'll either make something happen or someone will do something off camera."

"Perhaps you're right... Care to place a small wager on the outcome? I say there will be no shenanigans now, but later, they will add special effects."

I grinned at him. "You're on. Winner gets ice cream." I turned back to look carefully for any evidence of shenanigans. "We'll have to figure out when the show will air."

The antics of the man now became a spectator sport and we avidly watched the action unfold. He stalked theatrically in front of the church, proclaiming all the while the failings of the bride spirit. Synchronized with the panning of the cameras, Zackie's muzzle pointed first left and then right as the man paced back and forth. Eventually, to make her disdain plain to all, she sneezed mightily in his direction and began to circle before lying down for a nap. Just as she was really getting comfortable, the man bounded down the steps and proceeded to the far side of the church to enter an old graveyard. Forcing Zackie to her feet, we moved along the edge of the stone wall to keep the man in sight. A wrought iron gate stood in front of the cemetery. It was elaborate in the Victorian style and bore the words 'Moravian Cemetery Hope, NJ' in a twisted metal banner at the top. This gate was strangely familiar to me, but I couldn't at the moment place it in my memory.

While we watched the man slap at the gravestone of what was undoubtedly the bride spirit, Zackie suddenly stiffened and stared intently at something in the nearest corner of the cemetery. Her alert drew our attention to the figure of a man who sat hunched on the ground. Around him were roughly three rows of what looked like a path of footstones. The figure had its arms tightly wrapped around itself and rocked to and fro with its head bowed, unaware of the idiot man ranting to his camera crew. Gasping slightly, I froze when I saw the dead man, fearful that all hell was about to break loose.

"Don't worry," Cam murmured. "Zackie will shield us until we're ready to make our move. What you need to understand is that these spirits are like drowning people. They have no intent to do you harm, but once they notice people like us, they will latch on in their panic and desperation. They can drag you under if you are not prepared."

While the idiot droned on, we dared not approach

this spirit and draw attention to ourselves. Our difficulties were increased by the prospect of bringing a dog into the cemetery, so it appeared our best option was to wait this whole thing out. The sun was close to setting and the deepening shadows might afford us the ability to enter the graveyard unnoticed, if only the film crew would leave.

I groaned quietly as the idiot man asked his crew to hand him a spirit box, so he could try to hear what the ghost had to say. This was going to go on forever. As usual, dinner time was approaching and it seemed likely that I would miss another meal. My stomach growled in protest.

Cam chuckled and tried to distract me by asking what I noticed about the dead man. I looked carefully and told Cam that his coat was dark blue and he had a white stock around his neck. I could see buckles on his shoes and dark stockings that met his breeches slightly below the knee. Aside from clothing that placed him in the eighteenth century, I saw nothing from my vantage point that offered any additional clues.

As I shifted my gaze back to the idiot, I noticed him watching us as he fiddled with the spirit box. As amusing as it was for me to see a ghost hunter oblivious to what must be his heart's desire, I felt a bit of sympathy for him as the spirit box emitted nothing but static. You would think that at least a word or two from radio broadcasts might leak through and give him something to substantiate communication with the bride spirit. Luck was just not with him this day.

Eventually, the idiot turned off the spirit box and faced the cameras squarely. "While we tried everything at our disposal to make contact with the ghost of the bride, we failed to find evidence that she is here." Turning to show his good side to the camera, he continued. "We will carefully review our tapes and recordings to see if we captured anything that can only be detected by electronic devices. Sometimes, this is the way investigations go and you just have to roll with the punches." At this, he made a slashing motion across his throat and the operators shut down the cameras. Cam waggled his eyebrows at me, since it appeared that he would win the bet.

The idiot and the crew packed up their belongings and headed to the parking lot on the far side of the church. Cam and I lounged on the stone wall as we waited for their cars to depart. As night embraced the graveyard, Zackie kept watch on the spirit. She had the attitude of a herding dog, relaxing on her side while maintaining an air of alert surveillance. When the last car pulled out on to High Street, Zackie got to her feet and began leading us to the dead man.

As we approached, I recognized the path of footstones as tombstones that lay flat to the ground. Dates of death ranged from the mid seventeen hundreds to the early eighteen hundreds. Each of the stones was numbered, beginning with the number one in 1768. Apparently, the Moravians were an extraordinarily orderly people with a penchant for good record keeping.

Trusting that things would be different with Zackie and Cam present, I followed them to the man, but my gut felt tight. I steeled myself and tried to remain calm. Our man sat beside a tombstone that read 'John Lewis Luckenbach, born Jan. 27, 1758 in Germany, departed this life March 4, 1799.' The man raised his eyes and gazed balefully at us. His face was a mass of raised and crusted reddish-purple sores. Tears streaked down his cheeks from swollen eyes.

Cam approached and knelt near the spirit. "John, why do you stay here?" I heard a mumbled response. His tongue was swollen and he was sobbing. It was difficult to understand him. Cam glanced at me. I was squinting hard and cupping my ear in an effort to understand. "Do not listen with your ears. Not all of them will speak, but you must hear them nonetheless. Look into his eyes and feel his words."

I swallowed my unease and concentrated to go beyond revulsion for the man's appearance. Taking a deep breath and relaxing, my mind began to focus as I held John Luckenbach's gaze. "Smallpox," I said. "He died of smallpox. He suffered fevers and could not keep his meals down. His body ached horribly... But this death is not the source of his suffering." I held my breath and tried to go deeper, to get to the cause, but I began to feel feverish. Nausea was making my stomach roil. "I can't.... I can't anymore!" My tongue swelled and my skin felt like it was on fire. Looking at my hands, I saw pus-filled boils erupting from my skin. "Cam! Cam, help me!" I stared in horror at the lesions and was close to screaming when Zackie suddenly jumped up and slammed her front paws into my chest. I was knocked a few steps backwards, but managed to keep my feet under me. That broke the spell. Panting and rubbing my chest, I slowly returned to myself.

"Remember what I said about them dragging you under?" Cam examined my hands for the pustules. "You need to maintain your sense of self when you have discourse with them. The experience of dying is extremely powerful and it can overwhelm. Accept the experience, but let it wash over you. Do not internalize it. Hold on to your reality. Can you do that?"

I gasped and rubbed my hands, trying to make them feel clean again. "I don't know… I don't know if I can do this!"

"Look, this won't come all at once. It's going to take time and you will need to take things a little farther during each attempt. You did well this first time." Cam looked closely at my face. "Are you ready to finish this?"

"You have to lead. I'm done." But I squared my shoulders and stepped in closer.

Cam nodded and returned to kneel near the spirit. "John, tell me what happened. Why do you weep?" As John Luckenbach raised his hands in explanation or supplication, it was clear that there were no hands. The spirit garbled something through his swollen tongue and I caught the word 'Lenape.' The sobbing and rocking started again in earnest and Zackie sat down directly in front of the spirit. Putting her muzzle into his pocked face, she licked his tears and he clung to her. Cam stared intently at this scene. "He feels guilty for the death of others." He nodded his head and then continued. "The Moravians sent missionaries to the Lenni-Lenape, the tribes that lived along the Delaware. John was among those who were chosen to go. He fell sick during the mission. Many from the tribe died from smallpox afterwards." Cam frowned and now shook his head. "John feels that he is responsible for killing them."

I stared at the spirit's coat sleeves. "Why does he have no hands?"

"What becomes of someone who has no hands?"

"They can't touch? They lose the ability to do things? They need help from others?" I had no idea what the right answer might be. "Could he have lost his hands to amputation, maybe from infection?" This didn't really answer the question, but might account for missing body parts.

"All possibilities." Tilting his head, Cam thought for a moment. "In the context of this particular case, I would say that John feels helpless to make things right. The emotion is translated to his spirit body." Turning back to the spirit, Cam queried him. "Do you hold the one who made you ill responsible for your death?"

The spirit vehemently shook his head no and he conveyed the words, "God's will." Zackie laid her head on his shoulder and it looked like he took strength from her touch. The spirit sighed and leaned into her body, wrapping his arms around her.

"Watch his hands," Cam muttered to me. As the spirit of John Luckenbach seemed to calm and the tears ceased to flow, I saw a faint glow where the hands should be. We stood quietly and after a few minutes, the glow became brighter and hands emerged from the light.

"You're ready, then?" Cam looked closely at the spirit for confirmation. "Stand and follow Zackie. She will take you home." I saw the spirit rise and take hold of Zackie's collar. As the dog led the spirit away from the grave, Cam said to me, "They need to move quickly now, before he relapses back into his former state of mind. Shield your eyes. Do not look into the place Zackie goes." Turning away towards the church, I remembered the last time this happened and I hoped not to be blinded again.

A massive flash of light erupted behind me at the

same time that I detected a red blinking light near the church wall. Squinting into the darkness, the shadow of a man was revealed holding what was probably a camera. "Cam! There's someone here." We both stared at the blinking red light and then began walking towards it.

Cam bellowed as he advanced on the man. "Hoy! What are you doing there?"

The camera lowered and I detected maybe a moment's indecision on the part of the person filming. The man holding the camera stood his ground and did not move. "I saw everything you did. I have it on film."

As we got nearer, I recognized the idiot man. Cam folded his arms across his chest. "What exactly do you think you saw?"

"You were talking to something out there. I saw the girl almost fall."

"We were only paying our respects to one of my ancestors," Cam improvised. "The dog jumped on the girl and she almost fell. I'm afraid my dog is not as well behaved as she ought to be." As if a demonstration were necessary, Zackie took that moment to appear out of the darkness and to jump on Cam. She then proceeded to stick her nose in the idiot man's crotch. As I shook my head in disbelief, she turned to look at me with a grin that showed the tips of her canines. Cam had not lied about her sense of humor.

The man backed away from Zackie. "No, I don't believe you. I saw a light just now. It flashed on and then off. I can show it to you." The man pressed some buttons on the camera and a replay of what we'd just done came up on the screen. The recording was infrared and showed shapes outlined in red, yellow and purple moving about on the screen. Fortunately, the recording lacked a clear sound. He had been too far away from the action and none of our words had been captured.

Cam pointed to the screen just as the recording showed a dog shape jumping on a human shape. "What did I tell you?"

The man narrowed his eyes. "Keep watching." The film concluded with a small flash of white light and then reddish yellow shapes that must have been us approaching the camera. I wondered at the small flash of light, given my experiences with the real thing. Apparently, technology could not capture what I sensed.

Cam snorted. "You saw a firefly. What of it?"

"It's too early in the season for fireflies. I know what I saw." The man's jaw set stubbornly as he flipped the camera closed. "You were talking to something out there. This is interesting footage and I'd like to use it for my show. I'm willing to pay you."

Cam shook his head. "I'm sorry, but no."

The man scrubbed at his face with his free hand and looked up tiredly at Cam and me. I stared at his smeared eyeliner. "I'm sorry. We've gotten off on the wrong foot. My name is Lucas Tremaine. I'm not trying to embarrass anyone here. You can see from the footage that no one can tell who you are. Would you please allow me to use this clip? I promise, I won't reveal your identities."

The last thing I wanted was publicity. "We won't sign the release. You can't use this recording." He was right in saying that the infrared recording could not easily identify me, but this feeling was not rational. This was stark paranoia. What if they could augment images or voice on the clip and things became much clearer in the broadcast? My family was convinced I was a danger to myself and anything that had the potential of helping them to locate me was out of the question.

Lucas's face darkened at the rejection and I steeled myself for further arguments. Instead, he surprised me by just giving a curt nod, turning on his heel and walking away.

I shook my head and kept my eye on the retreating figure. "That seemed too easy."

Cam put his hands on his hips and also watched the man. "I think we have to keep an eye out for that one."

I chewed on my cuticle and worried. "He seems way too interested in us, but I'm not sure what we can do about it."

"Let's just be sure he's not around when we're out and about. We should go and find out what he drives." Cam began walking towards the parking lot at the far side of the church and I followed mutely.

Just as we rounded the corner of the building, a red Nissan pulled out of the parking lot and into the street. Zackie proceeded to chase the car a small way down the road.

Cam threw his hands up in disgust. "Would you cut

that out! Enough already with the bad dog behavior!" Returning to us from the road, Zackie again flashed the wolfish grin. "Honestly, I don't know where she comes up with this stuff!"

Cam's huffing and irritation were interrupted by a vengeful growl from my stomach. I patted my belly to calm the beasts within. "What do you think of getting something to eat and doing a debrief?"

To his credit, he only looked slightly put upon to endure another meal with me when I was so obviously ravenous. "I suppose we ought to." I resolved to try to do better with my table manners this time.

CHAPTER 5

We met at the Blairstown Diner and as was becoming habit, Zackie was fed first and allowed to sleep off the day's events in Cam's truck. Once in the diner, I ordered the breakfast for dinner, since it appeared to have a fabulous amount of food. The plate came stacked high with eggs, hash browns and toast. I dug in with gusto, temporarily forgetting my resolution to improve my table manners. I was soon dabbing at my shirt, which had become stained with coffee and jam. Cam had a cheese steak with a garden salad on the side and managed to avoid looking embarrassed on my behalf.

After the meal, Cam cast his gaze about the restaurant. "Did you know that they filmed a scene for *Friday The 13th* right here in this diner?"

I slapped the table with my palm. "And the Moravian Cemetery! That's why the gate looked so familiar to me." My eyes drifted around the room as I thought over the day's events. There was a lot I didn't understand. "How come the bride did not make an appearance and why was there only one spirit in the cemetery? I would have thought that given the chance to get someone's notice, every soul on the premises would be clamoring for attention."

"Who comes through depends largely on the sibyl present and his or her state of mind."

I cocked my head. "What's a sibyl? I only know the term as a priestess and oracle in the Greek myths."

"I think that was the original meaning, but this term has been used in my family for generations to describe those with the gift. As a male in the lineage, I was always a little affronted with the sexism so blatantly displayed in this naming convention. We might be few, but there have always been males in my family who could sense the dead. I'd really much prefer a more gender-neutral term."

Obviously, this was a sore point for Cam, but I had too much on my mind to pursue this line of discussion right now. I tried to steer the conversation back to the lessons of the day. "Okay, back to what you were saying... Which one of us made it possible for John Luckenbach to come through? And also, you asked me to call out the bride. How was I supposed to do that? I don't think I have anything in common with her."

"From what I can tell, there are both passive and active mechanisms to allowing spirits to come through. When I asked you to call to the bride, this would be actively seeking out a spirit. I gave you a short description of how she would appear and the general area where she tended to materialize. Even weak sibyls can call forth a spirit if he or she knows what to look for. John Luckenbach appeared, I think, because of your state of mind. You may have lingering guilt over how you interacted with the dead in the past and your emotions resonated with his."

I nodded my head. I could not disagree with this assessment. We sat in silence for a moment while I collected my thoughts.

Cam pointed delicately at me. "Would you mind very much removing the ice cream from your hands? I find it distracting."

"Oh, sorry." I dipped my napkin in the water and began scrubbing my hands. I didn't recall eating the ice cream with my hands, but based on the evidence, something of the sort must have happened. "So, the dead boy appeared because…?"

"His most prominent emotions were feelings of isolation and a longing to go home. Perhaps you were experiencing something similar."

"Home is the last place I would want to go. I'll admit to feeling a little lonely out here in- the-middle-of-nowhere-New Jersey, but you know how it is. It's impossible to have friends who won't eventually think you're crazy. It's just easier not getting too close to people."

"Why did you join a SAR team? There is quite a bit of inter-dependency among team members in this work. You wouldn't be able to remain anonymous for long."

"It was mostly an escape from New York. I made the deliberate choice to live in a more rural area because I thought I'd have fewer encounters compared to the city. I joined a wilderness response team because I thought this would make it easier to find friends if I were in the empty woods and there was nothing to draw out my more erratic behavior." I smiled ruefully. "I didn't realize there were mutual aid agreements and we'd be called out into the suburbs and cities. It's also not like the woods were really empty, anyway." Between murder victims who were heartlessly dumped in the woods and all the lost who would never find their way out, the woods were far from empty. The deeper I ventured into the woods, the more time I spent under the trees, the more dead I found waiting for me.

Cam grunted an agreement. "So, what happened when you arrived here?"

"At first, I thought I had finally found a solution. I was left alone for quite some time before it all started up again. God, that was depressing! 'Just when I thought I was out... they pull me back in....'" I smiled sadly, mimicking the line from *The Godfather*. Clearing my throat, I continued. "Some of the dead were people who got lost and were never found, like the boy. Others were suicides who were furious that I found them. There was also a murder victim. Someone dumped her body in the deep woods. She was the only one I did something for, but it was completely unintentional. She found me as I was hiding for a dog that was cross trained in human remains detection. The dog gave his handler the alert they use for HRD and the body was found." I looked down at my hands and sighed. "Cam, I feel awful about these spirits now, what I did to make them leave me... They're still out there."

His eyes were sympathetic as he tried to give me comfort. "You did the best you could. If you remember today, there are dangers to the sibyl during interactions. I think in the absence of proper training, your instincts for self-preservation kicked in. You understood the risks of interacting with them from hard experience. Fighting them off would seem the only natural response." I looked at him gratefully as he continued. "We can maybe do something if you can recall where you encountered them. I'll consider it part of your training."

My heart leaped as I realized that we would be able to help them. "I marked them all on my GPS, so I could avoid them in the future. I can find them again!" I thought a little and then a question struck me. "Why can't we just summon them? Instead of going to where they are, why can't they come to us?"

"From my experience, there are three factors involved: time, distance and emotion. The longer someone is dead, the less chance that a sibyl can detect them. They seem to fade in time. If you think about it, you hear about the occasional Roman soldier in Britain, but it's really rare that anyone sees one of our Paleolithic ancestors." Cam began ticking off the points he was making on his fingers. "Also, the spirits are often emotionally tied to the area where they died. They can sometimes be fearful of losing contact with what remains of their bodies. So the farther away you can get, the less likely that they will follow. Also, the less likely they'll hear you if you summon them. The exception to this is if there are high emotions involved, emotions that can overcome their bonds of place. I'm sure you've had the experience of being followed. They can be awfully persistent about having their needs met and desperation can give them energy that they wouldn't otherwise have."

I was starting to fade. This was a lot of information to take in, I had a full belly and it had been a long day. Tomorrow was Monday and I had to go to work. I asked Cam how we would manage my training during a working week.

"This will be kind of like SAR at times, except employers are going to be even less forgiving for any time taken. Just like SAR volunteers, you might have to take vacation days or call in sick when you're called out. Think about it... If you tell your employer that you need to find a lost child, in general, they will tell you to find the kid on your own time. If you tell them you need to free an earthbound spirit, I think that will go over even less well. For the planned work, we can try to schedule things during your off hours."

I bit my lip. "What about your job? Our hours may not coincide. I have a bunch of part-time jobs that I have to work to make ends meet. Sometimes, I have to show up on the spur of the moment when they need someone to work some hours."

"That's one of the benefits of being a genealogist. I, of course, have to be responsive to my clients, but my hours are my own."

"Wow, don't break a nail or anything." After thinking about it for a minute, I sighed dramatically. "Sucks to be me, I guess."

Cam mimicked an upper crusty accent. "The benefits of education, my dear."

I bristled a little at that. "I am educated. I went to college. The problem is that the world does not need another history major at the moment."

He looked thoughtful for an instant. "Well, we'll

see what we can do about that."

# # #

The day started off as you'd expect for a Monday. It was cool and raining and I desperately needed coffee. In truth, it was barely Monday. Getting up at 3 AM every day to prep for and deliver my newspaper route was a pill, but aside from the sleep deprivation this sometimes caused, this was not a difficult job. The upside was that it almost paid about half my rent every month. Since the other job was waitressing in a small family restaurant, I could sort of make ends meet most months. The downside was SAR equipment. This, along with gas money to get me to training and call outs, really cut into my discretionary funds. I had no illusions about saving for retirement.

I thought about the meals I'd taken with Cam and what a splurge that was for me. If we eat out again, I decided that I would have to convince him to pay by the ounce for ready hot food from a supermarket. We could eat it in his truck or go to a park with picnic benches. An alternative might be to actually cook, but I shuddered at the thought of my own cooking. This probably accounted in a large part for my near constant state of starvation.

Going through the motions of my day, I picked up and assembled my papers, delivered them by 6:30 AM and then went back home to shower, change and eat a peanut butter sandwich. My route was relatively small, so it didn't take me nearly as long as the folks who have several hundred papers to deliver in a morning. I was at the waitressing job in time to start the breakfast shift and just kept going through lunch. I hated split shift work. I would much rather work straight through rather than split up my hours between breakfast and dinner, but I don't always get what I want and I need the hours. When I didn't get enough hours, the paper route helped fill the gap. By 3 PM, I was done for the day and feeling a bit ragged. Could be worse, could have had a call out, I thought. I grabbed some leftovers from the lunch special that the restaurant was about to chuck and headed home.

After eating a quick lunch, I put the leftovers in the refrigerator and then washed my face of the debris from the meal. I next went to see the yellow and black labs named Heckle and Jeckle. Joel Armstrong, the landlord, gave me a break in rent for walking his dogs, but in addition to the monetary incentive, I also felt kind of sorry for the dogs.

The guy was a contractor and worked pretty long hours. By the time the dogs see me, they really need to get outside to pee. Just as Heckle and Jeckle finished dragging me around the block, I saw Joel's red pickup truck pull into his driveway.

I gasped out a greeting as the dogs hauled me to the truck. "You're home early today." Joel clambered out of the truck, not bothering to close the door. He looked at me with wide eyes and ran shaking hands through his graying hair. He was pale and his dark eyes were sunken. I thought that he looked like he might throw up. "Joel, are you all right?" The dogs could sense something was wrong and scrambled to be close to him, pushing the tops of their heads against his legs and whining. He finally squatted down and pulled the dogs to him, hugging them tightly and breathing heavily. I dropped the leads and just stood there uncertainly.

"I'm not all right." His voice was muffled as he pressed his face into his dog's fur. "I may never be all right again after that…"

"What's happened? Did someone on your crew get hurt?" Joel was a big man and usually pretty easy going. He was not someone who was easily shaken or intimidated.

Seeing his reaction, I was starting to get really concerned.

"No, nothing like that... at least, I don't think so." He sighed and looked at me with worried eyes. "You're not going to believe me."

"Try me. I've had my fair share of weird. This might not be as bad as you think."

Collapsing to a sitting position on the ground, Joel kept the dogs near him and began to explain. "We were working on an old house in Changewater. We're doing this one for free for that organization that builds homes for people who can't afford a place to live. We put in a few hours every day to get the place renovated and ready for move in. Nothing like this has ever happened before." Joel looked at me desperate for understanding, so I nodded my head for him to continue. "We were working on the oldest part of the house today – a stone farmhouse built back in the early eighteen hundreds. We're making the house handicap accessible and we were installing a wheelchair lift on the stairs to the second floor. The guy who's gonna live there is an Iraq War vet and he lost both legs to an IED. His wife is going to have a baby in a few months, so we wanted to have the house ready for them when the baby comes."

My impression of Joel just ratcheted up a few notches. I always thought he was a decent guy, but the work that he was doing really spoke to his true character. I knew enough not to say anything about what I thought, since it would just embarrass him. Instead, I just nodded again to let him know that I was following what he was saying and asked him to tell me what happened next.

"It started with this awful smell. It was so bad that the guys weren't even making fart jokes. The smell was like something dead and rotting, but worse. We opened up the windows and door to try to vent it out and that's when we realized that it was warmer outside the house. The room was freezing. We could see our breath inside, but if you went outside, it was cool but not freezing. We were a little freaked, don't get me wrong, but the guys on the crew are tough mothers and we promised that we'd have that house ready in few weeks. Everyone just got back to work. Me and a few of the guys started trying to find the source of the smell, so we could clean it up and make the house nice for the family. That's when things really went to hell."

Joel took a shaky breath and began to unconsciously rub the flanks of Heckle and Jeckle, who were nestled close to him. He swallowed visibly before going on. "We followed the stink upstairs and the light wasn't so good up there. We're working on the wiring, but there's no power up there right now. Anyways, it was pretty dim and we start looking around, just following our noses, so to speak. In front of one of the bedrooms, I notice these tiny footprints on the floor. The floors are still nice. They got those wide plank floor boards original to the house and they just need to be refinished and they'll look good. So, the planks are white pine and they're light colored and the little footprints are dark. They really stood out. I bent down to take a closer look and touched one. It felt sticky and I swear to God, it smelled like blood to me. The little footprints led into one of the bedrooms and the door was shut, but the footprints just kept going. If I was a smart man, I would've stopped right there and got out, but no, I had to freakin' open the door to take a look. Al was right behind me and he saw it too." He paused for a moment staring into the middle distance. When he continued the story, he began talking faster and faster. "There was this little girl, maybe three years old and dressed in a little white night gown, but the side of her head was caved in and there was blood all over her hair and it was dripping on the floor and she was crying, 'Papa! Papa!'" Joel stopped and put his face in his hands and rubbed hard, pulling on his short beard. The dogs began nuzzling his face, trying to stick their noses under his hands, all the while trying to lick the pain away.

When he finally looked up, his eyes were red and pleading. "What am I going to do? Even if I could get my crew to come back to work on it, I can't let them put a baby in that house. And how am I gonna explain that?"

My reflex reaction was to get angry. Here he was trying to do something nice for someone else and he was made to suffer for it. He was practically begging for my help and I knew that this was something I could do for him. I was built for this. I knew I could fix the situation. But then I thought of the dead boy. Was something similar happening to the little girl? I admitted to myself that based on my history, I really lacked the insight to handle this properly.

I heard myself say, "Listen, Joel, I know this guy who might be able to help you. Let me give him a call."

# # #

Standing outside the stone farmhouse a few hours later, we all agreed that Joel did not have to go back into the house. He would unlock the door for us and then just stay in his truck and wait for us to come back out. Zackie's nose twitched first at the house and then at the surrounding area. Even Cam looked a little worried, as he scanned the fields around the house. Everyone but Joel could feel it.

I kept my eye out for a graveyard because that would be a good explanation for why we sensed so many dead in this place. Not seeing anything, I finally asked Joel if there was a cemetery nearby or maybe a small plot for the family who built the house and cared for the land.

He shivered involuntarily. "Nothing I know about." As he fumbled for the key, my eyes swept the fields and empty windows of the house. "Found it. Here you go." He handed me the key and then walked briskly to his truck. Cam, Zackie and I approached the front door of the house and let ourselves in.

As I eased the door shut, we lost what little light we had from the setting sun and the house became dark. We turned on our flashlights to survey the room. The wheelchair lift lay in pieces near the bottom of the stairs, but nothing else seemed to be in disarray. The atmosphere felt charged, but the rank odor that Joel complained about was absent. The air was definitely dank, but not fetid.

Looking deeper into the foyer, I was distracted by quick little sounds of something small slapping on the floor upstairs.

Cam cocked his head. "Do you hear that? I hear the patter of little feet upstairs, like a running child. Lets go upstairs and have a look."

Just as I was about to agree, we heard the sound of a commotion outside. I opened the door to take a peek and saw that several cars had pulled up, including a red Nissan. "Cam, I think we have company." A camera crew was setting up and Joel was out of his truck, speaking to another man on the front lawn of the house. Off to the side, I could see Lucas fiddling with an electronic contraption.

"Damn it!" Cam brushed past me through the door. Zackie followed him out and went straight to Lucas, immediately slamming her muzzle into his crotch. Apparently, this was the greeting she reserved especially for him.

"Crap!" Lucas said as he twisted to dodge another greeting. "Would you call your dog off?"

Cam ignored the command and instead went on the offensive. "Just what do you think you're doing?"

"Let me explain," Joel interrupted. "Al over here called these guys in. He heard they were filming over at the Moravian Cemetery and thought they could help."

Lucas looked at Cam and me. "And why are you two here?"

Joel shrugged. "I asked them to come to help. Fia said Cam had a way to clean the house of the ghost. I gotta keep the renovation on schedule for the family, so we're ready when the baby comes. I don't have time to waste on this, so I don't care who does the clean up. Either or both of you guys can do the work."

Lucas narrowed his eyes at us as he listened to this. I glared back. I did not want this clown dealing with the little girl in the house. As I was about to weigh in with my recommendation on how to proceed, the text alert went off on my phone and simultaneously, Cam's phone gave an alert.

Cam gritted his teeth as he looked at his phone. "We have another call out. Perfect damned timing…" Checking the text, it said that our teams were needed to locate an overdue hiker at Merrill Creek Reservoir. The missing woman was an epileptic and it was possible that she had a seizure somewhere on the trails.

"I have all my equipment in my trunk." I pulled out my car keys and started walking. "I'm going straight to staging."

"Me too. I'll meet you there." Cam turned to Joel and spread his hands helplessly. "Joel, sorry, but our SAR teams are needed to find a hiker. We'll be back in touch directly, once the search gets sorted out." As we left, I saw Cam give Lucas an uneasy look. I felt the same way, but there was nothing we could do, given the situation.

CHAPTER 6

Arriving at staging, we dressed for the woods and equipped ourselves with packs and lights after signing in. The briefing indicated that the missing woman's name was Marina Rosenfeld and she had been out for a day hike with a friend. Lucy, the friend, was waiting anxiously on scene for news of Marina. I could see their car near the front of the parking area. It had been surrounded by flagging tape to prevent anyone from accessing the vehicle.

Cam and Zackie had been tasked with determining which trail Marina may have followed. I was added to the task to flank them. According to Lucy, she and Marina stopped outside of the visitor center when she noticed a broken shoelace on her hiking boot. She told Marina to go ahead and she would catch up, since it looked like there was only one trail to follow from that location. When Lucy had finished adjusting what remained of her shoelace to make it work well enough for a short day hike, she hopped on the red trail and entered the woods only to discover that it quickly diverged into a red trail and a blue trail. Lucy called out and received no answer. She next tried to call Marina on her cell phone to ask which trail to take, but Marina did not answer. It was discovered later that Marina had left her cell phone in the car. Lucy tried following the red trail and did not find her friend. She back tracked and then took the blue trail, again with no results. It was still early, so she figured they'd meet up at the car when it was time to head home. When the sun started setting and Marina had still not appeared, Lucy became worried and called 911 to report what happened.

Cam approached Lucy and introduced himself. "Has anyone been in the vehicle besides you and Marina?"

"Just the cop who came after I called 911. It's Marina's car, so he wanted to look in the glove compartment to see if she had taken her meds with her. He also checked her cell phone for emergency contacts."

Cam nodded and then asked another question. "Did you or Marina drive?"

"Marina usually drives, but today I drove her car part way because she needed to take a call from work."

Cam turned to me and asked if I could find Lucy's cop and bring him to the car. I headed to the visitor's center where they had set up incident command and after asking around, located Officer Jakes. We returned to the car and found Cam and Lucy still talking.

Cam broke off his conversation with Lucy and began to fill us in. "Lucy says that Marina had a number of seizures in the last year. I think it's likely she's had another, so she may be out there and incapacitated." He pointed to Zackie and explained what was going to happen. "Zackie is going to show us which trail Marina took, but to do this, she needs to know Marina's scent. Since the car and pretty much everything in it have been touched by both of you, she'll need to rule you out. I'm going to give her an acclimation circle around the car and then let her sniff both of you. I'll then put her in the car and tell her to take scent. When she comes out, she'll take us along the route Marina took."

Officer Jakes looked at Cam with naked admiration. "Damn! You mean to tell me that dog can subtract?"

"Indeed, she can." Cam proceeded to carry out his plan and when Zackie emerged from the back seat, Cam took her in a circle around the vehicle. When she hit

Marina's scent she took off, pulling Cam behind her. Leaving the police officer and Lucy behind, I trotted after the canine team and radioed in that our task was departing.

Zackie and Cam headed towards the back of the visitor's center and then made a beeline for the trail head. We followed the red-blue trail southwest towards the reservoir and then broke right to follow the blue trail northwest. After a short distance, we found ourselves near the ruins of the old Cathers farmhouse. All that was really left was a stone foundation that was protected by a split rail fence. Zackie suddenly stopped dead and raised her head, scenting the breeze and turning towards the stone foundation.

"Uh oh." Cam looked uneasy. "This is not Marina. This is Zackie's version of crittering." Cam unhooked Zackie from her harness and we both looked intently towards the ruins of the farmhouse, reaching out with all of our senses to find the cause of Zackie's distraction. A shadowed presence close to the ground loped out of the darkness. It was not illuminated by our headlamps and it came directly to Zackie and then lowered itself in front of her. We could now make out the shape of a dog and as Zackie touched the shadow with her nose, more features became evident to us. The face had a black and tan mask that was framed by short, floppy ears. The fur was short and mostly white with a black saddle, but the frame was too lean. This was an old dog with a gray muzzle and wasted muscles. It was also clearly not a living dog.

Cam put out his hand. "Hand me the radio." I gave him my radio as I watched the ghost dog in wonder. Of all the dead I've encountered, I've never seen an animal spirit.

"Incident Command, this is Task 11. Do you read me?" After getting confirmation that IC received his transmission, Cam continued. "Our dog has lost the scent. We were following the west side of the blue trail. We're currently at the Cathers farmhouse. Send in an air scent dog to check the east side of the blue trail. We'll take a break and then try to recover the scent trail from where we are."

Turning to me, Cam handed back the radio and then tilted his head towards the old dog. "This will be a challenge for you. Animal thoughts are not like human thoughts. Tell me what you sense."

I concentrated on the black and white dog and after a very long minute, I finally got something. "He's alone. His owner left and he stayed and waited. That's all I'm getting."

"Not bad. Try to see the owner through the dog's eyes."

Closing my eyes, I forced my perspective to be closer to the ground. Instead of sight, I 'saw' scent and this crossover of senses really confused me. The scent made me feel like home and gave me a sense of safety and security. The dog definitely craved the scent. I caught earth and livestock in the scent and the feeling of happiness. The scent then changed and I sensed something else that was familiar, but stronger than in the dog's past. Gun powder? I thought I sensed gun powder and then all the scent went away. Shaking my head, I told Cam what I experienced.

"Very good. You'll get better information the more you do this." He nodded his approval and then launched into the dog's story. "So, Sam over here was the resident farm dog many years ago. His owner enlisted to fight in the Great War. I got a sense of the uniform, so I think this is correct. He was dressed as a doughboy. To prepare for the fight, the man did quite a bit of target practice with his hunting rifle before he left for basic training. That's why you sensed more gun powder towards the end of the read. The man never returned from the war. I assume he was killed in action. Sam grew old waiting for him to return and eventually passed. He will not leave here because he continues to wait for his master."

"Can we do anything for Sam? Or is he going to have to stay here waiting forever?" I watched as Zackie groomed the new dog like a puppy. Sam made soft, mewling sounds and I felt sorry for him, but I didn't know what to do to help. He had been here for such a long time.

"Zackie will take care of Sam, don't you worry," Cam said. I bent down and ruffled Sam's ears. It felt odd. I sensed fur, but there was almost a static charge against my hands. I stroked his face and wished I had someone in my life who was that faithful.

As I pulled back to give the dogs some room, there was a sudden crashing through the woods and Merlin emerged, his bell clanging brightly. He sniffed briefly at Cam and me and then gazed at Zackie and Sam before retreating back into the woods. We next heard five short barks and some more crashing sounds. In short order, Merlin re-emerged from the woods with Steve and a flanker in tow. Keeping his head low, Merlin made his way to Zackie and delicately licked her muzzle when they made contact. I saw Sam's ears perk at this, but otherwise, he didn't react and just remained lying at Zackie's feet. It was odd watching Merlin's gentle behavior when there was such a size disparity between the two living dogs. The Belgian Malinois breed is a favorite of the police and military, so I was expecting a more assertive presentation. I also found it interesting that while Merlin had acknowledged Sam, there was no interaction.

"Oh, it's you guys," Steve said. Turning his attention back to Merlin, he thumped the dog's flank in approval. "Good boy, Merlin! Go find another!" I watched as Zackie touched Merlin with her nose, releasing him to go do his job. Steve kept an eye on Merlin's path as he ran off again and then looked back at us. "How's it going?"

"We're good, just taking a break." I reached for my water and took drink. "We'll try to recover the trail once Zackie reboots."

"Okay, let me go catch up with Merlin. I'll see you all later." Steve forced his way through the brush as the flanker reporting Task 14's new heading to IC.

I watched as Steve and his flanker departed."If Marina is out there, Steve and Merlin will find her." Cam just nodded. While this was reassuring for the search, I think we both felt slightly disoriented by the constant distractions and interruptions we were experiencing. "ADD anyone?" I shook my head slowly from side to side. "What do you think the odds are of finishing just one thing tonight?"

Cam sighed his agreement. "Let's just stay put a moment and let Zackie sort this out. Have a seat." Cam sat down with his back to a tree and I followed suit. We watched as Zackie continued to minister to the old farm dog. As she licked and murmured, I could see her strip away the years. The gray muzzle began to darken and the dog's frame filled out. The muscles on his back legs became strong again and his eyes cleared. Amazed, I saw Sam grow younger and younger until he became a fluffy black and white puppy. Sam yipped at Zackie and put his hind end in the air, punctuating his joy by furiously wagging his tail. Nudging him first with her nose, she picked him up by the scruff and carried him off.

"Look away," Cam warned. I averted my eyes just as the bright white light blazed behind me.

Smiling broadly, I looked to where the portal had been. "Wow, that was worth the price of admission!"

Cam grinned back at me. "Truer words were never spoken." He stood up and hoisted his pack. "Let's continue on the trail and see if we can spot Marina. Zackie will catch up."

Walking slowly down the trail and looking closely into the brush, we made our way past the old farm house. Every few steps we called out for Marina and gave her a chance to answer. As I checked a muddy area for evidence of footprints, I queried Cam about Zackie's history. "Where did Zackie come from? I know she's been with you for a number of years, but was she ever a puppy?"

"For as long as I've known her, she's been as she is." He paused for a moment to think. "That's going on thirty years now. She came to me from an old woman who lived in the hills of North Carolina. Lummie was what they called a sin-eater."

"Sounds ominous, but just about right for someone who associates with Zackie." My monkey brain engaged and I cocked my head at him. "So, tell me, what's a sin-eater? And why were you in North Carolina?"

"I was looking for relatives. A number of Scots ended up in North Carolina after the Rising in 1745."

"But I thought you were British! You don't have a Scottish accent."

"Ramsay is a Scottish surname. I grew up in the Cotswolds and that's in England. Anyway, back to Lummie. Lummie was a sin-eater, so she would attend funerals among the hill folk and consume a ritual meal that took away the sins of the departed. This was done so they would not walk after death. The lifestyle pretty much put her on the outskirts of that society, even though it was really Zackie who kept the dead from walking."

"Was Lummie a sibyl?" I asked.

"Yes. She was also a distant relative of mine, so this was not surprising to me. Zackie had been with her since she was a girl and she was near ninety when we met."

"How did Lummie and Zackie get together?"

"Zackie had been passed down through the female line in that family for many generations. As far as I could tell, Zackie originally came to the New World around 1760 with the Plott brothers and a slew of Hanoverian Hounds. Johannes and Enoch Plott were the sons of one Elias Isaac Plott, who was master of hounds for a local aristocrat in the Black Forest of Germany. Seeing no real future for

Johannes and Enoch in the Old World, Elias counseled them to depart for the American colonies and make a new life for themselves in a new world. Depending on who you believe, the boys were either gifted with hounds upon their departure or they simply helped themselves to some dogs from the baron's kennels on their way out." Cam gave a conspiratorial wink as he continued the story. "Either way, they set sail for the New World laden with dogs. Enoch did not survive the journey, but Johannes made it to North Carolina where he bred these hounds with native stock to arrive at today's Plott Hound. For a while, they were known as Plott Bear Hounds. Their ancestors had hunted boar in the Black Forest, so their strength was in hunting big game and both bear and boar were plentiful in the hills. Lummie's line married into the Plott line and somewhere along the way, Zackie became something of a family heirloom."

"So, Zackie is originally German?"

"Well, the Germans have the bargeist, meaning spirit of the funeral bier. It's supposed to be a monstrous nocturnal dog with huge teeth and claws. Anyone who saw it would die soon afterwards. I think Zackie has been around for a long, long time, and Germany might be somewhere more recent in her travels. One of the oldest gods of Egypt is Anpu, the Jackal God, Guardian of the Veil and Guide of the Soul. I can't help but think Zackie had some involvement there."

I guess my face must have screwed up and betrayed my thoughts, because Cam just said, "What?"

"So, Zackie is this immortal creature pretending to be a search dog and she goes around sticking her nose in people's crotches? There's something of a contradiction here."

"The world is full of contradictions. I've stopped being disturbed by this. And Zackie does not just pretend to be a search dog, she is actually quite good at it. She works hard at trailing, in fact. I think one of the problems with being immortal is that you have to continually find ways to keep yourself entertained. This is probably why we joined SAR. I think this is also where the crotch business comes in. I'll wager she finds it funny."

I considered this as I searched the underbrush and deer paths for any sign of Marina. As I crouched down to shine my flashlight along another muddy patch, the radio crackled and announced that Task 14, Steve and Merlin, had a find. We held our position and waited to find out the subject's condition and if a carry out was necessary. As Task 14 requested a stokes basket and a team for carry out, Zackie appeared out of the woods and joined us on the trail.

The radio crackled as IC tried to reach us. "Task 11, Command."

"Go for Task 11," I replied.

"Proceed to coordinates and join Task 20 for carry out. Prepare to receive coordinates." The speaker paused to give us time to respond that we were ready to record the location. "Coordinates: Easting 491951.7 Northing 4509822.1. Read back and confirm."

I scribbled down the UTM coordinates on the pad I carried in my chest harness, read them back to IC for confirmation and then advised IC that Task 11 was clear from the communication channel. Plugging the values into my GPS, I determined our heading and began walking with Cam and Zackie to the location of the subject.

By the time we arrived, Marina had been secured by straps into the stokes basket and volunteers were taking up positions for the carry out with three to a side. Each person was partnered with someone of similar height to make the ride as smooth as possible for the subject. As the team moved out, Cam and I began clearing brush and obstacles that could trip the litter bearers. The progress was slow, but sure. When a woman of about my height raised her hand to request respite from carrying the litter, I came in behind her, grabbed the handle near her hand and tapped her on the back to let her know she could release the basket and move away. She replaced me in clearing the brush, while I now helped to carry Marina back to the visitor center.

Just as I began to settle into the rhythm of the walk, a man at the front of the litter near the subject's head suddenly cried, "Drop right!" I was on the right, so I dropped to my knees and did my best to immediately bring the edge of the litter down to the ground quickly and gently. Those on the left tipped their side of the litter up and held it in position so that Marina was now on her side, but still held in place by the straps. She was vomiting and would have choked had the command not been given. The man who told us to drop was speaking soothingly to Marina as he cleared her mouth and cleaned her face. When she was ready, we righted the litter so that she was again resting on her back and we continued the walk back.

When we reached IC, the EMTs from the

ambulance took over and Marina was prepped for the ride to the hospital. Lucy was right at her side and I could see the relief wash over her. With the search completed successfully, we debriefed and signed out, each of us heading to our vehicles. All in all, the search had been quick and efficient. It was only 10 PM and while I envied the folks who didn't have to get up until sunrise, I was happy to get what sleep I could before I had to work the paper route again.

Before I managed to stuff my gear in the trunk of the car, Cam tapped me on the shoulder. "Let's talk with Joel tomorrow to see how things fared with Lucas and his toys."

"I'm off work at three tomorrow and Joel usually comes home around five or six. Let's aim for a debrief with him around seven, okay? I'll slip a note under his door before I turn in tonight."

Cam nodded his agreement to the plan and ambled off to his own vehicle. Zackie was already making herself comfortable in the back of the truck, unperturbed by the night's activities and the things left undone.

#

I stretched luxuriantly in my bed and tried to relax into a sleepy state. My belly was full of the second round diner leftovers and I should have felt drowsy. No good. I flipped and tried again. Still no good. I was too keyed up from the search and sleep was evasive, so I did what all the experts on insomnia rail against: I turned the TV on and tried letting the droning of the broadcast lull me to sleep.

Just as I my eyelids started to droop and I could feel the pull of sleep, I heard a familiar voice. "While we tried everything at our disposal to make contact with the ghost of the bride…" I immediately sat up, wide awake again. This was the end of the show Lucas had taped on the weeping bride ghost. When I heard him end the commentary with, "Sometimes, this is the way investigations go and you just have to roll with the punches," I waited for the credits to roll, but then realized that he wasn't done yet. "But sometimes, investigations become more interesting with a reanalysis of events," he continued. "Watch this infrared footage of the church's graveyard. Keep a close eye on the upper right area of your screen and you'll see an orb that our investigators captured."

At the word "infrared," I grabbed my phone and hit

the speed dial for Cam. "Cam! Turn on channel 38 – hurry!" I watched as the infrared footage was looped again and again with arrows drawn in and pointing to the small flash of light. While it was confusing to me why high tech gadgetry could not capture the magnitude of light released from the true event, it was infuriating to me that Lucas dared to use this footage without our consent.

"Baah-stard!" I heard Cam yell over the phone.

I was too riled up to be amused at his choice of pejorative. "This guy is really starting to piss me off, Cam." I watched again as the scene looped a final time. "The only good thing is that no one can tell that's us in the clip."

"Well, this time, anyway. There's no telling what Lucas is willing to do for ratings. He knows we'd probably only sue as a last resort, because that would just bring us to the attention of the media. Even if we tried filing anonymously, I don't have faith that our identities wouldn't be leaked. The show is too popular and journalists can usually find a way to get information. "

I took a slow, deep breath and then blew it out. "So, what exactly are our options?"

"Avoid him, if possible. The problem is that we've

piqued his interest. Between the Moravian Cemetery and the Changewater house, he won't just chalk it up to coincidence." Cam yawned mightily over the phone. "I'm going to bed. There's nothing we can do about this right now."

CHAPTER 7

When I returned from my paper route, I found a response from Joel slipped under my door. Appended to the note I left him the night before, Joel had scribbled a request to meet at the Changewater house at 7 PM. Before taking a shower and changing, I sent a quick text to Cam to let him know where we'd meet that evening. I had no doubt Lucas was still on the job and we'd run into him. I spent the entire day at the restaurant spoiling for a fight and my tips took a nose dive. I could not wait to confront that twerp.

Arriving at Changewater that night, I saw Cam had gotten there first. Fortunately, there was no sign of Joel or any of the other construction guys. Cam was yelling at Lucas and appeared to be absolutely livid. I got out of my car and walked to his side, presenting a united front.

"And this is in no way legal! Do you know for how much we could sue your show? Not to mention you personally?" Cam yelled. His face was red and his fists were bunched at his sides.

"So, sue me," Lucas responded. He was leaning against his car and picking at his nails. His eyeliner was perfect. It was clear he saw through the bluster and knew that Cam and I would not risk exposing ourselves to the media by bringing a legal suit.

"We don't have to sue you," I retorted. "What makes you think there aren't other ways of evening the score?"

"Well, you'd have to be careful about that," Lucas said as he reached into his car to pull out some sort of ghost hunting device. "Cross the line and I will sue you. We'd all get attention from the media and I'd get free advertising for my show. Same result for you and I'd get some giggles out of it."

"I will clear the area wherever you want to work," I told him. "You'll never get anything on film again to entertain your viewers and your ratings will plummet."

Lucas tilted his head and raised his eyebrows as he looked at me. His unqualified skepticism was unmistakable. "Oh, please, be my guest," he said.

I could feel the color rising in my face and my jaw clenched. This was the last straw. I spent my life trying to avoid letting people know about my abilities. The one time I speak honestly about it and this guy dismisses me as a fraud or a liar. Cam saw the brewing storm and tried to prevent any more revealing statements, "Uh, Fia, I don't think—"

"You don't believe I can do it?" I screamed at Lucas.

"I don't believe anyone can do it!" Lucas roared back at me. "This stuff isn't real! There are no spirits of the dead waiting to be either interviewed by me or banished by you!"

"Whoa, you don't actually believe that the dead come back?" I was stunned. "You're deliberately lying to your viewers! I cannot believe that you'd exploit a basic human fear of death to make profit!" I gaped at him, staggered by his admission. "People may have lost someone or may be dying and they watch your show because they're desperate for hope. How can you take advantage of vulnerable people like that?" In some ways, I felt jubilant to expose him like this, but in other ways, I felt disgust. This was the most cynical thing I've ever encountered.

"I never lie to my viewers," he said in a more normal volume as he fought to regain control. "I show them exactly what the instruments produce. They draw their own conclusions. I have never, never told anyone that an instrument reading is evidence of a ghost." I could almost hear the missing sentence, that there's a sucker born every minute.

I looked at Cam and he looked back at me with a mirror of my own expression. We were both shocked and too disturbed by Lucas's callousness to speak. Anything for ratings, anything for money and he had the perfect alibi. The silence stretched, more uncomfortable than the screaming had been. Joel pulled up just in time to fill the conversational void.

Joel climbed out of his truck and looked closely at each of us, as if he could size up the amount of discord based on facial expressions. "What's happened?" Joel asked. "Something's not right…"

"Just a minor disagreement," Cam replied.

"Feels kind of major, if you ask me," Joel said.

Trying to defuse the situation, I turned to Cam and said, "I thought you were going to go all Monty Python on him."

"What is that supposed to mean?" Cam asked, quirking an eyebrow at me.

"You know, call him a malodorous heap of parrot droppings… Or tell him that his mother was a hamster and his father smelt of elderberries."

"You're too young to know those skits," Cam said with a slight smile.

"Apparently, I watch a lot of subversive television."

"If you'll all excuse me, we have a lock down to do," Lucas interrupted.

"What's a lock down?" asked Joel.

"We're going to lock ourselves in the house and prevent anyone else from entering. We'll record whatever happens without the possibility of contamination from unknown persons," Lucas explained.

"I suppose that sounds reasonable…" Joel hesitated. "Are they going with you?" Joel indicated Cam and me.

"Why not?" Lucas replied. He was smirking and appeared pleased by Joel's suggestion. What better footage could he get than unwilling subjects forced to participate in his sham operation?

Cam considered that smirk for a moment and then said, "I think we're better off investigating the outside of the premises. We'll leave the interior, for now, to Lucas and his team." Lucas shrugged and motioned to his crew to join him in the house. I went with Cam to his truck to retrieve Zackie.

As Lucas and his team shut and secured the front door, I turned to Joel and said, "If you have a moment, we'd like to hear about your experiences with Lucas so far."

"Not much to tell, really. Lucas poked around the house yesterday and took a bunch of readings with his instruments. Nothing happened worth mentioning."

"Did he in any way try to provoke the spirits?" Cam asked. "You know, did he yell insults or do anything in the house to try to anger them?"

"No, it was all pretty quiet," Joel said. "He just walked around and took readings. I honestly thought there'd be fireworks or something yesterday. I know what I saw, but nothing like that happened to him. That's what I told my crew and it made folks feel better about returning to work today."

"And nothing happened during the work day?" I asked.

"Not a thing. No smells, no cold… everything seemed pretty normal. Maybe Lucas fixed something with his gadgets."

"No, I don't think so," Cam said as he scanned the fields. "Let's head up the road a bit."

"I don't think anyone needs me for anything and I'm okay with never seeing anything like that little girl again. I'm going to head home. I'll to talk to you all tomorrow," Joel said, climbing back in his truck.

Preoccupied by what we sensed across the field and up the road, we gave Joel a distracted wave goodbye. As he went on his way, we also took to the road. Zackie had her nose in the air and based on her behavior, she was scenting strongly what we could sense weakly. As we got closer to whatever was drawing us all forward, Zackie quickened her pace and became more animated, emitting a series of low whines and projecting a sense of urgency.

"The more duress experienced by the dead, the more anxious she becomes to rescue them," Cam offered. "She does not abide their suffering."

We eventually reached a depression in the ground about a hundred yards from the house. As I leaned over to take a look, the depression became a pit and I was struck by a sense of double vision. It was making me dizzy and I quickly sat down before I fell.

"Cam, I'm seeing two things at the same time. There's a slight depression in the ground and there's also a pretty deep pit. I can't tell which one is real," I said as I rubbed my eyes.

"All right, keep a grip on your reality. Concentrate first on the slight depression. See only that when you look straight on. Only allow the pit into your vision if you look peripherally," Cam advised. I did as I was told and was soon able to discern a body lying face down at the bottom of the pit. "The pit is from the past and what the dead man remembers."

"Oh, no… he's hurt!" I said. Zackie had leaped down into the pit and was gently nosing the man who lay in the earth. I could hear him moan and saw blood ooze from various gashes. The back of his head had been crushed by a heavy blow and there was little of it left. He was unable to see and was in horrible pain, but he kept trying to push himself up. "My wife… my child…my wife, my child," I repeated, compelled to convey his thoughts as his distress crystallized in my mind.

"Poor man….he's been struck multiple times by a hatchet," Cam said. Zackie was working hard to nose her way under the man to try to lift him or to get him to hold on to her. We watched to see if the man could get himself up by clinging to Zackie, but he soon collapsed back into the pit.

"Maria and Mary need help," I repeated as the man moaned and tried again to get up. "What can we do, Cam?"

Cam climbed down into the pit, somehow mastering the contradiction in perception between our time and what the dead man perceived. I could only watch him out of the corner of my vision. I felt useless, but I could not make the images diverge if I looked at them straight on. It was as if I existed in both times simultaneously and the sensation was akin to a fast drop on a roller coaster. I was really starting to feel nauseous with this constant shift in perspective.

Breathing deeply, I kept my eyes trained on the horizon, only peeking to the side as my roiling gut would permit. I watched as Cam tried to turn the man over. His ruined face had one eye that was still intact and it was pleading with us to help Maria and Mary.

"Maria and Mary have gone over," Cam said as he held the man. "You need to follow them. Zackie can take you to them."

"No, still here…need help… save them…" I intoned, repeating the man's thoughts. His mind burned with the need to save them. If his body were whole, he would have walked from this grave to find them, but his spirit perceived the damage his body had taken and it could not rise from where he died. He was condemned to lie here, repeating his dying thoughts over and over again. We had to do something. Tears of frustration were running down my face and I needed his pain to end.

"Can Zackie take him?" I pleaded with Cam.

"He won't go," Cam answered. "He is adamant that Maria and Mary are still here."

"What can we do?" I repeated.

"Nothing right now," Cam said. "I need to figure this out. This will not be an easy one." Cam climbed out of the pit and I felt the weight of the man's despair as Cam left him. Zackie stared hard at us and stayed by the side of the man. I could hear her barking loudly and incessantly from the pit, clearly frustrated by our failure.

"I'm sorry," Cam said to Zackie. "There is nothing I can do here and there is still at least one more out there," he said as he pointed across the field. "Please be reasonable!"

Zackie continued to grumble, but she touched the man once more gently on his shoulder to let him know that this was not over before leaping from the pit. Leading the way across the field, she did not make eye contact with either of us. I wiped my face and exchanged a look with Cam before stating the obvious. "She is really pissed." He just nodded as we both followed Zackie across the field.

We walked silently for almost a mile until we reached the road. At the crossroads where McCullough and Changewater Road intersected the Asbury – Anderson Road, we came to a halt. All was quiet, but we could sense a disturbance. It was full dark now and I reached into the side pocket of my cargo pants to pull out a small, but powerful flashlight. This was one of the perks of being

SAR – ready for anything and I had the equipment to prove it. The flashlight beam cut through the darkness like a fine, steel blade and I was able to quickly survey the roadside. Cam had put on a headlamp and was doing the same.

Slightly pulled back from the road and within a stone's throw of a residential area, our lights hit upon a low marker. We soon discovered an identical marker only a short distance from the first. Walking to the objects, we shone our lights down to get a good look. Both markers were roughly rectangular with a gentle arc near the top that softened the shape. The inscription on the first marker read *Peter W. Parke 1813 – 1845*. A smudged shadow sat between the years. Cam shrugged his shoulders and we walked closer to the second marker to have a look. This one read *Joseph Carter Jr. 1813 – 1845* and where the first marker bore a smudge, this one showed a small metal wreath.

"What are these graves doing here on the side of the road?" I asked. "Maybe there used to be a family farm here? But the dead men aren't related – they have different last names." I looked around with my flashlight. "And where is the rest of the family buried? These are the only markers."

"If it's not a family graveyard, what is this?" Cam said as he looked back and forth between the markers.

As we stood there trying to figure out the meaning of the graves' location, we both heard a loud and emphatic *No!* emanating from some point behind us. Whirling around at the sound, we saw Zackie standing in the middle of the road. She was poking her nose first left and then right at something. I immediately thought she had found some road kill, but that did not jive with the sound we had heard. Jogging to her location, the flashlight's beam bounced around erratically in front of me and I was thankful that there was no traffic. Cam arrived seconds later and we both stared at what Zackie had found.

Two dead men lay side by side. As Zackie urged them with light touches of her nose to stand and leave this place, we again heard the word *No!* and this time it was certain where the noise had come from.

"Peter and Joseph?" Cam asked. I could feel the acknowledgement and a certain relief that they were recognized and not forgotten. Cam looked from the dead men to the markers and then said, "They moved the markers, but left the bodies when the road changed. These men are buried beneath the road."

"And they won't listen to Zackie because they need us to right this situation?" I asked, but just as the words left my mouth, I knew this was not the source of their anguish. "Okay, so it's not about proper burial…" I concentrated, but only got a jumble of emotions, from regret to fury and rebellion, but lacing through it all, there was a deep sense of injustice. I could not make sense of what I was feeling from them and I shook my head to clear their emotions from my mind. I looked helplessly at Cam and said, "I'm not getting anything that I can understand. I don't know how to help them."

Cam edged closer to the dead men and closed his eyes. Glancing at me, he gave a small shake of his head to let me know that he was also baffled by what he read from them. Staring intently at the dead men, he studied them closely for several minutes. Finally, he looked back up and said, "These men were hanged. I can see rope burns on their necks and the cant of the head is wrong on both of them."

"That would explain why they are buried at a crossroads," I said. "The people of their time would not allow someone who was executed to be buried in hallowed ground. They were kind of vindictive, as if execution were not punishment enough. Burial at a crossroads would also bring constant disturbance from travelers and not allow those executed to rest in peace."

Cam nodded and added, "And perhaps they weren't guilty of whatever crime brought them to the gallows. If that's the case, then I can understand why they would feel such a strong sense of injustice." Tilting his head as he thought, he continued, "But what are we supposed to do about this? The crime took place so long ago that there is really no hope of justice at this late hour. We can't un-do the hanging and realistically, we're not going to be able to name the true guilty party. How are we going to get them to move on? They are hell-bent on staying."

Zackie began to whine anxiously as she walked in agitated circles around the dead men. Cam stared at his feet and his shoulders slumped. I relied on him as my mentor and if he didn't have a solution, I didn't know if one could ever be found to remedy this situation. Feeling defeated, I hung my head.

"Maybe we should – CAR!" I said as I spotted headlights in the distance. Moving quickly, Cam and I made our way back to the side of the road and stood next to the markers. Zackie took off to the other side of the road and I sensed that debilitating flash of light that signaled her departure. "She left us?" I asked Cam.

"I think she's feeling pretty lousy after tonight's work and she needs to lick her wounds," he said to me. "I wouldn't worry about her. She'll come back in her own time."

Staring at the inscriptions again, I commented, "Both men died in the same year and were buried next to each other. I think it's obvious that whatever happened to them involved both of them. They were probably both hanged for the same reason. Something this exceptional should be easy to find in the historical record."

Cam nodded and scrubbed his face with his hands. "This is at least a starting point... Look, it's getting late and so far tonight, we've been pretty useless. Let's call it a night and reconvene tomorrow. I think we need to start fresh."

"You're right. Let's go home," I said. I turned back towards the field and walked along slowly with Cam, trying to shake off the stink of defeat. Tomorrow was another day and maybe if we understood more about what happened to the two men buried at the crossroads, we could at least help them to find rest. There was nothing solid in my thinking and I felt pretty unsettled by the lack of anything definitive. Just as I was about to ask Cam about doing some library research tomorrow, a sound roared through my head. Falling to my knees, I clapped my hands protectively over my ears. Cam was still standing, but he also held his hands over his ears.

"Bloody hell! It's coming back," he screamed over the noise. As I felt it whip back toward us, the roar increased in volume and both Cam and I were knocked flat to the ground with the impact of its presence. "Fight it!" he screamed at me. "Get up and fight!"

He did not have to tell me twice. Every nerve was on edge and I was itching for a fight after being thrown to the ground. It was frighteningly easy to revert back to my old ways. I gathered the force in my hands and feeling for the presence, I slammed it with everything I had been repressing since I started working with Cam. I could feel it stagger back, but I still could not see it. When Cam hit it, I felt it totter. On the heels of this strike, I immediately sent out another bolus and hit it again as hard as I could and I could feel it go down and then, just as quickly as it had come, it was gone.

Panting and bending forward with his hands on his knees, Cam said, "You are so much better at that than I." I tried to smile, but the adrenaline was still rushing through my body, so the best I could do was grimace. Sitting on the ground sweating and panting with my head between my knees, I tried to recover.

After a moment, I finally gasped, "I've had a lot of practice."

"We need to get out of here. Whatever that was could come back," Cam panted. He straightened and began to walk stiffly toward the house. Staggering upright, I caught up to him and we limped back together, both of us with our guard up and breathing heavily.

"What the hell was that all about?" I whined at him when I at last caught my breath. "What happened to the gentle approach? I thought it was all about singing Kumbaya and holding their hand and then they'd go away." Unfairly, I was blaming him for the feelings of cognitive dissonance that were swamping me.

"I never said that," Cam said quietly. He was subdued and seemed deeply disturbed by everything that had transpired during the night, so I did not press him. In all honesty, as confused as I was by how we dealt with that last entity, I had used up my reserves and I was done for the night. Exhausted from the confrontation, my only thought was that I needed to get home. Conversation right now would help no one.

When we reached the house, everything was dark and quiet. The red Nissan and the crew cars remained nearby, so I assumed that the lock down was still in progress and nothing of significance was happening. "Not my monkeys, not my circus," I again muttered to myself. Apparently, floating around in my tired mind, this was the catch phrase associated with Lucas. I mumbled a quick goodnight to Cam, fished the keys out of my pocket and walked to my car.

# # #

The next morning, I managed to deliver the newspapers, but I was still a mess from the previous night's fiasco with the entity in the field. I had a killer headache and generally felt weak, so I called in sick to the restaurant. Crossing my fingers that someone else could cover for me, I said a quick prayer that I would be able to manage without the day's pay. That done, I immediately fell back into bed and went to sleep.

A few hours later, I woke up feeling slightly better, but still a bit woozy. The headache continued to pound away and I rubbed my temples. Dehydration and calorie deprivation, I thought, and so went about trying to fill my belly. I was fortunate to find some eggs and cheese in my refrigerator, so I fixed an omelet and made some coffee. Feeling much better after eating, I picked up my phone and was about to call Cam when feelings of uncertainty from the previous night began whispering in my ear. I put the phone down again. Had he been withholding information about the true nature of the lingering dead? If so, for what purpose? Another possibility was that he just had things wrong, he was not the expert I took him for and it would be dangerous for me to continue learning from him. I pressed my fingers on my eyelids as I thought. My head continued to throb, but blocking the light helped a little. It was clear that we needed to meet to figure out the mess from last night. It was also clear that my interactions with the dead were significantly more controlled under his tutelage, so despite my current misgivings, my gut feeling was that I should continue working with Cam. What was not clear to me was why I was led to believe that my actions in the past took completely the wrong approach, only to be encouraged to regress to this behavior last night. Perhaps I was being too simplistic, thinking that a 'one size fits all' approach was the lesson Cam was trying to teach. Sighing, I hit the speed dial to call Cam.

"Hmmmph," he said when he answered. I was not the only one feeling under the weather.

"Don't go anywhere. I'll be right over," I told him.

Twenty minutes later, I pulled into his driveway. The house was small and non-descript with white vinyl siding that looked crisp and clean in the late morning sun. Tempering the sterile white, blue-gray shutters surrounded the windows and a matching door completed the look of a tidy, well-kept house. Just as I was about to lean on the doorbell, Cam pulled the door open and stepped aside to give me entrance. His eyes were bloodshot and his face had a sickly pallor. I could faintly smell the fumes of alcohol leaching from his skin. Zackie stood at his side and was also not herself. Her head hung down and her tail drooped noticeably.

"You're drunk," I accused Cam as I entered the house. The rooms I could see contained the bare necessities and were absent of both decoration and the normal clutter expected in a home. It was so much like my own rooms that I could not help but notice.

"Nonsense. I was drunk last night. Today, I am hung-over," he mumbled as he closed the door and headed left into his kitchen. "Coffee? You can have the next pot. This one is mine," he said as he poured a huge white mug full with the steaming liquid. While he perched on a stool at the counter and cautiously sipped the coffee, I started the next pot brewing and hunted through his cabinets for another mug. Zackie lay on her belly nearby with her chin on the floor and looked up dolefully at us. No one does that mournful look like a hound.

"Is that your coping mechanism? Drinking?" I asked while I searched.

"Very rarely, but it tends to be a good start," he replied.

I grabbed another white mug and sat on the stool next to Cam. He looked at me out of the corner of his eye. "Don't worry," I said, "I'm not going to lecture you for something done 'very rarely.' Whatever gets you through the night…"

"And what got you through the night?" he asked.

"Plain and simple exhaustion," I said rubbing my temples. "I can't stay awake long enough to do anything that might help alter my consciousness." I folded my arms around myself and leaned forward. With my heels planted on a rung of the stool, I slumped into what must have resembled a fetal position. The stool felt hard and not quite uncomfortable under me, but I felt secure that at least I would not fall back to sleep. When I saw the carafe had finally filled with the dark liquid, I got up, poured myself a cup and took a moment to swallow a healthy mouthful before sitting again. Cam's coffee was excellent. I sat there inhaling the aroma and getting a caffeine buzz.

"You have some coffee..." Cam said and pointed to his upper lip. He handed me a paper napkin from the countertop and continued while I wiped absently at my face. "I think the events from last night took a toll on each of us," he said. "She probably had a worse night than either of us," he mumbled, thrusting his chin toward Zackie. "In addition to the expected wear and tear following an encounter, you seemed pissed off before driving away. Would you care to enlighten me?" He looked at me with concern and waited for me to respond.

Cam's direct approach took me by surprise and my hands involuntarily balled into fists. I consciously opened and flexed my hands and took a deep, steadying breath before I spoke. Even with preparation, I did not succeed in controlling my temper as I vented my frustration. Looking Cam directly in the eye, I said, "I took you on as a mentor and I completely accepted your version of things. I was made to feel like shit for dealing with the dead as I had. I was working hard to reform myself. But then last night, the dead seemed to be in need of an ass kicking. So, maybe I'm not quite the asshole you made me out to be." Cam's concerned expression never wavered and the anger went out of me. He was not playing me. He was acting in good faith and he did not deserve my harsh words. Hunching my shoulders around my mug, I ducked my head and hid my face behind my hair. I did not want to look at him. I stared at the dark liquid instead as I tried to express myself in what I hoped were more gentle words. "Look, I had the sense from you that most of the time, the dead need only a small prompt to help them to move on. I was also under the impression that I had handled things badly my entire life and that there was no need for me to use force. Am I wrong on both counts?" I asked.

There were a few moments of silence following my

rant, so I peeked through my hair to see if Cam was now in turn angry with me. His eyes were downcast and he appeared to be thinking. Maybe he gripped the empty coffee mug a little tightly, but his posture was relaxed and he did not otherwise seem agitated by my outburst.

"I'm sorry that I gave you the impression that you need to do penance," he finally said. "Let me say it plainly for you… You are not to blame for how you handled things in the past. You did the best you could under the circumstances." He blew out a breath and continued, "The core of this work is improvisation, because what we encounter resists easy classification. Your approach is not always wrong, but it's mostly wrong. Let me get some more coffee and I will try to explain." Cam stood up and shambled over to the coffee machine, pouring the remaining liquid into his mug. As he sipped, he gazed into the middle distance and mumbled to himself, "Where to begin…" I waited patiently in silence as Cam put his thoughts together.

"As in life, so in death," he started. "Think of this as the guiding principle. In life, we have free will to make decisions for ourselves, for the good or the bad. The dead cannot be forced to pass over. They must freely consent to this act. In general, it is in their best interest to move on, but have you ever tried to convince a living person that something was in his or her best interest? You need to select just the right argument to convince them and even then, it may take some time if they are not yet ready to commit to change. In general, there is something unresolved – an action, an emotional conflict, a trauma – that holds the dead paralyzed in this existence. If you can provide them with some sort of resolution or completion, Zackie can accomplish her task and escort them to the other side."

He paused and took another sip of his coffee as he considered how to proceed. "As for your previous *modus operandi* for dealing with the dead, yes, it is usually unnecessary to thrash them into submission. If I were to assign your behavior to an analogous situation in life, you would be the tough guy in a bar who beats people to a pulp for the smallest of offenses. In that particular context, your behavior is viewed as antisocial in the extreme."

I flinched at this comparison and a reflex argument formed on my lips. In some ways, I must have agreed with him or I would not feel so guilty about everything. Instead of arguing, I turned to face him and said only, "Go on."

Cam took a breath and continued. "I believe that I will ultimately be able to convince you not to indulge too frequently in a little bit of the old ultraviolence," and here he winked at the reference to *A Clockwork Orange*. "Given our encounter last night, I think I start to see you more as my slightly misguided bodyguard. I have never seen a power like yours and, used correctly, it could be life saving. So, back to our guiding principle... If someone is a bastard in life, unless there is some epiphany that leads to a sudden conversion before death, it is likely that he will also be a bastard in death. I think this is what we're dealing with for that entity in the field. For those singular bastards, a rapid and forceful response is not only acceptable, it is highly recommended if we are to survive."

"A few more questions," I interrupted. "Has something like this ever happened to you before?"

"Nothing so intractable. I have had stubborn spirits in the past who refused to depart until some issue was resolved, but the solution was usually fairly obvious. And definitely never two in a row who were steadfast in remaining earthbound."

I closed my eyes and started rubbing my temples again. This was like a specialist doctor telling you that he's never seen anything like your symptoms before. What you want to hear is that what you have is routine and he's cured people with this same disorder hundreds of times before.

After a while, I paused in my ministrations and asked, "Have you ever seen so many of the dead in one place? In all my experience, I have encountered them one entity at a time over a much longer timeframe than what we saw yesterday." I shrugged my shoulders and added, "It's almost as if they have their own territories or maybe they're waiting in line to see me."

"Last night was an anomaly," Cam said nodding. "One at a time with a break in between – that's the usual occurrence." Turning from the counter, Cam faced me to gauge my reaction as he said, "I have a theory that we're like a power source to them. I think they may be in a stasis until they encounter a sibyl or someone with a little bit of power that they can draw from. Once they are animated, they pursue whatever their particular obsession may be. But like a battery, we run down with use, so another entity is unable to immediately draw from us, leaving us with the scenario of a single entity appearing at a time."

"This makes sense to me. This stuff drains me like nothing else," I agreed.

"I think maybe when the two of us work together, we have a gestalt situation and we are able to animate more of the dead across a shorter interval of time because of it." Tilting his head to the side, he added, "Just another theory. We'll see if it bears out." Cam paused and rubbed his face with his free hand. Closing his eyes briefly, he sighed and then continued, "Right then. Just as in the SAR world after a mission, we should debrief. To sum it up, we had multiple disincarnates in a small geographic area, one of whom was extremely violent. We failed in every respect to send any of these spirits on to the next world."

"So, why do you think we failed?" I asked. "What could we have done differently?"

Cam's brows knitted as he thought and he chewed his lip. "I wish there was an easy answer," he began, "but I don't think that there was anything that we could have done to make this work. I do think that this problem is complex and it's going to require some thought and digging to properly understand it before we can work out a strategy on what we're supposed to do to right things."

"That's what I was afraid of," I said. "It would be a whole lot easier if we had just made a mistake last night and we could go back and fix it." I took a moment to rub my gritty eyes as I thought. "If we accept that the dead originate from the limited area associated with their death, the spirits we encountered yesterday at least died in close proximity to each other. Now, is that just geography or also temporal?"

"The hanged men were definitely associated temporally based on the dates on their markers." Cam paused and then asked, "Do you think what's going on in the house and the three dead men are somehow related?"

I tried to recall the details from last night before answering. "I don't know what era the little girl is from, but the three men wore similar clothing and could be from the same time."

"It would be a huge coincidence, don't you think? It would be more plausible that three separate events occurred that led to three separate hauntings. The past was fairly violent and it wouldn't surprise me if death stalked that place for different reasons."

We both went quiet for a moment while we thought. I glanced at Zackie and she was now sitting up and staring at us expectantly. You'd think we had food that she wanted. Just as she stood up and began to stretch, Cam broke the silence.

"Let's do the easy thing and start with the internet," Cam suggested. "I loathe the mold and dust when I'm forced to dig through some town hall's archives. For the most part, I find that it's possible to make serious progress using online tools. We have names and dates from the markers and that should get us started."

Zackie and I followed Cam to his study and I was struck again by the similarities in how we lived. Our homes were controlled areas and this was probably a common thread for people like us. We had few possessions and little clutter in our lives. The only exception to that rule was the SAR equipment nestled in my trunk. Every other aspect of my life seemed unintentionally designed to present as little disorder and distraction as possible. Given the entropy that the universe threw my way on a regular basis, maybe my brain just needed a break from the chaos and so, subconsciously, I kept things simple where I could.

Cam took up his position in front of the laptop and adjusted the rolling office chair to a suitable distance from the desk. Zackie curled up under the desk and yawned mightily at us. The room had a futon and one overstuffed beige chair that had seen better days, but I was happy to relax into it after balancing on the stool for so long. Cam booted up his laptop and after about a minute, a handful of icons organized themselves on the screen. Cracking his knuckles, Cam set to work and double-clicked on an icon that looked like a sinuous dragon. "I'm pulling up a search engine that will access a genealogy database that I use for work," he told me. Typing quickly, Cam entered in the text fields Peter Parke's name and the years that bound his short life. In less than a second, a page appeared with a picture of the marker we had found near the crossroads and a short biography of the man.

"He was indeed executed by hanging," Cam said. "The crime was murder and it looks like a pretty gruesome tale."

Peering over his shoulder, I read out loud, "Hanged for the Changewater axe murders, which occurred on the evening of May 1, 1843 in and near the home of John B. Parke." Scanning the write up, I confirmed that Joseph Carter was named as his accomplice.

"Look here," Cam pointed to a paragraph on the screen. "According to this bit, the guilt of the two men remains doubtful. Even in their time, the public was not convinced of their role in the murders, but they were hanged anyway at the Belvidere Courthouse on August 22, 1845."

"I don't think they did it. Nothing slipped through in their thoughts that even remotely suggested that they were guilty of murdering anyone," I said. Cam just nodded at this. He also didn't get anything from the hanged men to make him think that they were axe murderers. Something that dramatic would be hard to hide from us.

"Let's see if there's any information on the Changewater murders," Cam said as he brought up another window to do an internet search. Typing in the town's name and the word 'murders' brought up nothing relevant, just a write up on the history of Changewater. We tried all the synonyms for murder and still came up empty.

"Go back to the link for the history of Changewater. Maybe it had another name in the eighteen hundreds," I suggested. We pulled up the article and found that Changewater was the oldest town in Washington Township and had used this name at least as far back as 1769. There was just no specific information on the murders that we could get from an internet search.

"We know when the murders occurred and we

know when the men were executed. We should be able to pull up some information from old newspapers," Cam said.

"Okay, so we go to the library and start digging through microfilm?" I asked standing up.

"No need for that. I have access to a newspaper archive online for the genealogy work," Cam said. I sat down again and made myself comfortable. "You have no idea how much easier life became for me when we entered the digital age." Cam clicked and typed some more and I let my mind wander. The next thing I knew, I was awakened by my phone signaling an incoming text. Poking groggily at my phone, I accessed the text. My landlord was in the ER and he needed me to feed his dogs after their afternoon walk.

"Cam, I think something happened at the house. Joel is in the ER. He just texted me to help with his dogs."

Cam looked up from the computer monitor with a worried frown. "Let's go," he said. "I will tell you about the murders later."

CHAPTER 8

Cam was searching through a milk crate packed full with various small items when I pulled up next to his truck and parked. It was mid afternoon and we were still hours away from drive time traffic, so I had made good time getting to the hospital after stopping to walk and feed Heckle and Jeckle. Zackie stood at Cam's side nosing briefly at the items as they dug through an assortment of neatly coiled leashes, flagging tape, orange webbing tied in a daisy chain and other things that were pushed aside too quickly for me to identify. The whole collection had a faint odor of insect repellent, which I surmised must also be in there somewhere.

"Ah, there it is," he said as he pulled out bright red dog vest from the crate. As he fitted Zackie into the vest, the words 'therapy dog' showed in large letters on her flanks.

"You're kidding me, right? She's not a trained therapy dog too!" I said shaking my head in disbelief.

"Well, it's not unheard of for a search dog to also be a therapy dog. Do you know K9 Simber?"

"The Shepherd-Husky mix? She's a trailing dog, right?"

"Yes, that's the one. She's also a therapy dog. Her handler takes her to VA hospitals to cheer the veterans," Cam informed me. "As for Zackie," he said as he lowered his voice and gave a conspiratorial nod, "let's just say there are times when it is convenient to appear to be a therapy dog." Cam finished adjusting the vest and then said to her, "I'll call you when we're ready." He then straightened and walked the two steps to my side, turning me away from the dog just as the blinding light flashed. "It's more convenient this way," Cam said to me as he led me to the emergency room entrance. "Zackie can come to us once we're past any check in point where we'd need credentials. We'll need her if anything followed Joel from the house."

I felt my hackles start to rise the closer we got to the building. Hospitals were a no-go zone for me because of all the confused souls and without Zackie to shield me, I felt vulnerable to attack. Biting my lip, I stayed silent, but my gut was clenching as my muscles took over the blood supply. Everything I looked at came into sharper relief as my body prepared for a fight. Cam could sense my unease and he paused, grasping me by the arm. "Hoy, stand down, Fia," Cam said. "Visualize a cage around yourself, like the shark cages divers use. The dead can pass around you, but they cannot get to you." I did as he said, concentrating hard on making the bars of the cage thick and plentiful. When I had created an unbreakable cage, I nodded to him. "Right then," he said and we continued to the ER entrance.

The reception desk was staffed by a middle aged woman who had a calm, capable demeanor and appeared to be the epitome of efficiency. When we asked her where we could find Joel Armstrong, her fingers flew around the keyboard as she accessed his information. As we waited for her to review the output, a biker staggered by us dragging a broken leg. He was carrying his helmet and blood was dripping steadily from his mouth. His left side was an exposed mess of road rash and deeper wounds. I averted my gaze to give him no reason to notice me, but I felt guilty about it. The nurse at last informed us that Joel had been admitted to the hospital. We were provided with a bewildering set of directions that we were assured would bring us to the reception desk of the main hospital.

"I hope he's all right," I said. I began to chew on a cuticle as I looked for the landmarks the nurse had described, while strategically avoiding eye contact with the wandering souls. "I hope…" But I let the thought trail off because I was helpless to do anything for these souls.

"They don't all need our help, you know," Cam said softly. "The biker is only momentarily confused. He'll find his way." Gazing at the spirits who milled about in the hall, Cam said, "These too. Some of them will take a little longer to adjust, but none of them are stuck."

After a few false turns, we found ourselves at last at the main reception desk. The irony of having trained search and rescue workers lost in this labyrinth of hallways did not escape me.

As if reading my thoughts, Cam grumbled, "We should have taken the flagging tape from the milk crate to mark our way."

We were told by the receptionist that Joel was in the cardiac unit and he gave us visitor's passes and another series of instructions to reach that area of the hospital. As we set off again, I allowed myself to hope that it was an unrelated cardiac incident and that I was working myself up for nothing. I went back to chewing on my cuticle and looking for landmarks.

"At last," Cam said pointing down a long hallway. "Those must be the elevators to the cardiac unit." I pushed the up button and we waited patiently for the elevator to arrive. We had the good fortune of having the elevator to ourselves on the ride through the upper floors. Just as the elevator doors began to open and we prepared to exit, Cam whispered, "Zackie, now," and the three of us stepped smoothly from the elevator. I had to admire his technique. If there were security cameras on the elevator, there would be no record of Zackie coming up with us. The staff on this floor would assume that we had proper clearance for a dog, since we had made it past the main hospital reception desk.

We made our way past the nurses' station without incident and followed the room numbers down the hall until we reached Joel's room. I peeked in to make sure that he was not asleep or otherwise occupied and that it would be okay to enter. The room was a double and another patient was watching television behind the separating curtain. Joel looked up at me with surprise and greeted me with a warm smile. He seemed genuinely pleased to have visitors, so we stepped into the room and approached his bed. The muted colors of the walls and the bedding did little to create a sense of comfort. It was just gloomy and depressing in the room. Zackie was twitching her nose at the scent of disinfectant, which appeared to be used liberally on the floors and in the bathroom, but there was no overt reaction that a discarnate had attached itself to Joel.

"How are you feeling?" I leaned on the cold railings surrounding the bed as I looked him over. Joel had an abrasion that was darkening into a really standout bruise along his right cheek and temple. More concerning, he was wearing a heart monitor tucked into the front pocket of a blue standard issue hospital gown. The wires crept from the pocket over the neckline of the gown and disappeared under the fabric.

"Not too bad, everything considered," Joel answered. "They're keeping me overnight just as a precaution."

"What exactly happened?" Cam asked. His brow was creased with worry and mirrored my own feelings.

Joel cast a glance towards his roommate and lowered his voice. "The shit really hit the fan today.

Whatever you guys did last night riled things up in the house." Cam and I both winced. Anything that Lucas unleashed in the house with his shenanigans wasn't really our doing, but we felt responsible nonetheless. Lucas was really starting to grate on my last nerve and I was going to give him an earful the next time I saw him.

"I was the first one at the site," Joel continued. "I thought it would be safe to work inside by myself after you guys had been through the place." He gave us a slightly accusatory look before going on with the story. "The house felt really cold again and that should have tipped me off. I was trying to ignore it because we got that deadline to move the family in, so I started mounting the chair lift to the stairs, but it just kept getting colder and colder. I was hell bent on working through it, but then the stench started up and that was hard to ignore. I was about to take a break when I saw a shadow out of the corner of my eye. Nothing too bad, just something flitting across a wall." As he said this, Zackie lifted her nose towards the door and someone who belonged in the morgue walk by and continued down the hall. Tugging on her lead, Zackie pulled Cam out the door.

"Sorry, I'll be right back," Cam said as he stumbled

after her.

"What's that all about?" Joel asked.

"I think there's someone they know who walked by," I improvised. "Please go on. What happened after you saw the shadow?"

"Nothing much at first. I went and I propped the door open to get some fresh air in the house. I was just standing in the doorway taking a smoke, when something went flying and hit me in the head. I went down and then… and then…" Joel rubbed the tender flesh on his temple as he tried to remember what happened next. "I think it was the tools that it threw. It was something heavy... I kind of remember the sheetrock on the wall near me getting wrecked. The guys found me outside. My head was bleeding, so they called 911. I must have dragged myself out of there before I passed out."

Cam and Zackie reappeared and came to the bedside. "What did I miss?" Cam asked.

"There was some poltergeist activity," I said. "Joel got hit by a flying tool. The crew found him and got him to the emergency room."

"I should have been good to go," Joel said. "It was just a thump to the head, after all. I guess the stress had got to me and my chest started to hurt while I was waiting to see a doctor. That pushed me straight to the front of the line and I ended up here." Joel waved his hands expansively at the hospital room. "My dogs okay?" he asked after a pause. "If they don't let me out tomorrow, I'm going to need you to take care of them until I get out."

"Heckle and Jeckle are fine," I said. "Don't worry about them. I'll walk and feed them until you're back home." I looked at my feet and said, "I'm really sorry you got hurt, Joel. That shouldn't have happened."

"Naaah," he said waving his hand dismissively at me. Ever the tough guy, Joel said, "I've had worse." As a sign of trust that warmed my heart, he followed up with, "You guys gotta keep working on that house. They always blame the contractor when things get behind schedule and I got a reputation to uphold. Do your job, so I can do mine. Deal?"

Cam and I shook his hand and agreed that we would not give up.

# # #

Heading towards the elevator after wishing Joel a good night's sleep, Cam was again yanked along as Zackie suddenly changed direction towards a door leading to the stairway. We followed her down two flights of stairs and into another ward before she slowed in front of one of the rooms. Glancing in, I saw a pale woman. Her head was bald and she lacked both eye lashes and eyebrows. Stark blue veins were clearly visible around her temples through nearly translucent skin. She was lying limply in the bed with her eyes half closed and a man was holding her hand as he leaned against the safety rails.

"I'll get you some ice chips," I heard him say as he turned from the bed and moved to the doorway.

He was not wearing the eyeliner or the Goth clothes and it took me a moment to identify him. "Lucas," I said as I recognized him. He looked up and at first, I don't think he saw me. He was disoriented and had a look of abject misery etched into his face. As soon as he recognized me, his eyes hardened.

"What are you doing here?" he demanded looking from me to Cam. "This is private. You need to leave." He planted himself solidly in the doorway, protectively blocking our view of the woman.

Cam and I stood dumbfounded, not knowing how to respond to his hostility under these circumstances. Like deer caught in the headlights, we continued to stand there frozen for another beat as Lucas glared at us. Zackie finally ended the spell by grabbing the lead with her teeth and freeing it from Cam's grip. She pushed past Lucas, entered the room and went straight to the woman's bedside.

Lucas was first surprised, but then furious. "You get that dog out of here!" he hissed at us. "Can't you see how fragile she is?"

As Lucas stormed towards Zackie intent on grabbing her collar, Zackie balanced her front paws on the edge of the bed and shoved her nose under the rails and into the woman's hand. The woman started and looked up to see the source of this new sensation. Seeing the dog, she smiled and gently touched Zackie's head.

"No, please Lucas, let the dog stay," the woman whispered. Lucas immediately dropped his hand and stepped back. "Would you please get me some ice chips?" she asked him.

"Okay, Hannah. Just be careful with that dog," Lucas said as he inched towards the door, his eyes locked on Zackie. Grabbing Cam by the arm before he went through the door, he said, "You stay here and keep an eye on that dog. Don't let it hurt her."

Cam nodded and put his back against the wall, staying in the room as requested, but staying out of the way. After a moment of standing there awkwardly, I followed Lucas down the hall to the ice machine to apologize to him. I found him near the machine leaning with his back against the wall and his face in his hands. Hearing me approach, he looked up and I could see how exhausted he was. Lucas was a different person when he wasn't dressed for ghost hunting. He was just a guy with a huge burden to carry and, at the moment, all the fight had gone out of him.

"She's the reason I do it," he said to me.

"Do what?" I asked.

"The show. I do the show even though it's a load of bullshit." He scrubbed his face again and then looked at me. He was so tired. "I was trained as a real scientist, you know. I have a Ph.D. in pharmacology. I'll never be able to

153

work in that field after this show ends. I've lost all credibility."

"But you do the show because of Hannah?" I prompted.

"The drug regimen she's on is experimental. The insurance company won't pay for it. She's failed every other course of chemotherapy they tried." He sighed and a tear trickled from his eye. "The show pays for her treatment. I have to keep the ratings up no matter what or she's going to die." He looked at me with desperation in his eyes. "The drugs are helping. I know they're helping." I heard the plea in his voice and then he sobbed, "She's my wife... I can't lose her." Lucas buried his face in his hands and wept.

I touched his shoulder and tried to comfort him. Lucas didn't want comfort. He wanted me to confirm what he said, that she was going to get better. With all my heart, I wanted to give him these reassurances, but I thought about how Zackie went straight to Hannah. I was sure that Hannah already belonged to her, but I could not tell this to Lucas. I was unable to lie and I could not tell the truth. Instead, I did the best I could. I grabbed some paper towels from the counter near the ice machine and handed them to

Lucas and then looked for a way to give him a moment to regain his composure. Turning towards the ice machine, I took a Styrofoam cup and placed it under the dispenser. Keeping my eyes on the machine to give Lucas some privacy, I pushed the button for chipped ice and filled the cup. When I turned back, he was almost back to normal and I handed him the cup. He nodded his thanks and walked down the hall back to his wife.

I followed slowly as I thought about what Lucas had told me. By the time I reached the room, I still had come to no conclusions, other than that I needed to talk to Cam about it. Zackie was now on the bed lying close to Hannah, who lay quietly with her eyes closed. Lucas stood near the nightstand where he had deposited the cup of ice. His mouth was set in a thin line and his arms were crossed, but because Hannah had her arms wrapped around the dog, he said nothing. Glowering at Cam, he shot his eyes from the dog in the bed to the would-be handler. Cam shrugged his shoulders, dismissing the silent accusation and did nothing to remove the dog. Under different circumstances, the pantomime would have been amusing.

"What's her name?" Hannah asked, her eyes fluttering open to half mast.

"She's called Zackie," Cam answered.

"I like Zackie," she murmured. "Will you let her visit me sometimes?"

Cam looked at Lucas and said nothing, only raised his eyebrows. Lucas closed his eyes and exhaled briefly. At last, decision made, Lucas spoke up. "Sure, Hannah. Zackie will come to see you. How about you get some rest now?"

"Okay," she said and closed her eyes again. After a few minutes, her breathing became regular and her arms went limp. Zackie slowly eased herself up and then gracefully moved from the bed without disturbing her.

We all stepped into the hallway and Lucas drew the door partially closed behind him. He motioned towards a lounge at the end of the hall and we quietly followed him to the collection of comfortable chairs and sofas. Lucas collapsed into a chair. Hunching forward, elbows on his knees and his hands folded in front of him, he stared at the ground and avoided looking at us for a moment. Finally, he turned his gaze up as we took seats on the couch opposite him.

"Will you come back with Zackie? For Hannah?" he asked, a tremor in his voice and his eyes pleading. "You have absolutely no reason to do anything for me after how I treated you…."

"Of course we'll come back," I interrupted him.

Cam nodded his ascent. "Hannah told me that your show pays for her treatment. I know this is not your chosen profession."

A muscle in Lucas's jaw twitched and he looked steadily at Cam before replying. "It's not a sacrifice."

It was Cam's turn to look away. "All I'm saying is that I understand why you aired the film clip. Now that the reasons for your actions are clear, I'd like to offer to help."

My eyes widened a little at this proposal. "What are you saying, Cam?" I asked slowly. It was all well and good for Cam to go public, but my family could not be given a way to find me. I might have been thinking along the same lines myself earlier, but things were moving a bit too fast suddenly.

"What I'm saying is that we can allow Lucas to film us, provided that he distorts our voices and obscures our faces. We can't have people know our identities." I breathed a small sigh of relief at this requirement. Cam turned to Lucas and asked, "Will you agree to that, Lucas?"

Lucas considered the plan for a moment and then nodded. "This could work in our favor. The public might be drawn in by the idea of mystery psychics. Whatever you are doing, it is active and attention-grabbing and will keep people watching. I think the format of the show has gotten stale and something new like this could perk people's interest again." He paused and glanced at each of us before saying, "I have some ground rules too, if this is going to work. I have no right to ask, since you're both doing this out of kindness, but I could not accept your generosity without getting agreement on this."

"Go ahead and ask," Cam said. "We need to know now if this is at all feasible."

"I know you two believe that you are somehow interacting with the great beyond. You know that I do not believe in any of it." We both agreed that this was true, so Lucas went on. "I feel strongly that the viewers be told only the objective truth. There will be a multitude of interpretations of what is seen on the screen and I don't want to lie to people by giving them a single, self-serving analysis of the data. It would be so easy to say that every anomaly is attributable to a ghost. The viewers might eat that up. I would know better. You can't control for everything and all sorts of noise in the environment could distort a reading...." He let his thoughts hang for a moment. Opening his hands, he said, "I just don't want to lie. That's important to me."

"Take the footage and use it however you see fit," I said. "You be the narrator and interpreter of events. It's maybe best all around if what we do can never be concretely pinned down to something paranormal."

"Okay, looks like we're on to something," Lucas said. "I'll see about getting you guys some kind of salary for your efforts. It won't be anything much, since the budget has already been set."

"We weren't expecting compensation, but I'm certainly not going to turn it down. Something is always better than nothing," I quipped with a huge smile on my face. With zero expectations for pay, this was a windfall and might help ease some of the constant strain of trying to make ends meet.

Cam looked thoughtful. For a moment, I thought that he was going to decline, but eventually he said, "That's very generous of you."

Lucas lowered his eyes, maybe still feeling guilty for unauthorized use of the film footage. "Let's start with the Changewater case."

"We should probably fill you in on recent events," I offered as I thought about Joel. "Something happened in the house this morning." Just as I was about to say more, my stomach grumbled like a grizzly bear coming out of hibernation, so I suggested we grab some dinner and talk.

CHAPTER 9

"I think we both know that helping Lucas won't save her," I said as I took a big gulp of my beverage. To soothe my caffeine and sugar jones, I had ordered a large coke while we waited for Lucas to show up. He had wanted to make a last check on Hannah before leaving the hospital. If it weren't for us, he probably would have stayed there all night watching her sleep.

"Yes…. But Lucas needs saving. He's on his last legs," Cam said. Sipping his coffee, he added, "Let's at least take the burden of the show off of him."

"Sorry I kept you waiting," Lucas said as he approached the table. He pulled out a chair from the small round table and sat down heavily. His face was drawn with fatigue and he gave my coke a look of longing.

We made small talk after the waitress took our orders. Once the food arrived, there was no time for discussion as I tucked in and filled my belly with fries and a cheeseburger slathered in ketchup. Lucas, unfamiliar with my eating habits, paused in the middle of his meal to gawk. At some point, he must have decided that staring was rude, cast his eyes to his own food and resisted looking back until the meal was finished. I was simply too starved to be embarrassed.

Cam automatically handed me a pile of napkins as he began telling Lucas about Joel's experience. "What went on in the house last night, Lucas?" he asked. "You didn't… provoke the spirits, did you?" Cam's mouth turned down as he posed the question.

A faint smile tugged at Lucas's mouth and he immediately suppressed it. Was he amused at Cam's distress at taunting something that did not exist, but he wanted to be polite? Lucas paused for a beat and then said, "No, that wouldn't make good television. The viewers would think we were harassing a little girl. It wouldn't play well, so we just went from room to room taking instrument readings and trying to record EVPs." I nodded to myself. Lucas was sticking to the facts from his perspective and not drawing attention to the differences in our opinions. After he drained his coke, he asked, "Are you sure Joel didn't just get spooked by something and hit his head in a panic to get out?"

"No, that wouldn't be like Joel," I answered. "He's a tough guy. He doesn't spook easily. I once saw him at a dog park step between his labs and a huge, really nasty dog that was trying to pick a fight. The other dog had its teeth bared and hackles up, but Joel didn't flinch."

"We were told that the flying tools destroyed the sheetrock near the front door. We can check it out to make sure Joel remembered this accurately. Any damage to the wall could not be attributed to just his imagination," Cam added. Lucas just shrugged his shoulders, obviously not convinced by either of our statements, but not willing to debate the matter. He was probably just cataloging our reports, so he could script the next show in an enticing way.

"You might want to film the two graves we found last night," I said to give him some fodder.

At this, he perked up and tilting his head, he said to me, "Do tell…" So, I told. He was intrigued by the hanged men, but felt that the man in the pit could not be adequately substantiated in some way for the audience. Overall, I thought that he was accepting our impressions and observations as another piece of data, but it was clear that he was having trouble giving much weight to this type of evidence.

"Maybe if you reference the historic record in addition to what your 'mystery psychics' found, that will fill in the story for the viewers," Cam suggested. Directing his gaze at me, he said, "I was able to get the full history of the axe murders just before we ran off to see how Joel was doing, so you haven't heard this part yet."

"Do tell…" I prompted him, tilting my head and mimicking Lucas.

"At the time, they called this the crime of the century," Cam began as he settled into telling the story. "In the modern vernacular, it was a home invasion. On the night of May 1st in 1843, some person or persons went to that house in Changewater and murdered four people. Three bodies were found in the house and one person was murdered outside. They were all killed with a hatchet or axe." I shuddered a little at this. Actually seeing the wounds on the man in the pit did not allow me to have any distance from the story. I ought to be immune to brutality by now, but it still got to me.

"Was this just a random act of violence or was there a motive?" Lucas asked, leaning forward. Taking out a small notebook from a back pocket, he began jotting down notes.

"It's believed that the motive was robbery. The man who owned the house, John Bowlby Parke, earned his living investing in real estate and loaning money to his neighbors at interest. He was known by the community to have stashed a substantial sum of money in the home."

Lucas was thoughtful for a moment and then asked, "Did either Peter Parke or John Carter owe him money? That could also have been a motive. Maybe they just didn't want to pay up."

Cam shook his head and responded, "There was no mention of any debt owed to John Parke by either of the hanged men. But that is a good point. Anyone who owed money could have been a suspect." Yawning widely, he covered his mouth with one hand and signaled for the waitress, lifting his empty coffee cup with the other. "That's the crux of the problem," he said after she filled his cup. "There were probably a lot of possible motives beyond robbery that were never considered. And without these alternative motives, how many suspects were ignored? The more I learn about the case, the more I am convinced that this was a rush job and two men were railroaded into a conviction."

"What caused the rush?" I asked as leaned an elbow

on the table and propped up my head up. It was getting harder to keep my eyes open. "Were they afraid that there would be more murders?"

"No, nothing that innocent," Cam said. "The bloodlust started during the burial of the murder victims. The funeral was held at the orchard at the back of the house in order to accommodate the crowds. The caskets were afterwards transported by wagons to the Mansfield cemetery." Cam's eyes narrowed as he retold the story and his mouth compressed in distaste when he paused. The tale disturbed him, but we needed to understand what led to this miscarriage of justice.

"Some years earlier," he continued, "the Mansfield Church had split into two congregations, some worshipping in Bethlehem and others in Washington Township. To avoid arguments among the surviving family, the reverends from both churches were asked to officiate at the funerals. Each one tried to outdo the other in convincing the crowd that the guilty party stood among them." Cam shook his head in disgust and took another pause to fortify himself with more coffee. I stole a glance at Lucas. He was caught up in the story and had stopped taking notes.

"The Reverend Jacob Castner from Washington

166

won the battle of the preachers in the end," Cam continued. "He delivered a deeply divisive sermon during the interment, encouraging neighbors and family members to scrutinize each other as suspects in the killings and to root out the guilty parties. He was particularly hard on the family members. Many people removed themselves from the burial, so that they would not have to listen. For those that remained, the good reverend whipped them into a frenzy for revenge," Cam concluded.

"So, that's when things must have really started to go south for the criminal investigation," Lucas murmured. "Law enforcement was probably under an even greater pressure to pin the crime on someone after the funerals." He sat back, folding his arms across his chest. The fingers of one hand began to drum on his upper arm as he considered. "Any errors that occurred then are now made fixed and immutable by the passing of time. There's no correcting it. Everyone who was a possible suspect is long dead and any evidence of the crime no longer exists for us to examine." He looked grim and tired. "We're not going to be able to solve this to anyone's satisfaction."

"I think we all agree on that front," I nodded. "How about, for now, we focus on just trying to corroborate the history with observations from the present?" Both Cam and Lucas shrugged an agreement. This was the best we could do at the moment. "The man in the pit was fatally injured and was located a few hundred yards from the house, so that might jive with the victim killed outside. Was a little girl killed in the house?" I asked.

"The man outside of the house was likely John Castner. It appeared that he had been lured away from the house and was possibly the first to be murdered. His body was found in a sinkhole not far from the house. Castner was married to John Parke's younger sister, Mary. They both lived in the house, with him working the farm and his wife keeping house with the help of another sister. Mary and John Castner had a little girl named Maria Matilda. She was only three, not that it made a difference to the murderer. The little girl's body was found in a bed lying in her mother's arms. Both had severe gashes and deep puncture wounds to their heads. The murderer had pulled a blanket up over the bodies and covered the face of the mother with a pillow."

We were all silent for a moment. Cam added softly, "The little girl was buried in her mother's arms." I think it was at that moment that I resolved to help this family if I could.

Lucas said nothing, only raised his eyebrows. These people were probably just characters in a story to him. I could almost hear the wheels turning as he sought a rational explanation for these correlations between the past and the present. While he thought, I asked another question. "The mother and little girl were found in an upstairs bedroom?" Cam nodded, so I continued. "Okay, this was also where Joel encountered the little girl. That accounts for two bodies in the house. Who was the third?"

"John Parke, the homeowner, was also killed that night. He was the most viciously attacked. His skull was broken into pieces by the force of the blows. He was found in his bed and was probably killed as he slept. The murderer put a pillow over his face as well."

"What happened to the sister - the one who helped keep house?" Lucas asked yawning. "How did she escape?" He rubbed his face and then started jotting notes again.

"Sister Sarah was tending to the sick child of a relative and was not at home that night. Oddly, John and Mary's six and nine year old sons were in the house, but the murderer passed over them. A field hand named Jesse Force was not so lucky. He slept in one of the rooms and had also been attacked, but he survived. Unfortunately, or maybe fortunately for him, he didn't remember anything."

"So, we have four people murdered and two people executed." I counted on my fingers as I summarized what we knew. "We have encountered four of these to whom we can provide a tentative identity: Peter Parke and Joe Carter were the executed men, John Castner was the man in the sinkhole and his daughter, Maria Matilda was seen in the house." Lucas scribbled away and held a finger up to ask for a moment to catch up with his notes. He gave a nod my way when he was ready and I continued, "We have two murder victims yet to be positively identified in an encounter, Mary the mother and John Parke the homeowner. There is another unnamed entity in the field, who may correspond with one of these victims."

"All right," said Cam as he signaled for the bill. After we each threw down some cash, he continued. "Next steps. Fia and I need to go back into the house and rummage around to find out who remains there. It's possible some of the murder victims have moved on and we won't have a full house to contend with." He stretched and yawned again before saying, "But this won't happen until tomorrow night. I am completely wiped out." I had been a little worried that the two men would decide to white knuckle it, ignore our sleep deprivation and try the house that night. I was delighted when Cam admitted his exhaustion and scheduled us for the next night.

Lucas rubbed his face and hunched forward, balancing his elbows on the table. "I'll let the film crew know to get ready. You'll each receive a contract tomorrow night that will stipulate that we do nothing that could in any way identify you. I'll also have the crew sign confidentiality agreements to keep your identities secret."

Cam and I agreed that this sounded good and we all stood up from the table, stretching and stifling more yawns. To make the drive home less daunting, I decided to hit the ladies room and splash some cold water on my face to wake up. I told Cam and Lucas that I would meet them outside. By the time I made it to the parking lot, Lucas had already gone back to the hospital, leaving his good night wishes for me with Cam.

CHAPTER 10

Another day, another dollar. I was starting to think that this was probably my real going rate, despite working two jobs. By the time we ate the previous night, I was feeling pretty hypoglycemic and I really needed the food. In the harsh light of day, I was berating myself for incurring the additional expense. Nothing I did involving delivering newspapers was going to earn me any additional remuneration, so I tried being extra friendly to my restaurant customers. That did not seem to produce bigger tips, so I was maybe not so good at being insincere. By the time I went to walk and feed Heckle and Jeckle, I saw that Joel had made it home from the hospital and stopped in to see how he was doing.

"I'm a free man!" Joel declared. He was grinning ear to ear and the trauma of the previous day was already behind him. The thought flashed through my mind that real tough guys are resilient.

"Good for you! I'm glad they let you out," I said as I leashed the dogs. "Enjoy your freedom and rest a little more while I walk these guys for you." I brooked no argument and insisted that this was part of my rent agreement.

When I returned from being dragged around the block, Joel was sitting on his front steps eating a bowl of ice cream. He ran back inside and came back with another bowl for me, complete with a stack of napkins. "I'm not even sure why I bother giving you a spoon," he teased as we settled down on the steps. The day was unseasonably warm and after being exercised by the dogs under the hot afternoon sun, the strawberry ice cream tasted deliciously creamy and was pleasantly cold in my mouth. I won't say that I set a land speed record finishing off the ice cream, but Joel was still eating as I contemplated licking the bowl. Maybe he read my mind, since his next words were, "Let me finish my ice cream and then each dog can have something to lick out." Pretty much caught in the act, I repressed my natural asocial behavior and waited for him to finish. As he slowly ate the ice cream, Joel looked contemplative, staring silently into the distance. He looked like he was deciding whether to say something.

Breaking the silence, Joel finally said, "I can't stop thinking about the little girl." A shadow passed over his face that even the bright sunshine could not dispel. Maybe he wasn't as over it as I had thought.

My body stiffened and I looked at Joel from the corner of my eyes. "Did you make some kind of connection with her?" I asked. That would not be good for Joel. He needed his home to be a safe place if he was going to recover.

"No… She just reminded me a lot of my kid." He looked at his hands and began rotating the empty ice cream bowl. "The little girl had the same colored hair as my Ginny."

"You have a daughter? I had no idea." I relaxed again and looked at him fully. The bowl stopped spinning and his shoulders slumped. He stared at the bowl and he sighed softly before answering.

"I had a daughter. She died when she was about the same age as that little girl."

This at least explained why the little girl was drawn to him. "I'm so sorry, Joel. What happened?"

"It was a long time ago. We were in a car accident. A drunk driver T boned us running a stop sign. My wife blamed me even though she said she didn't. Losing our daughter was pretty much the end of our marriage."

I touched his arm and said, "None of it was your fault. You can't control everything that happens in this world. But losing your family really sucks. I'm so sorry this happened to you."

"I wish it had been Ginny I saw," Joel said softly. After a few minutes of silence, he looked into my eyes and said, "You're really lucky, you know."

"How's that?"

"You know they're there. I never believed. All this time, I thought Ginny was gone, that she doesn't exist anymore." He gave me a sad smile and then started fiddling with the bowl again. I sat quietly and considered what he said. It was definitely a different perspective for me. I never felt lucky that the dead sought me. I always thought of it as more of a curse. Eventually, Joel grabbed my bowl and went back inside to get us some more ice cream. We ate companionably for a while, talking about this and that, just letting things settle.

Clearing his throat, Joel asked in a strong voice, "What will you guys do next?"

"We're going back to the house tonight," I answered him. "Cam and I got a good feel for what's going on outside. Now, we need a better understanding of what we're dealing with inside." Thinking the storm had passed and that Joel was back to being a tough guy, I described the history of the house and lands and the murders committed there.

Joel's eyes opened wide with alarm and he sputtered, "Jesus… we're putting a family in this house?" Shaking his head and looking down, he clutched his bowl tightly and muttered, "Oh, this ain't good at all…"

I instantly regretted being so honest with my history of the place. This agitation couldn't be good for his heart. Ducking down to catch his eye, I said, "Hey, we're going to try to make it better. We can't put a family in a house like this, but if we can clean it up…"

He looked up and gulped a breath. Nodding at me, he said, "I hope you can clean it up. That family has nowhere else to go right now." His brow knit and he continued, "You just be careful. Whatever it is in there, it wasn't the little girl that came after me. Whatever it is took down a big guy like me and you're just a little bit of a thing."

"They'll miss me if they start throwing things. I'm too short to make a good target," I said grinning impishly. "It'll be like putting a little person at bat – no strike zone," I added, deliberately bringing up Joel's favorite baseball story. Grateful for the diversion, Joel told me again about Eddie Gaedel, a little person immortalized in the record books after batting for the St. Louis Browns in 1951. Laughing, he described how Eddie was strategically signed as a pinch-hitter just days before a double-header against the Detroit Tigers and how he has gone down in history for having one game, one plate appearance, one walk, and a perfect on-base percentage of 1.000.

Joel was still smiling as we offered the bowls to the dogs and I congratulated myself for bringing him out of his worries. The dogs licked and slurped while Joel told me funny dog stories. I wouldn't admit it to Joel, but I was also worried about our next visit to the house.

###

The stone house looked no different in the setting sun, but I was fairly vibrating with the tension. Maybe ignorance was bliss. It was easier walking into that structure when I knew nothing about the deaths.

As promised, Lucas brought the contracts. As expected, they were long, unwieldy things, stuffed with legalese. I skimmed through the text to understand all the conditions imposed. The gist of it was that we were being signed on as contractors, our identities would not be divulged and then my eyes bulged when I came to the section on compensation. The pay being offered stunned me. I looked up at Lucas, my jaw slack, and just said, "Are you sure? I thought you said we weren't getting much."

He looked uncomfortably at Cam for a moment and then said, "Well, last night in the parking lot, Cam said we should give you his share." Cam glared at Lucas and gave small, rapid shakes of his head. "Sorry, she asked and I don't want to start off our partnership with dishonesty," Lucas told him.

"Cam, thank you!" I threw my arms around him and gave him a big hug. I supposed I could have been proud and demanded that we each get only our own share, but Cam had a decent job and this pay would allow me to drop the newspaper route and still have some to spare. I was ecstatic and for a brief moment, I didn't feel anxious about going back into the house. I signed the contract and its duplicate, putting one in my car and handing the other to Lucas.

The anxiety returned when we stepped over the threshold and entered the house. Lucas began filming and narrating, while other crew members held microphone booms, lights and other cameras that tracked our progress. Our ease at being filmed was a measure of how the trust had grown. Our unease at fully entering the room was a measure of how the house, or perhaps knowledge of the house, was influencing our mood. Cam glanced furtively around and I joined him, looking for any signs that we were not alone. Zackie extended her neck, stretching her nose into the room and sampling the slight currents that were wafting through. In a sudden move, having caught some scent, she whipped back around towards the entrance and began examining the holes in the sheetrock. Standing on her hind legs to reach the damage higher on the wall, she looked like a hunting dog that had just treed her quarry. As she dropped to all four feet again, she nosed the tools lying near the ruined wall, inhaling and huffing as if trying to reach some conclusion about cause and effect. The film crew was eating this up, taking footage from different angles to make the most of the moment.

"Er, we never explicitly discussed this," began Cam, "but can we also have Zackie blurred out? She's a rather distinctive looking dog..."

"Really?" Lucas said, "The dog? Really?"

"Please," I chimed in. "Cam has a point. People in the search community would know her on sight."

"Should I also distort her bark?" Lucas asked, dripping with sarcasm.

"Well, that would probably be best," Cam answered stone faced.

Lucas was nonplussed and looked at us as if we'd lost our minds. We stared back and shuffled our feet a little, only slightly embarrassed that we were putting him in a tough position with his producers. He had to film something, after all. After a long moment, Lucas scrubbed his face with his free hand and finally said, "Fine. We'll blur her."

Zackie took the moment of agreement to start sneezing. She then shook herself several times before pushing through the group and heading up stairs. "She's clearing the scent from her system," Cam explained as he followed her. "She does that when the scent is thick on something and she wants to move on."

We charged up the stairs in time to see Zackie perform a door ID on the first room on the left. Standing on her hind legs, she slammed the door with her front paws. Just like on a search, she was indicating that her subject was on the other side of the door and she wanted to get into that room. I cautiously cracked opened the door and Zackie squeezed past me. The rest of us stood warily outside as Lucas kept up the play by play narrative and informed his viewers that we were experiencing a terrible odor emanating from the room. He ordered the crew to go to night vision and turn the lights off.

Moderating my breathing so as not to inhale the stench too deeply, I opened the door fully and stepped into the room. Cam was on my heels and the film crew crowded around the doorway. Zackie had her front feet on the bed and had flung a pillow to the floor in her pawing. She was nosing back the covers as I stepped lightly behind her to see things from her vantage point. A woman with a child clutched to her breast lay on the bed. Both were grievously wounded, with blood flowing from jagged cuts and punctures on their heads and upper bodies. The child reached a bloody hand towards Zackie and the dog responded by inching closer and touching the little hand with her muzzle. The mother lifted the little girl towards the dog and I heard the words *'Please, oh please!'* echo in my head. Grabbing the child's white nightgown in her teeth, Zackie pulled the little girl from the mother's arms and bounded off the bed, half carrying and half dragging her towards the far corner of the room. Cam and I immediately turned away and shielded our eyes.

Standing just inside the doorway, Lucas panned a camera across the room and uttered an exclamation as he reported detecting a small flash of light through the camera's viewer. With his lens trained toward the far corner of the room, he did not see the gathering of a dark and oily mass near the ceiling. It was roiling like a thunder cloud and both Cam and I instinctively raised our hands in defense as we turned to face this threat. The mother's deafening screams reverberated in my head and I covered my ears even though that did nothing. She levitated above the bed, all her limbs kicking and striking out to protect herself. Cam shouted *'No!'* as her arms and legs were ripped from her body. The force of the dismemberment sent her limbs flying in every direction and her screaming went on and on. She would not have the mercy of death, only the torment that accompanies it.

We had no time to help her as the bed now rose and crashed against a wall, pinning Cam behind it. The metal frame split from the impact and jagged pieces broke off and would have killed Cam, but I aimed my energy against these and forced them to the floor. As an old dresser shifted towards the doorway, I caught the movement out of the corner of my eye and threw my energy against it to prevent the crew from being injured. It shattered harmlessly against the door frame, but I could not react quickly enough to shield myself from the splintered wood now directed towards me. The front piece of a drawer caught me in the temple and I went down, seeing flashes of light. I could feel blood dripping down my face and I thought crazily that Joel would be unhappy to learn that I wasn't short enough. I was on my hands and knees, trying to crawl away and blinded by the blood in my eyes. Another object struck me in the side and I rolled with the force of the blow. As I curled up to protect myself, I tried to focus beyond the pain and strike out at the entity. Just as I was about to lash out, something heavy hit me in the back and my ribs shattered. Writhing in pain, I felt someone – Lucas – cover me with his body against the maelstrom of flying wood and metal. Shielded, I rallied my defenses and fought back, knowing I was fighting for my life. I struck out at the dark mass with all the pain in my body and for the first time in this battle, it took a hit. Not letting up, I pounded and pounded away with my mind as I felt my body being dragged out the door. The entity was weakening. Even injured, I believed I was stronger than this thing and I could feel it retreat as I aimed blow after blow into its center. At last, it was gone. As soon as I'm better, I promised myself, I'm going to hunt this thing and tear it into bits. Maybe in a hundred years, it will find all its parts and make itself whole again and I hoped that there would be enough of me left after that time to do it again.

As the rage dissipated, I could feel Lucas holding me and wiping the blood from my face. He was muttering something, telling me he'd take care of me and that I'd be all right. Maybe it was shock, but cradled against his chest, for the first time in my life, I actually felt safe. Looking at the concern in his gray eyes, I felt a spark of connection, but I couldn't or wouldn't give it credence. Instead, I said, "Is Cam all right?" I didn't hear the response. I was fighting to stay conscious. Right before passing out, I managed to say, "I was sucker punched, you know."

CHAPTER 11

The smell of disinfectant filled my nostrils and I turned my head to try to find some fresh air. Turning too far to my right hurt. I forced my eyes open and looked around to get my bearings. I lay on a gurney and a light blue curtain created a small perimeter of privacy around me. My hand touched the gauze bandage at my temple and I felt a tug of pain from my back as I made this little move. I was exhausted and I think I fell asleep again.

"Can you hear me?" I heard Lucas say. He was a little fuzzy, but he was there next to the gurney. As he came into focus, I noticed a dusky purple bruise on his cheek. "Do you know where you are?"

"Yeah, I'm in the hospital. Probably the ER," I muttered. "Where's Cam?"

"Cam's been admitted. He had a severe break in his arm and he's going to need surgery for it to heal properly."

Lucas looked at me with a furrowed brow and both his eyes and lips slanted downward. He would not quite meet my gaze as he said, "I am so very sorry this happened to you. It's completely my fault."

"It's not your fault," I murmured. "We would have gone into that house with or without your film crew." I felt so weak. Just talking was taking it out of me.

He went on as if he hadn't heard me. "They think you may have a concussion or possibly an intracranial hemorrhage. You lost consciousness for a while and wouldn't come out of it. They're going to give you a CT scan." He swallowed hard and then raked his hair back and away from his eyes. "Your ribs are broken and you have stitches," he pointed towards his right temple. He gestured with an upturned palm as if he were going to say more, but then just dropped both his hands to his sides and remained quiet for a minute. "I'm sorry," he finally said again.

"I'm not concussed," I told him. My voice was weak and I could barely get the words out. "I'm just drained. I've been through this before." I did not tell him that it was never this bad before. But a CT scan wasn't going to help me. All these tests were just going to cost me. The greater worry was spending more time in a hospital in

186

my debilitated state. I had nothing left to build a defense and I was apprehensive about all the dead roving the halls in this place. Trying to sit up, I said, "I can't afford this."

Lucas put his hand on my shoulder and gently urged me to lie down. "The show will pay for your medical expenses. Don't worry about that," he said. His hand was warm and my skin tingled where he touched me. His eyes showed concern and as I gazed at him, I thought that the eyeliner he was forced to wear for the show really did him a disservice. The thick, dark lashes complemented the silver gray of his irises and he needed no artificial enhancement to make his eyes beautiful. I felt like weeping because I was weak in so many ways in that moment. I should not be noticing these things about him. Giving in to the failure of my body was the least of all sins, so I closed my eyes and let myself drift off.

It was dark and I was no longer in the ER when I woke again. I sensed that I was not alone and there was a moment of panic. My companion did not feel human. As I struggled to rise, I felt the pull of an IV in my arm and heard a faint clicking sound on the linoleum that was somehow familiar. Something wet and cold touched my exposed thigh and I shrank away from this surprise. When

Zackie's head emerged into my field of view, I expelled a breath of relief. There was some additional clicking of her nails on the floor as she positioned herself and leaped into the bed with me. She must have been under the bed keeping vigil and I felt a wave of gratitude for her protection from the wandering dead.

"Thank you," I said to her, uncertain about how to proceed. I reached out to her with all my senses as I tried to make deeper contact. "But what about Cam?"

She cocked her head and gave me an unwavering stare. I gasped and my head rocked back as my mind flooded with images, scents, sounds and emotions. She was funneling down an animal's integrative awareness combined with an immortal's perspective to something plainer and less rich, but my brain felt like it was sizzling on a hot grill. I could not manage the information content even though I was careful to go slowly as I sorted through. I felt a sharp pain behind my right eye as I assembled the pieces that said that Cam was all right. He could fend for himself. This was a relief to me. I would hate it if my incapacity diverted Zackie's attention and left him unprotected. I already failed him once back at the house and it almost killed him. These dark thoughts and feelings of inadequacy gnawed at me and I wanted to see for myself that he was truly all right.

Rubbing my eye, I croaked. "Can we go and see him?"

Taking mercy on me, Zackie looked up and pointed her muzzle to the open door. The sound of someone approaching reached my ears. The nurses would come and check on me soon. We'd have to wait.

"Is Lucas with Hannah?" I asked her, not sure if she would know the answer to that one and really not wanting to engage the full communication channel again. My head was starting to pound and I was feeling a little nauseous.

She turned her head slightly and looked at me from the corner of her eyes. Her paw slapped me gently on my good arm as she made a quiet 'Ymmmph' sound. Was this really my concern? I suppose it wasn't and my face reddened as I looked away. As I pressed my fingers harder against my throbbing right eye and took deep breaths against the rising nausea, I felt the mattress rustle as Zackie departed and tucked herself under the bed just before a nurse walked in.

"You're awake," she said as she grabbed my chart.

"That's good. My name is Martha. How are you feeling?"

"Better," I said, surprised that this was true despite the Zackie-inspired symptoms. "I still feel a little tired and achy, but I'm otherwise okay." No sense complaining about the newest symptoms, since I knew these would stop as soon as I stopped trying to communicate with Zackie.

"Good," Martha said again as she checked my vitals and updated my chart. "You don't have a concussion or any other brain injury, but your ribs are broken and you have some stitches on your head. We won't do anything for the ribs and just let them heal on their own, so just take it easy for a while, okay? Your major problem is that your electrolytes are really whacky. The pharmacy had to do a special mix for your IV. Never seen anything like it…"

She raised her eyebrows and let the sentence hang to see if I would explain myself, but the best I could do was express consternation. "Huh," I said. Not exactly erudite, but there was nothing I could say that would make any sense to her.

Shrugging her shoulders noncommittally, she continued. "I'm going to draw some blood to test your current levels, okay?" I nodded and presented the arm with

190

the IV. A cannula was in place that greatly simplified things for both of us. Before she took the blood, she checked the hospital bracelet and asked me to verify my name and date of birth. Wishing me a good night, Martha walked briskly out the door to her next patient, narrowly missing the young man with a Y incision on his chest. Thankfully, both continued walking down the hall unaware of each other.

Ignoring the nausea and pain in my head, I pushed out of the bed and looked for an obvious place where they might have stored my clothes. The closet seemed like a good bet and I dragged my IV stand over to it to have a look. Zackie crawled out from under the bed and stuck her nose in the closet as I opened it. Inside, I found my clothes and more importantly, my cell phone was still in the cargo pocket of the pants. I called the restaurant and the newspaper to leave messages, so they had a fighting chance of finding replacements for the next few days. Next, I searched the nightstand for another hospital gown. I first found a pair of socks with non-slip treads in the drawer and immediately put the fuzzy footwear on my cold feet. Continuing to rummage, I finally found a spare gown and put it on carefully to avoid disturbing the IV tubing, positioning the closed side of the new gown to cover the open back of the one I was wearing. Feeling much more secure, I grabbed the stand with my fluids and wheeled it towards the door.

"Zackie, we need to go to Cam." Zackie immediately took point and paused at the door frame to check for the scent of anyone coming our way. Having determined that the coast was clear, we hurried down the hall towards the elevators. A man at the nurse's station was preoccupied with a phone call and had his back to us as we passed. The faint ding as the elevator opened did not draw his attention and Zackie and I stepped aboard.

"What floor?" I needed the information, but I was cringing and trying to ready myself for the onslaught from her mind. My brain felt like it was bleeding and scorched after she communicated his location to me. I absently touch my nose, thinking that there must be blood dripping. We rode up five floors, emerged from the elevator and headed down the hallway, avoiding the nurse's station. I followed Zackie into a darkened room and spotted Cam sitting up in a bed with his left arm suspended by a cuff that attached to a Rube Goldberg contraption involving cables, a weight and some pulleys. I pulled the door partially closed, so that our voices wouldn't travel. Zackie gently balanced her

192

front feet on Cam's bed and he touched her head affectionately with his good hand.

"About time," he said as Zackie withdrew to lie on the floor. "What took you so long?"

"Oh, you know, the usual," I said trying to keep it light. Careful with my back and the IV, I sat gingerly in a chair near his bed and tried to normalize. "How's the arm?"

"Peachy," he growled. "They'll operate tomorrow and put a metal rod in." Cam was grumpier than usual and this worried me. Maybe the break was worse than he was letting on. I should have done a better job protecting him from the entity's attack. We both looked away and did not speak for a spell.

Wanting to break the silence, I finally asked Cam, "How did Lucas explain our injuries to the EMTs and hospital staff?"

"He said we were filming in an old, dilapidated house and a structure gave way." He shrugged. "They seemed to buy it."

The sheets rustled slightly as Cam used his good hand to fiddle with them. Finally looking up, he took in the bandage, the bruises and the IV. "I've made a right mess of things," he said softly. "I did not protect you properly."

"I thought I was the body guard," I tried to joke. I didn't want him to feel responsible for what happened to us. I really was the superior fighter when it came to subduing the agitated and unruly dead. It was my responsibility to protect the team. Zackie snorted as she sensed my thoughts and I looked crossly at her. Well, sure, maybe she could have done something more effective, but I was there at the time of the attack and she was not. The blame still fell squarely on my shoulders.

"You could have used some help," Cam explained. "I wish I could have done more to control that entity, but being pinned to the wall by the bed crushed my arm. Things would have been worse, but the mattress absorbed a good deal of the force. Still, I'm sorry. I could not focus through the pain to lend you any help."

"It should never have come to that," I replied. "I should have been on guard for the attack, but I was paying attention to the wrong thing. I was wrapped up in the agony of that poor woman...." My thoughts wandered back to that traumatic moment and I shuddered.

"The entity was furious that we got the little girl away," Cam said slowly, recalling the experience. "I think the entity may be at least part of the reason that the others cannot move on." He paused and frowned. "I would have liked to help that poor woman...We should have done better." Eventually, Cam waved his good hand, ready to let it go. "We can go round and round with the self-blame game," he sighed. Zackie snorted again at this comment and Cam rolled his eyes at her. "Yes, yes, we both suck. Thanks so much, Zackie." Bringing his attention back to me, he said, "Anyway, it's clear that this entity behaved in a non-random way. This was not your typical poltergeist phenomenon. It was tactically brilliant in how it distracted and inflicted damage. There was intelligence and deliberation behind the attack. I think it learned from the first attack in the field how we work together, so it took a divide and conquer strategy." He paused and gathered his thoughts before continuing. "Another thing that emerged from this encounter is that you appear to have a bit of the berserker in you."

"I have what now? You're joking, right?" He could not have been serious about this remark. We would be in a bar right now toasting our triumph if I had that kind of warrior instinct.

"I'm perfectly serious. I was fully conscious, if useless, during the whole thing. While I could not focus my mind and respond because of the pain, it appeared that your abilities increased with pain. You used it to your advantage somehow."

"Berserkers were supposed to be impervious to pain. They fought in wolf pelts without any armor and went into bloodlust-induced trances during battle. They were killing machines." I started to gesture when I felt the pull of the IV and dropped my hands to my lap. "That was nothing like what happened. I was writhing on the ground trying not to die. The only reason I was able to do anything was because Lucas protected me long enough to launch a counter attack."

"Maybe so, but pain does not shut you down, don't you see?" He was working through the implications and I could almost hear his mind clicking as the pieces of a plan fell into place.

"Oh, hell no!" I said. "Whatever you're thinking can't be good for me…" Occasional self-sacrifice was one thing, but my finely tuned sense of self-preservation warned me that intentional pain might be in the offing. And I was no masochist.

196

"It's not what you're thinking," Cam was quick to correct. "The entity now knows that if it hits you, you will hit it back even harder. It will be in a quandary the next time we face each other. It needs to take you out on the first shot, but we know how it operates now, so that will be nearly impossible to do when we work together."

"Well, let's hope that's true," I said.

Cam went on, ignoring my misgivings. "The other thing I was thinking is that this is like a hostage situation. The entity might be keeping these spirits trapped in this plane of existence. If one tries to leave, the others will suffer. Look what happened to the mother when the little girl was set free."

"That fits," I nodded as I spoke. "The problem in using this analogy is that hostage negotiations require building a rapport with the perpetrator. Did you get any desire for communication from the entity? All I felt was rage."

"True enough," Cam responded and then paused while he considered. "So, we're down to a tactical incursion to rescue the hostages."

My brows knit as I concentrated. "Our hostages are

in four separate sites. As far as we know, there is only one perp. Can we plan a diversion and at least clear one site at time?"

He frowned and tilted his head as he thought. "With four sites, we lack the resources to adequately protect the hostages. We might succeed at clearing a site a time, but the remaining victims will suffer for it."

My expression hardened as I said, "Maybe that's the price of doing business. I don't like it any more than you do, but that might be the only way."

Cam compressed his lips and looked away. It went completely against his grain to allow the dead to suffer. Zackie made a disgusted sound and then stood and nudged my leg. It was time for us to go.

"We need to get back to the room before anyone notices." I stood carefully and tested my balance before moving towards the door. "Let's keep thinking about it. Maybe there's another solution."

# # #

The next morning, my electrolytes were back in the

normal range and I was judged to be in good enough shape to be discharged. Zackie had disappeared, so I built my defensive cage and then contacted Joel to collect me while I waited for the hospital staff to get my paperwork organized. This was the fastest recovery for me ever after a confrontation with a spirit. Before I was put in a wheelchair and taken to the hospital lobby, I was told how to care for the stitches and advised by the doctor to drink raw coconut water to counteract any future bouts of electrolyte imbalance. Such a simple solution. I should have gotten a diagnosis years ago.

Joel was waiting in the lobby to take me home. "So, what are we, like taking turns visiting each other in the hospital?" he started. "What in the hell happened to you?"

"I'm okay," I said shifting my eyes meaningfully toward the attendant. "I'll tell you all about it on the ride home." I got out of the wheelchair and thanked the attendant before heading to the exit. Feeling an uncomfortable pull on my ribs, I climbed into the truck and buckled myself in. As soon as Joel started the engine, I began filling him in on the previous day's adventures.

"I'm really glad the little girl is free, but geez… the rest of this ain't good at all," he said when I finished. His face was lined with worry and his knuckles grew white as his grip tightened on the steering wheel. "I don't think you or Cam should go back there. We'll figure something else out for the family."

"Like what?" I asked. "Do you have another property that is ready for them?"

"No, nothing close to habitable. The Changewater house is as close as we've got, but it's not safe. That guy has been through enough, what with losing his legs in the war. I don't want to bring more trouble to him."

I nodded and said, "I absolutely agree with you. But it's going to cause trouble for him if he has no housing for his family in a few months. The best option is that we clear that house and make it safe for the family."

"I don't like it," he responded doggedly. "You guys could have been killed. You shouldn't go back there."

I could tell he was torn by the situation, so I said, "Look, my car is parked at the house. I have to go back there no matter what. Can you take me there after lunch?" He started shaking his head and was about to argue. "Nothing's going to happen in the middle of the day," I said before he could say anything. Joel clamped his mouth shut and looked dubiously at me, so I added, "We'll bring Zackie. You know how animals can sense things before people can. She'll let us know if there's anything we need to worry about." Still, he would not agree until I started layering on the practical side of things. After I mentioned that I there was no way I'd be able to hang on to my jobs without the car, he finally caved in.

When we opened the door to my apartment, Zackie was there to greet me. Her presence didn't appear to faze Joel. Maybe he assumed someone brought her there late last night. After Joel left to attend to his lunch, I asked Zackie about Cam and was relieved to learn everything went well with his surgery. We would visit him after I got my car back. While wolfing down a sandwich, I made a note to buy some raw coconut water next time I went shopping, checked for mail and then prepped myself for some much needed personal hygiene. Using a plastic grocery bag and duct tape, I improvised some head gear that would cover the stitches and took a quick shower. My hair would be greasy for the next five days until they took the stitches out, but such was life.

During the trip to Changewater, I mentioned to Joel that I would go to visit Cam after retrieving my car. Joel said he would be busy violating his doctor's orders and visiting construction sites that afternoon, so he said he would see Cam that evening. For the remainder of the ride, I tried to keep him from getting stressed by asking about baseball trivia. In the end, the operation was mercifully easy and uneventful. Zackie shielded me from detection by any of the revenants and it was a quick thing to get out of Joel's truck and hop into my car. I could see Joel finally relax in my rearview mirror as we drove away, our vehicles diverging as we each headed to our separate destinations.

As thrilled as I was to be back at the hospital, it was still better being a visitor than being a patient. Zackie made her way ahead of me through whatever wormhole she uses for these purposes and I took the conventional route, checking in at the main desk and receiving directions to Cam's room. Roaming the halls with my defensive cage in place, I was irked to discover that after all my recent experiences, I now had a familiarity with the layout and it was becoming easier to navigate the hospital. Upon reaching the room, I was met by a groggy Cam and an excited Zackie. She appeared pleased that we were all together again.

"Would you please stop wagging so hard?" Cam

grumbled. "I find it irritating."

"I'll try if it makes you happy," I responded. Taking the seat near the bed, I took in the new cast on his arm. "Will you let me sign your cast?"

"What, right now? Are you mad?" Cam clumsily grasped at the covers and tried to draw them up around his injured arm.

I felt a twinge of guilt for messing with him when he was still a little out of it, so I asked, "Can I get you anything? Water maybe? Or something to read?"

"No, I'm quite all right. Just do me a favor and distract Zackie for a bit. She's flooding my mind with her nonsense and I'm not up to it. Maybe take her to Hannah and let me get some sleep."

"You heard the man," I said to Zackie. "Meet me outside of Hannah's room." I shut the lights off as I left Cam and listened for a moment for his steady breathing. There's nothing like seeing someone up close and personal to check their well being. He really was going to be okay. I felt a weight drop from my shoulders as I headed to the elevators.

Zackie and I entered Hannah's room together. She was delighted to see Zackie again and it was good to see that she had more energy than the previous night. Lucas was beaming when he looked at her. He had a really nice smile. It made the corners of his eyes crinkle in an attractive way. When he turned that smile on me, I felt a little flutter in my chest and the beginnings of a blush on my cheeks.

"You've been released – excellent!" he said.

I could feel Hannah's eyes on me as I sputtered a response. "Yeah, can't keep a good woman down, I suppose." I instantly regretted my choice of words, since Hannah remained trapped in her situation, and presumably, she was a good woman if both Lucas and Zackie had taken to her. I looked at her as my face reddened and I tried to think of something to say to fix this. Her eyes narrowed almost imperceptibly as she stared back.

The tension was interrupted as Zackie dove under the bed moments before a young nurse's aide entered the room. "How are we doing today?" she asked Hannah as she went about taking a pulse and blood pressure. She was so young, she still had acne on her cheeks.

"I'm feeling better today," Hannah answered her.

"That's good... that's good," the girl responded absently as she updated the chart. Looking at Hannah after she finished her scribbling, she said, "You keep up the happy thoughts. I had a neighbor who had cancer and she had a real positive attitude. She's doing great."

"Um, I know you're trying to help," Hannah said, "but what you're saying really puts all the responsibility for the outcome on the cancer patient." Hannah struggled to sit up and her voice rose as she said, "What about all the people who didn't make it? Are you blaming them for not being positive enough? They didn't try hard enough, so they don't get to survive?"

"Oh no, honey! That's not what I'm saying at all," the nurse's aide said, her eyes widening as she backed away. Looking distinctly uncomfortable, she said, "You take care, now. I've got to go."

As she rushed from the room, Hannah called after her, "Cancers aren't all the same. Some of them are more lethal than others." Sobbing, she said, "The patient doesn't get to choose!" She was clearly upset and Lucas immediately went to her side to offer comfort. Zackie crawled on to the bed from the other side and pressed her body against Hannah. I stood where I was, shifting uneasily, feeling useless and appalled with myself for being attracted to this woman's husband.

"I'll get her some fresh water," I said, grasping at this excuse to get out of the room. I walked down the hall with my eyes on the floor, avoiding eye contact with everyone. Hannah was suffering. She knew she was dying. She didn't need me to add to her distress, but with Cam out of commission, it was up to me to be Zackie's escort to Hannah. I resolved to control my attraction to Lucas. I had to stop reacting to him. *The heart wants what the heart wants*, a small voice murmured in my mind. *Shut up*, I thought and I slammed my hand against the button to dispense ice and water into the Styrofoam cup.

By the time I returned with the cup, Hannah had calmed down. Lucas and Zackie remained where they were, flanking her protectively. I set the cup down on the night table and tried to make myself inconspicuous, sitting in a chair against the wall. I chewed on my cuticles and waited until Zackie was ready to leave. Staring determinedly at anything except Lucas, I fought my own exhaustion as it crept over me, like waves lapping the shore. Definitely too much, too soon. My ribs ached dully and my eyes were starting to feel gritty. When I rubbed my eyes, it pulled on my stitches. But I had no right to complain. Some people had it much worse. *Here's a straw, suck it up*, the little voice said. *Shut up*, I thought again.

Hannah eventually began to doze and both Zackie and Lucas retreated gently from the bed. "I have to go back to work," Lucas whispered as he made his way to the door. "Thanks for coming by."

I nodded silently, avoiding his eyes. After he left, I gave him a few minutes to get well ahead of me. The last thing I needed was to be trapped in an elevator with Lucas. I eventually got up from the chair, feeling stiff and weary. Looking at Zackie, I tilted my head towards the door and she joined me as I went through. I emerged alone and walked slowly to the elevators.

# # #

"What?" I said as Cam scrutinized me. I felt better after getting some sleep in my own bed, but my current mood reflected the weather. I had woken to pouring rain and skies that were gray as a corpse. Both employers were not expecting me back for another two days, so I ate, dressed and went to visit Cam at the hospital.

Cam was alert and irritable, which I took as a sign that he was healing well. He gave me another once over and then said, "There's something wrong. What's changed?"

"What's changed is that I have broken ribs and stitches on my head," I muttered.

"No, that's not the whole of it," he said crossing and then uncrossing his arm over his chest when the cast interfered. He continued to give me a penetrating look and Zackie poked me with her nose, as if to prompt me to spew my innermost thoughts.

"I don't want to talk about it," I forced out between gritted teeth. To change the topic, I said, "When do you want me to pick you up tomorrow?" The hospital was going to discharge Cam the next day, provided all went well and he showed no signs of infection after the surgery.

"I should be processed before eleven," he said. Sweeping his gaze around the small room, he rolled his eyes and sighed dramatically. "Meanwhile, I'm bored out of my mind. The nurses said it would be good if I walked around a bit. Fetch me another gown to cover my bum and then let's go visit Hannah."

Of course, I thought glumly to myself, but I did as he requested and found another blue gown that I draped around his shoulders. After helping him to put on some hospital socks with non-slip soles and adjusting the sling for his arm, Zackie burrowed behind Cam as he sat up and leveraged him out of bed and on to his feet. My ribs thanked her for this. While Zackie took her shortcut, we shuffled down the hall and to the elevators.

Lucas was in the room when we arrived, so I went to the seat near the wall to keep my distance from him and ground my teeth. Cam sat near Hannah and Zackie took up her position in the bed. Hannah seemed to be in good spirits today and chatted amiably with everyone. I mumbled a few responses to her pleasantries, but otherwise chewed my cuticles and kept to myself. While Hannah and Cam laughed over some joke, Lucas came and kneeled in front of me. I felt that fluttering sensation in my chest again and I almost held my breath.

"Are you okay?" he asked. I looked at him, but said nothing. He touched my face near the stitches and tried again. "You're not in pain, are you?" Gazing into his face, my eyes were drawn to the mottled bruise on his cheek I had noticed before. Clasping my hands together, I resisted the urge to touch his cheek.

I put on the best poker face I owned and said, "I'm fine. Really." Cam caught my eye as he looked from me to Lucas and back again. He and Hannah had stopped chatting and I felt her eyes on me as well. I got up and moved away from Lucas. "See? Legs work and everything," I said as I went to the windows to gaze out.

"All right," Lucas said uncertainly as he stood again. "Let me know if I can do anything for you."

You could do a lot for me, I thought to myself, but you're off limits. I nodded at him and forced a smile and then pretended interest in something outside.

"So, I'm to be discharged tomorrow," Cam said, drawing everyone's attention. I sighed softly, grateful for his diversion. "You can all sign my cast. I'm even going to get a paw print from Zackie."

Resolving to try to deal better with this situation, I squared my shoulders and turned back to the group. In what I hoped was a normal tone, I chimed in, "Hey, cast signing was my idea."

"And you may have the privilege of signing first," he said. After that, the conversation bounced around with ideas on how to better decorate the cast and the chances of coming up with a method to tie die it. After a while, Hannah began to tire, prompting Lucas to check his watch.

"I better get back to work," he said. He looked tired and wrung out. I don't know how he kept up the constant schedule of work and hospital visits. Kissing Hannah on the forehead, Lucas moved toward the door. Before he left, he turned to thank Cam and me for bringing Zackie for a visit. We waited until we heard the soft ding of the elevator in the distance and then also said our goodbyes as Hannah drifted off to sleep.

In the elevator, Cam said to me, "Do not ever play poker."

I scrubbed my face until the stitches pulled and said, "Is it that obvious?"

"To everyone but him, I'd say," Cam answered. He looked at me kindly and not without pity. "When I was a young man, I faced a similarly impossible situation."

"What happened?" I asked, just as the elevator doors opened. We walked silently to his room to continue the conversation. I looked at my feet and tried to imagine what Cam went through that could be similar to my torment.

Cam eased himself into the bed and smoothed the covers before he began his story. "He had been dead for nearly three hundred years before I was even born." His eyes looked a million years old and he focused on a point on the wall rather than look at me. "His name was William and he haunted a warren of underground tunnels in Edinburgh. He was among the three hundred plague victims who were sealed into Mary King's Close in 1645 to prevent the contagion from spreading." Cam ran his good hand over his eyes, disturbed by the memory. "They weren't actually bricked up in the close, that was a myth, but they were quarantined. William sewed himself into a shroud of his own making when he was close to death. He was so concerned that he wouldn't be decently buried." He smiled briefly, as if this was a foolish thing.

"Was Zackie with you when you met William?" I asked.

"Yes, we had returned from the States and were living in Scotland at the time. Those were good days."

"What brought you to Mary King's Close?" I prompted to get back to the story.

"A friend of mine worked for the Town Council in the old Royal Exchange building. This structure was built right over the close in the mid eighteenth century. Anyway, there were complaints about cold spots and objects moving and levitating in the offices. They were having a hard time holding on to workers, so my friend asked if I'd have a go at making things more hospitable."

"It was William, then? He was haunting the offices?"

"William was just inquisitive. He'd never seen anything like a stapler before and he loved the fine, white paper that lay everywhere in the office. I spent days trying to talk to him about why he did not want to pass to the next world and he kept diverting me with questions about modern life. For a seventeenth century lad, he had a wonderful curiosity about the world." Cam reached for the Styrofoam cup on the nightstand and took a few sips on the straw. He looked wistful as he continued, "Days turned into weeks and I got caught up in his enthusiasm for learning about the world. He just had so much vitality! I know that sounds odd about a dead man, but he really gave me an appreciation for the things around me and I began looking on everything with new eyes. I took him on trips around the city and countryside."

"Hold on just one minute... I thought you told me that spirits tend to stay in an area. A spirit can travel that far from the area they haunt?" I was floored by this new understanding.

"Most spirits don't, but this one did. He would share my senses when we left the close. We –"

I interrupted at this point because I was really disturbed by what I heard. "You let him possess you? Cam, that is incredibly dangerous and irresponsible! How could you do it?"

"This was not possession," he barked at me. "William would never do that to me. I was in full control at all times. How could you think such a thing of me?"

"I'm sorry," I said softly. "Help me understand exactly what was going on."

"He would just experience things through me. William could taste chocolate for the first time this way. The colors were more vibrant to him and sounds were more complex. Even touch could be augmented and he could discern the subtlety of textures and temperatures."

I paused for a moment and thought about it. "That sounds more intimate than sex," I said taken aback. "You must have really loved him."

"I did love him. That's the whole point of telling you this story," he said sweeping his good arm towards me. "Do you want to hear it or not?"

I nodded my head and kept my mouth shut until he continued.

"We went to museums especially, since he could see how time changed everything and what had happened after his death. I think because he died so young, he had missed out on so many of life's experiences. I tried desperately hard to make up for that during those weeks." He looked away and was lost in thought for a moment. "As it turns out, this was not the reason William did not want to move on, but I'm still glad I did it. He eventually confessed to me that he felt cursed to walk the earth because he did not receive last rites. He thought this was purgatory." He rubbed his eyes with his good hand and muttered, "Bloody man… half the people were dead of the plague. There were no priests. And why would he need to be cleansed of his sins? What sins could he have had? He hardly lived long enough."

"What did you finally do to help him to move on?" I asked gently. This was tearing open old wounds and I really felt for Cam.

"I paid for a mass to be said for him." His face was flushed and there were unshed tears in his eyes, yet still he went on. "I asked the priest to say a prayer beseeching intercession, asking God to forgive William and grant him a place in heaven. William needed to hear the words said. He came with me to the church to hear the mass and then he said goodbye and went with Zackie."

We sat quietly together for a few minutes. I finally said, "You loved him so much you let him go." He just shrugged and kept his silence, staring down at his cast.

Eventually, he cleared his throat and said, "I think I'd like to rest now."

"Thank you for telling me about William," I said before Zackie and I walked through the doorway.

CHAPTER 12

I picked up Cam and Zackie from the hospital the next day, and per his request, we drove straight to the Changewater house to get his truck and then arranged for an afternoon rendezvous at his house. The man wasted no time.

When I arrived at Cam's house that afternoon, aside from the irritation of my greasy hair, I felt happy to get back in the saddle. We convened in Cam's kitchen and fueled the synapses by consuming large amounts of coffee. Zackie lay comfortably on the floor, but her ears were alert as she listened to our conversation. I was more than ready to discuss what we might do to cleanse the house and lands at Changewater, but my enthusiasm came to a screeching halt with the first words out of Cam's mouth.

Looking at me over the rim of his mug, Cam said, "You know, Lucas is not going to request a meeting with us to resolve this situation." I felt a small pang at the mention of his name, but I willed myself to keep my mind on task.

"He considers us on the injured list and probably has unjustified feelings of guilt over it."

"Yeah, that's true enough," I said as I fidgeted slightly. On the one hand, I didn't particularly want to see him because of the effect he had on me, but on the other hand, I craved his presence. I hated feeling so conflicted, but I knew I had to listen to that little voice and suck it up. It was time to be professional and not let emotions wreak havoc with the work. "How about we decide on a plan of action and then make the request ourselves? If we're driving the process, he won't be so skittish about having us back in that house."

"My feelings exactly," Cam said and raised his mug in a small toast.

"Okay, so to begin... I know you're not a big fan of attempting a blitzkrieg from site to site and trying to release these souls regardless of what the entity might do," I began, "but that might be the only way."

"You're right. I'm not a fan," he said. "You seem a bit too easy with the fact that the remaining spirits will be tortured in retaliation."

"Well, it's not like they can be killed. They will

suffer, but they will reform," I said.

"Did you think that maybe we won't be able to move them on? They might not consent to the others being harmed," Cam warned. "Look how well we did that first night."

"Maybe it's a matter of order," I said tapping my finger on the mug as I thought. "We freed the little girl, so maybe the mother would want to join her. Once they are both gone, the man in the pit might be willing to cross over. He did express concern about his wife and child."

"Or maybe the mother will refuse because her husband in the pit will become a target for the entity's rage," Cam countered.

"Do you think it's possible that we could find just one of them who doesn't give a rat's ass about any of the others?" I said exasperated.

"Unlikely," Cam said as he took a sip of coffee. "Really, they've had more than a century to make a move and they all chose to stay and protect the others."

I made a face, disgruntled that we could not do a fast, clean operation. I put my elbow on the counter and

Reyna Favis

rested my chin on my hand while I thought. Cam leaned his back against the counter and cradled his coffee, staring into its black depths for inspiration. "Crazy thought..." I finally said. "We need more boots on the ground to cover the sites. Can we get help from anyone? You said your grandmother taught you. Is there anyone else in your family who can lend a hand here?"

Cam shook his head. "Granny is long gone and her talents were not identical to what we do. The same goes for the rest of my family. Everyone's gifts are different."

"How so?" I asked, sitting up and genuinely curious. I had no idea there were different flavors of this ability.

"My sister sees past lives. She actually covertly counsels people who have not gotten over some trauma from a previous existence. I also have a brother who works with spirit attachment."

"Past lives I've heard of. What the heck is spirit attachment?"

Maybe my eyes were bugging out a bit at this revelation, or maybe Cam thought we were straying from the point. He rolled his eyes and said curtly, "There's a lot

220

you don't know yet and we don't have time for this."

"Aw, c'mon," I whined. "You know I'm not going to be able to concentrate until you at least tell me what this attachment thing is."

He sighed and said, "Fine. Spirit attachment is the result of the dead being greedy for life. They attach to people with habits that can feed their obsessions."

"Like a dead alcoholic looking for someone who also likes to indulge?" I asked.

"Yes, like that. Except it might be someone who has the occasional beer and the spirit drives them to destructively drink more and more."

"Maybe that's what was going on with William," I accidentally blurted out. It was too late to take the words back, so I began back-pedaling furiously. "I'm sorry, Cam! I didn't mean—"

Cam curled his lip and I saw an angry retort forming as his face reddened. "No, he was just curious," he yelled. "How dare you say that William was just some tawdry attaching spirit?" His expression was angry, but I could see the shock of realization forming in his eyes.

I did not respond right away and I kept my voice low when I finally spoke. "I do not think he was just an attaching spirit," I said. "I know he meant a great deal to you. But I do think that he loved you enough to let you go."

He visibly sagged at my words, but he didn't refute them. The skin on his face drooped as he looked down and dropped his gaze from mine. Zackie whined softly as she watched him and then stood up to put her chin on his leg. They seemed to be having a private conversation, so I gave them some space and went to refill my coffee mug. I stared out the window over the sink while I drank it and my shoulders hunched around the mug as regret ate at me. Why did I have to say that out loud? Would it not be better to let Cam continue to remember William as merely curious? The fact remained that he did in the end release Cam of his own free will. In essence, he gave up what little life he had left in this world for Cam.

After a few minutes, Cam stood up and said, "Just give me a few minutes." He walked slowly to his bedroom and softly shut the door. Zackie slumped back to the floor and lay with her head between her paws, staring sorrowfully at me.

"Now, I've done it," I said to Zackie in a small

voice. A few minutes turned into an hour, but it didn't feel right to just leave. I spent the time pacing around the rooms and fretting, trying to come up with a way to make it up to Cam. I finally went to Zackie and said, "Will you open the way for me?" At first, she gave no response, but then she slowly stood to her feet.

I shielded my eyes with my left hand and turned my head from the blinding light. Stretching out my right hand, I felt my way towards the opening. While I expected the light to be searing hot, I instead felt a bone chilling cold the closer I approached. Taking a deep breath, I plunged my hand into the opening and reached out with my mind for William. I screamed with the sudden, consuming pain and threw myself backwards. It was all reflex. I had no thought other than the electrical pain that shot into my hand. Cam came running out of his room in time to sense the portal shut and see me writhing in agony on the floor.

"What the hell did you just do?" he screamed. He was frantic as he knelt by me, but I couldn't speak and I had stopped thinking. I was gasping and tears were involuntarily running from my eyes. My right hand was grasped protectively against my chest by my left and I had rolled on to my side into a fetal position. My whole body quivered with the aftermath of the ordeal and I felt like I was going to vomit. "Let me see your hand," he demanded as he wrenched my other hand away. My right hand was balled into a fist and at first it looked white, like something frostbitten. As he turned my hand and opened the fist, the dead white skin displayed marbling from burst blood vessels and it looked like putrefaction might be setting in. The hand belonged to a corpse. I watched in horror as my fingers extended of their own volition, revealing blackened nails. A small piece of parchment dropped to the floor as the hand opened.

"I did not… did not… do that," I croaked before I passed out.

# # #

Cam was sitting on a folding chair staring at me when I awoke. It was dark and the only illumination came from a lamp in another room. I still lay on the floor where I had fallen. Cam couldn't move me because of his broken arm, but he had brought a pillow for my head and a blanket to cover me. My hand was wrapped up to the wrist in a dish towel held fast with duct tape.

Seeing me stare at the wrapped hand, Cam said, "I did pretty well for only having only one hand." He paused and then said quietly, "It started moving while you were out. It was pulling on the blanket and touching the floor around you…" He swallowed hard and continued. "I couldn't stand to look at it, so I wrapped it in a dish towel." Getting a hold of himself, he took a deep breath and said, "Do you want to tell me what happened?"

My throat was full of phlegm and I had to clear it a few times before I could talk. "I was sorry for what I said about William. I thought if I could reach him, I could relay a message to you and make it all right."

"And you asked Zackie to let you through?"

I nodded. "I had no idea this would happen."

"Well, it's been a good dozen hours and the putrefaction hasn't crept up your arm. I really thought it would kill you," he said, his eyes shifting uneasily.

"Do you think my hand will rot?" I asked.

"I don't know. I've never heard or seen anything like this before. No one has ever been so foolish…" He let his voice trail off. "Don't you have any sense of self-preservation?" he said at last.

I looked down and did not respond.

After a short silence, Cam said, "For what it's worth, he did reach me." He held up the small piece of parchment.

"Was it worth it?" I asked.

He quirked his lips and responded, "For me, yes. For you, probably not."

"What am I going to do?" I whispered, helpless against the growing horror.

"A doctor probably won't help," he said. "Modern medicine can't cure dead." He thought for a moment and then asked, "Can you move it at all?"

I picked up my arm and put the wrapped hand in front of my eyes. I willed my fingers to move and was gratified when I saw movement under the towel. I was smiling and about to tell Cam that at least I had movement in my fingers, when the hand shot forward and began touching my face. I screamed and tried to get away, but it was useless. Cam lunged from the chair and wrestled the hand away from my face, forcing it down to my side. When it finally stilled, he cautiously moved away. He was sweating profusely and shaking his head. I lay there breathing hard and tried not to give into hysteria.

"I know this feeling," I finally said to Cam. "This is the way it was when I was kid." I kept my voice steady and quiet as I continued. "At least now, you're around to understand if I start screaming and can't stop. No one understood then." I felt a hot tear escape from the corner of my eye. "Oh God…" I breathed, turning my head away from him. "I'm going to end up in five point restraints again in some psychiatric facility."

"I promise you, I won't let that happen," Cam said.

I turned back and looked hard at him to measure the truth of his words. His eyes never wavered, but the decision to commit me might not be solely up to him if I really lost it. Cam was not a relative, after all. He had no legal say in what would be done with me. With the course of my life in the balance, I forced myself to stay in control, to think things through and to come up with a plan. "Damn straight," I finally said. Getting to my feet, I embraced the growing fury and went to the kitchen. I began rummaging through the drawers until I found the cleaver.

"Jesus God!" Cam exclaimed, jumping to his feet and rushing in behind me.

I went to the sink and placed the cleaver on the counter within easy reach of my left hand and began to unwrap the towel. "If this thing is going to try to strangle me in my sleep, I want to find out now." Looking at it was less of a shock now that I knew what to expect. I screwed up my courage and poked it hard with my left hand. It contracted the fingers a little, but otherwise didn't move. I poked it again several times rapidly and just as I was about to start swearing, the hand came up lightning fast and lightly slapped my poking finger. It then balled up the other fingers, leaving the index finger extended and shook this finger at my other hand as if it were scolding me.

Cam was slack jawed when I turned to look at him, incredulity etched in my face. I stared at him wild-eyed and bellowed, "What the fuck?" That was all I could say for the next few minutes. Non-expletives lacked sufficient dynamic range to cover the contradictions inherent in this event. Zackie took that moment of confusion and stood up at the counter to grab the cleaver in her jaws before disappearing into the house with it. Cam and I stared after her and then our eyes met as we understood her meaning.

The hand was not a danger.

The hand slowly reached towards Cam with the fingers extended and the palm open, offering a handshake of introduction. Eyes wide, Cam offered his own hand and accepted the gesture. Releasing Cam, it next came gradually up to my face. I automatically turned my head, flinching away with another loud expletive.

"I think it wants to know who you are," Cam said. "Come here and stand in front of a mirror." Grabbing my shoulder he guided me to the half bath in the hall, flicked on the light and stood there looking over my shoulder. Facing the mirror, I saw I wore a blank look of shock as the hand rose and delicately touched the reflection of my face. As it withdrew, the ring finger and the pinky curled into the palm with the thumb, leaving the remaining fingers erect.

I stared at the hand in the mirror and my brow wrinkled in confusion, "Two? What the hell does two mean?"

Cam's eyes crinkled as he said, "Not two. You're too young to know... Peace. It's saying peace to you."

My mouth became a firm, white line as my lips compressed and my eyes squinted angrily back at me. I raised my left hand with the middle finger extended. "Screw you!" I yelled. "Give me back my hand!" In response, the scolding finger returned briefly and then the hand dropped to my side. Swearing to myself, I pushed past Cam and left the tiny bathroom. I stormed to the front door and yanked it open, pulling the keys out of my pocket awkwardly with my left hand as I headed through the night to my car. Opening the trunk activated a small automatic light in the side of the cavity. I began rooting through the piles of SAR equipment until I found the gloves that I used to push through thick woods and briars. I swore triumphantly as I pulled on the right glove.

"And what good did that do?" asked Cam from the open door.

Blowing upwards to get the bangs out of my eyes, I said, "I don't know." The adrenaline from the amputation decision was dissipating and I slumped against the rear bumper, hugging myself with my left arm.

"Fia, come back inside and let's figure this out," Cam called.

I shrugged my shoulders and sat for a few minutes in the dark. Eventually, I stood and closed the trunk. He was right. There was no one else on the planet I could talk to about this and I knew I wasn't thinking straight anymore. I felt violated and I didn't know what to make of the hand and its offers of a peace between us. I re-entered the house and sat down on a kitchen stool, once again trusting Cam to explain how to behave in this bizarre world.

"I don't think this is reversible," he began after sitting next to me.

"You don't know that," I interrupted. "You said you've never seen anything like this before, so how would you know?" My right hand hung limply, while my left hand emphasized the words with a chopping motion.

"You're right. I don't know," he replied, his voice low and soothing. "What I do know is that this is a terrible shock to you." He paused and I took the moment to collect myself, to stop the panic and to think about what he was saying to me. "For now," he continued, "just consider what it would mean and how you would need to adjust if this is not reversible."

I closed my eyes because I didn't really want to think about what life would be like with this dead thing attached to me. Inhaling sharply, I opened my eyes and said, "Look, I can try training myself to rely on my left hand, but this thing has a mind of its own. I can't stand the idea of it touching my food. Even worse, what am I supposed to do about showering? I don't want some dead thing feeling me up." I was grimacing and starting to feel distressed again.

"Understandable," Cam said, his eyes widening. "Do you really think you'll be molested? It seemed mannerly and peaceful in our interactions with it."

"I don't know, but you said it yourself before – as in life, so in death. What do we know about this thing when it had life? Nothing. It could be capable of anything, including lying to us to convince us that we have nothing to be worried about."

Cam looked thoughtful for a moment and then said, "Okay, rather than try to argue the point....I used to scuba dive in the UK when I was younger. We used these heavy, thick neoprene gloves because the water was always so cold. You can't really feel anything through them. You could wear a right hand glove in the shower."

I looked at him stunned. Here we were, trying to problem-solve the minutiae while the bigger issue of owning a dead appendage remained an elephant in the room. As if he could read my mind, Cam said, "Hey, we do what we can do here. Let's not try to boil the ocean until we have a better understanding of what we are dealing with." He went to a closet near the front door and said, "Let me find those gloves."

I nodded and forced my brain into problem-solving mode. It's impossible to feel simultaneously out-of-control terrified and to think analytically, so the more I thought about how I was going to deal with the dead hand, the calmer I felt. Focusing on what I could do made me feel more in control and I mentally blessed Cam for his genius. As Cam rummaged in the closet, I raised my voice and said, "I can't ever let people see the hand. I'll have to keep it covered at all times." I thought some more and then added, "I can wear latex gloves at the restaurant. They'll just think I've become some kind of hygiene freak." I rubbed my jaw with my good hand and followed up with, "I'll find some fashionable-looking gloves to wear otherwise. If anyone asks, I'll say I have vitiligo."

"That's good," came his muffled response. "Ah, here they are." Emerging from the closet, he handed me a spongy-looking black glove. It was a little big for me, but it had a Velcro wrist strap that I could cinch down. "At least this will make you stop chewing on the cuticles of your right hand," he said as he sat down again.

I looked at him with disgust and then, still caught up in solving the little things, I asked, "How about mortician's makeup? Maybe I can put that on the hand and do without the gloves sometimes." He looked more relaxed now that I was taking command and coming up with my own solutions, so I suggested that we go online and order the makeup and some gloves and have it overnight delivered. After the shopping spree, I told him I should go home to get some sleep.

"Are you sure you'll be okay? You can always stay here the night," Cam offered.

"It's okay. This ain't my first rodeo," I quipped to put him at ease. The truth was, I felt uneasy about being alone with the dead hand, but there was also some truth to becoming numb to the weirdness that permeated my life. "I'll be okay. If there is any sign of trouble, I'll call." Actually, if there was any sign of trouble, I had a hatchet in my trunk. If the dead hand were some kind of homicidal maniac, I did not want Cam anywhere near the danger.

"As you wish," he replied in an obvious effort to match my insouciance. "I have a dog with a cleaver loose in the house somewhere, so this might not be the best night for a sleepover."

# # #

I made it home without the dead hand causing me to swerve off the road. It stayed quiescent and made no attempts to interfere, so I decided to push my luck and clean up a little before turning in. Putting on the neoprene glove, I took a tense and uncomfortable shower. Between the glove and the head gear to protect the stitches, I was starting to feel less and less clean after my washing off. The stitches would come out in another two days, so this discomfort was temporary. The dead hand was something I would have to get used to.

Since it refrained from groping me, I decided to make an overture of peace. After drying off and dressing in my jammies, I stripped off the neoprene glove and washed the dead hand with some soap in the bathroom sink. I couldn't tell if this was good, bad or indifferent to the hand, but I suffered no complaints and really, this needed to be done periodically. Touching the hand was a little creepy. I didn't really have much sensation, so it did feel like I was washing something foreign to me. The fact was, it was cold to the touch. If it were still my hand, it should have been the same temperature as the other hand. The hand was now definitively non-self to the rest of my body. Looking at the dead hand dispassionately as I dried it, I decided to paint the nails of my left hand black to match it if I found that I could mask the look of decomposition with mortician's makeup. Probably, this would be less weird than wearing gloves all the time.

Grabbing a pad and pen on my nightstand, I started a shopping list and included black nail polish as the final item. As I was about to put the pen down, the hand quickly wrote in the margin of the paper 'Thank you.' The words were written in an elegant and flowing script and it contrasted sharply with the block letters of my shopping list. I stared at the writing and began rubbing my lips with my good hand. Two thoughts came to me unbidden: we were not limited to just hand gestures in order to communicate and I was starting to think using the royal 'we.' Feeling in no shape to pursue any of these disturbing thoughts that night, I carefully put the pen down near the pad and placed the SAR glove on the hand before turning in.

If the dead hand did anything during the night, I had no clue. I slept deeply until the alarm sounded that it was time to deliver my newspapers. The SAR glove was still in place and I left it on. As I drove the route, my aim was as good as always and I landed the papers in the driveways with practiced ease. Once I returned home, I put the plastic bag on my head and replaced the SAR glove with its neoprene counterpart before hitting the shower. Feeling as clean as was possible under the circumstances, I got dressed in my waitress uniform, switched the gloves and then hunted through my cleaning supplies for some latex gloves. I put two pairs in my pants pocket and carried another pair with me as I left for the restaurant.

CHAPTER 13

"They fired you?" Cam's eyebrows contracted and his lips pursed. We were once again sitting in his kitchen and I was telling him about my day.

"Yeah, I took a bunch of sick days recently, but mostly they were afraid of a lawsuit." I shifted on my stool and slumped forward with my feet on the rail and forearms across my thighs. This was a good position in case I needed to hurl. "There was an incident in another state where servers wore gloves to supposedly protect themselves from contracting HIV from customers. Some customers were offended. The restaurant owners didn't want to stir things up."

"Well, the irony is that you might be able to sue the restaurant owners for unlawful termination. Maybe you have a disability." Cam waggled his eyebrows, challenging me to do the hipster thing and contribute to the irony load in this world.

I shook my head. "No way. If I claim I have a

disability and need to wear the gloves, I'll need a doctor's note or I might have to show the hand to prove it in court." I pushed the hair out of my eyes and sighed. "I can probably get another job just as menial without all the hassle." To change the topic of conversation away from my dismal future, I brought up the hand's ability to communicate through writing.

"Have you queried it?" Cam leaned forward and stared intently at me. His eyes were bright with the potential for new discoveries.

I shook my head again. "I don't trust it to necessarily tell me the truth. How can I test its veracity? There's nothing I could ask where I already know the answer. And how can I be sure it doesn't tap into my thoughts?"

Cam plucked at his chin with his good hand and sat back. "You have a point." He was quiet for a moment while he thought. "It might still be worth asking a few questions to better understand it. What it says might be true or false, but if we ask clever questions, there may be events in the future against which we could assess the truthiness of the answers."

I rolled my eyes. "You're going to have to be the clever one, then. The best I can come up with is, 'Are you a good hand or an evil hand?' And what if it just wants to chat and has nothing important to say? Honestly, I don't want to get into this right now."

"How about if we just hand it a pen and paper and see what happens? No questions." Cam raised his eyebrows expectantly and waited for my answer.

"You don't get it." I hunched over more and stopped looking at him. "I don't want to give this thing any more of a presence than it already has." I took a deep breath and tried not to redirect my anger at Cam. All of this was my own doing, after all. "Because I have this thing attached to me now, any hope for a normal life is gone. Maybe I could fake it to some degree before. At least I looked normal to other people. For a while, I thought that if I could learn how you do it, I would find a way to live with my abilities." Tears of self-pity were threatening to overflow and I cleared my throat angrily as I tried to explain myself. "I am cut off from the normal human experiences because of this." I held up the gloved hand to make my point. "Forget ever having a lover. Can you imagine going to bed with this?" This conversation had my face crimson with embarrassment, but I held up the hand and pulled off the glove to really make my point sink in. Revealed in the light of day, it showed itself in all its grotesque glory.

"I see." Cam's eyes were full of sympathy. I quickly looked away and pulled the glove back on. "If you were hoping to find that particular holy grail through my guidance, well, you know the William story." He sighed softly. "Still, I don't think it's beyond hope. My mother found my father, after all. It's just going to be harder in your situation."

I nodded and let the tears flow for a while. I didn't believe him. It wasn't harder in my situation, it was impossible. The only benefit was that this dead hand put another brick in the wall between Lucas and me. Eventually, I wiped my face on my sleeve and shifted in my stool to angle my body so that I was looking at the cupboard on the far wall. Clearing my throat, I made another attempt to change the topic and hoped for a better outcome this time. "It didn't sound like your family could help with the house in Changewater." I concentrated on making my voice light and it was almost normal.

Cam adjusted his body to also face the cupboard.

241

"My direct family would be of no help, but maybe Lummie's line…" I could hear Zackie's tail wag against the floor at the mention of the name.

"Lummie had kids? I thought she was a sin-eater and reviled by decent folk." I choked a little on the attempt at an Appalachian accent, but my mind was already leaping ahead. If someone had a child with Lummie, then maybe there was hope for me.

"She had a sister who had kids. No one in that generation was a strong sibyl, so this part of the family was able to keep their abilities better hidden. The subsequent generations produced a few individuals with striking abilities."

As I stared at the cupboard, I thought that springing eternally with hope was really self-defeating. Living this way was just draining. I forced my train of thought back to the Changewater problem. This was something actionable and I might actually be effective in helping to solve the problem. "Would any of them be willing and able to help?"

Cam tilted his head as he thought. "Maybe. I'd have to take a trip to North Carolina to know for sure." I could almost hear the wheels turn as he planned the trip. "Zackie should stay with you when I go. It might be awkward if she accompanied me."

"Why is that?"

"She was a bit of a stigma for the family, being associated with the sin-eater. I think they were glad to be rid of her." Zackie sneezed mightily from her position on the floor to let us know what she thought of that. "Anyway, you should probably take her to see Hannah a few times while I'm away. I know this is uncomfortable for you, but Hannah needs Zackie."

Still wrung out, I really didn't want to get into another emotional conversation, so I nodded in agreement. "Will do."

Cam grunted and adjusted the sling on his arm. "Driving long distance round trip is out of the question. I'll need you to take me into Pennsylvania tomorrow to catch a bus." He stood up and I followed as he moved to the study and sat in front of the computer. After a short search, he pointed to the screen with his chin. "There's a Greyhound station in Bethlehem." With a few deft clicks, he booked his trip and then settled in to write an e-mail to Lummie's kin.

#

I wore my new, fancy gloves when I drove Cam to the bus terminal. The FedEx package and a check from Lucas's ghost show had been waiting for me when I finally got home the previous night. I explained to Cam that instead of practicing with the makeup, I had deposited the check and gone grocery shopping, so he wouldn't be treated to my new Goth nails just yet. He was less interested in my nails than in catching the bus, so he mumbled something about it having to wait until he got back. He then exited the car and waved absently to Zackie and me as he headed into the bus station.

After dropping Cam off, I drove to the hospital to first get my stitches removed and then to visit Hannah. With a few snips and a little tweezing, the stitches came right out. The cut had healed nicely and I was left with a slightly raised, pinkish scar that the doctors assured me would fade in time. As I made my way to Hannah's room, I resolved to start looking for another job right after treating myself to a shampoo. First things first. My hair was greasy and lank and I was paranoid that it smelled bad. Still, I felt worse about the scar, so I arranged my hair to cover it and tried hard to avoid seeing the reflection of my loveliness in the dome mirrors at the hallway intersections.

Hannah looked pleased when I walked through the door with Zackie. I'm sure it had more to do with Zackie. Lucas was sitting on the edge of her bed, but rose to greet me.

"Excellent, your stitches are out." He smiled happily at me and shifted my hair to get a better look. Inwardly, I cringed that he was touching my disgusting hair and looking at the unsightly scar. *And what if he saw the rotting hand?* The little voice in my head chose that moment to remind me of my true power to horrify.

"I'm okay. It healed really well." I started backing away to get out of his reach, but my eyes strayed along the contours of his features. He gazed at me steadily, unaware how much I wanted to touch the slight stubble of beard on his cheek. He wore his hair loose and if I ran my fingers through it, it would feel soft and silky.

"How's Cam doing?" I turned my head as Hannah spoke, but my eyes were unfocused and I stared stupidly at her for a moment. "Cam. How is Cam?" Her brow wrinkled as she tried to get me to understand her. Hannah had her arms wrapped around Zackie, who was stretched out on the bed at her side. If animals could smirk, that's what she was doing.

I blinked a few times and put my brain back into gear. "Cam is doing well. He went to North Carolina today to visit some friends."

"How's his arm doing?" Lucas moved to Hannah's other side as he spoke and sat on the edge of the bed. I placed myself at the foot of the bed, so he wouldn't have to crane his neck.

"Well, um, he took a bus rather than drive. But he…that is…that seems to be his only concession to his injury. So, um, it doesn't appear to be causing him a lot of pain, but I'll bet it's still… uncomfortable." Just as Cam predicted, I also felt distinctly uncomfortable. I was trying hard to hold up my end of the conversation, but I found Lucas to be a distraction and it was difficult to keep my train of thought for these simple questions. I could feel Hannah watching me as I gazed at her husband, so I forced my eyes to look at her instead. "And how are you feeling today?"

Her eyes were hard as she answered me. "About the same, but at least I'm not falling asleep every few minutes." She sat up a little taller in the bed and Zackie readjusted her body so it pressed more fully against Hannah. "I like to stay aware of what's going on." Her eyes bore into mine and her lips compressed into a hard line. Obviously caught in the act, I unknowingly did my best deer-caught-in-the-headlights imitation.

"Would you like me to run to the lobby and bring you some newspapers?" Lucas shifted, ready on her word to run this errand.

Hannah's eyes softened as she looked at him. "No thanks, sweetie. I meant it in the larger sense." Her hand reached to gently touch his cheek.

Kissing her hand, Lucas stood. "Okay, if you don't need anything, I'll go back to work." Turning to me, he smiled. "Thanks for bringing Zackie for a visit."

As he left the room, Hannah turned her acid gaze back in my direction. "You're lusting after my husband."

"I—"

"Don't. Just don't." Hannah let her eyes drift away and she hugged Zackie tightly to her. "I don't have time for bullshit."

I released a deep breath, relieved that I no longer had to dissemble. "Okay. No bullshit." I was glad that she was looking elsewhere as I continued. "I am attracted to Lucas." Her eyes shot back to me and an angry retort formed on her lips. Before she could start in on me, I interrupted. "But he's your husband and I promise you, I will not make a move on him."

She tilted her head and studied me, but said nothing for a while. After she let me squirm for a full minute, she finally spoke her mind. "I play a game sometimes. I add the words 'while Hannah's alive' to a lot of the stuff I hear." She exhaled strongly and closed her eyes. "Once I'm dead, things will go on as if I were never here. Everything will change."

"The world has never stopped for anyone's passing and I don't think it will make an exception for you." This sounded harsh even to my own ears, but I was playing by her ground rules. I sat down in a chair near the bed and continued. "But you're not really worried about things in 'the larger sense.' You're worried about what Lucas will do when you die." Hannah nodded her head once, her eyes still shut. "He doesn't really notice me, if you haven't noticed. I notice the hell out him, but he has no idea." I waited for her to open her eyes, but she lay there stubbornly and did not look at me. Exasperated, I finally asked, "Am I lying?"

"No, you're not lying." She sighed and opened her eyes. "He wouldn't touch you in front of me if it meant anything." I nodded and she continued. "He's kind of oblivious to a lot of things. He thinks the treatments are helping and that I'm not dying."

"Do you want to continue the treatments?" I leaned forward to watch her face closely as she responded.

"There's nothing really to continue. I have one last round remaining and nothing's going to change, but it will make him happy if he thinks there's still hope." She gave a small shrug.

"Have you talked to him about dying?"

"I want him to have his hope for a little while longer." She smiled a little. "He still talks to me about the future sometimes." Her smile faded as she thought. "I'll discuss reality with him after the last treatment. Don't say anything, okay?"

"Promise." I stared at Zackie. She looked positively

blissful. "Can I ask you a question?"

"You can ask. I might not answer. I don't like you, after all."

"All right…" At least we were being honest. I thought for a moment how to phrase the question. "What does Zackie do for you? You always seem glad to see her."

Hannah stroked Zackie's flank in a repetitive, soothing motion. "When she's around, it doesn't hurt as much and I feel more peaceful about what's going to happen. It's one thing to be able to admit that I'm going to die, but it's whole other thing to actually go through with it." I nodded, but didn't say anything, waiting for her to continue. "I want you to promise me one more thing."

I tilted my head and scrunched my eyebrows. "I thought you didn't like me. Why are you asking me for favors?"

"I'm pulling the cancer girl card. Is that all right with you?" I raised my eyebrows for her to continue. "Make sure Zackie is there when I die." Her eyes were large and pleading and she swallowed hard as she waited for my answer.

"I'll do my best. Just don't go suddenly, okay? Give us time to get here." Hannah visibly relaxed. She must have known on some subconscious level what Zackie was and that, in the presence of such a being, she would be ensured an end without fear and without pain.

Contrary to Hannah's claim that she did not fall asleep every few minutes, her eyes grew heavy. "Okay… That's good," she murmured. In seconds, she was fast asleep, worn out by the effort of hating me.

CHAPTER 14

My hair dripped on to the classifieds, smearing the ad for full time and casual qualified truck drivers. I luxuriated in the feeling of my clean hair and tried not to focus too hard on the fact that there weren't any suitable job openings. I did not have a teaching certificate, and so was unqualified to be a part-time math teacher for an elementary school. I would not be able to maintain conveyors and PLCs (whatever those were) for a local dairy. I never poured concrete. Sighing, I flipped the newspaper closed. I had spent the afternoon filing for unemployment and then driving around to restaurants, diners and retail establishments, filling out job applications and trying to make a good impression. On the few occasions where I was able to submit the application to a manager, they had stared at the gloves as I handed over the paperwork. My guess is that they found it off-putting and I would not hear back from them.

To improve my hiring potential, I pulled out the mortuary makeup and spread out the contents of the kit on the card table where I ate my meals. Zackie made herself comfortable under the table. According to the label, the makeup was non-thermogenic. A Google search informed me that thermogenic makeup was for use on 'live' skin. Body heat causes it to break down, so it can be applied uniformly. The same makeup used on 'dead' skin just blotches. Airbrushing was probably the best way to apply makeup to the skin of the deceased, but I did not have the resources at the moment to invest in this. The rub-on makeup would have to do. Working on the hand was probably going to be harder than working on a corpse, since with a corpse, all you had to do was choose a becoming shade of foundation for the subject and go with it. With the hand, I had to match the complexion of my good hand. Just as I was about to try and figure out how to do this, the phone rang and the caller ID announced Cam.

"Cam! How y'all doin' down South?"

"Peachy. Negotiations have stalled, so I think it's going to take another day or two to convince them to come."

"Really? What do they want?"

"They want to not leave the mountains. They don't

trust us city folk and our city ways."

"Can you offer them some kind of inducement?"

"Working on that. I'm feeling them out at the moment, since I'm not sure what they'd go for."

"Cam, can you hold on for a second? I have another call coming through."

"No. I have to go. They've just come back. I'll talk to you later." With this, he hung up and I went to the other call.

"Hello?"

"Fia? This is Lucas."

The first word that came to my mind was 'crap.' Instead of blurting this out, I reverted to social niceties. "Lucas! How nice of you to call. Is everything all right with Hannah?"

"Hannah is fine. We're eating dinner in her room." A muffled few words sounded faintly in the background. "She says to bring Zackie back when you have a chance."

I rolled my eyes toward the ceiling and then glanced at Zackie. That girl was becoming an addict. "Will do."

"Listen, the reason I'm calling is that my producers want more footage. The last segment we filmed got a huge viewer response. They want more. I couldn't get through to Cam, so I left a message. I thought I'd call to see if you guys felt up to it and if you knew anything more about scheduling."

"Cam said he should be back in another few days." Since everything was not aligned with Lummie's kin, I needed to stall. "But I don't think we'd be ready to film anything at the Changewater house right away. How long do you think the producers would be willing to wait?"

Lucas groaned. "I don't know...they're impatient." There was a scraping noise as he adjusted the phone and then faintly, "No, finish your vegetables..." After some muffled words of complaint, there was another scraping sound. "Sorry...what was I saying? Oh, yeah... I'll try to convince them that we need to build the suspense, maybe do a little more historical background stuff, but I don't know if that will fly."

"Well, give it a shot. I'll try to come up with a plan B, just in case."

"Okay. Let me know as soon as you know

something. I'll talk to the producers tomorrow."

After hanging up, I rubbed my lower lip with my good hand and considered our predicament. Lucas must be under a huge amount of pressure from his bosses. He would not have tried to call us in so soon to do more filming if it were just up to him. Neither Cam nor I were ready for another showdown at the Changewater house, but I could really use another paycheck from the production company right now. Preserve life and limb or keep a roof over my head and food in my belly? Maybe I could land another job before things became too desperate.

Sighing, I turned my attention back to the makeup, since this was something I could probably solve. I sorted the various shades of foundation from lightest to darkest and then started with the primer to create a base on my good hand. This would prevent the makeup from rubbing off on everything I touched and even though I didn't need that now, I figured it might distort the foundation colors, so I needed to test it in combination with these colors. I next applied a streak of each of the foundations to my good hand over the layer of primer. None of them were the perfect shade. The makeup had to disappear on my good hand to be a good match to my natural coloring and all the foundation shades stood out pretty starkly.

While I considered how to mix the foundation colors to match my skin tone, my mind wandered back to Lummie's kin. Maybe Cam would be able to convince them to help. I had only the vaguest notion as to what they brought to the table, but I figured reinforcements could only be a good thing in our present state. Choosing the lightest and darkest foundation shades that were closest to my natural coloring, I used a blank region of my good hand to blend the colors. Better. A two to one ratio of light to dark might fit the bill. Frowning, I cleaned the hand with a makeup removing wipe and thought about what it would take to get those folks down from the mountain. Warren County New Jersey had large tracts of land devoted to farming and wilderness, so maybe they would feel more at home if they knew this. But what if this distrust of city life was just a ruse? What if they took one look at Cam's broken arm and thought better about this venture?

I replaced the primer and started my color mix again using the new ratio. Eureka! This was blending nicely with the rest of my good hand. I began repeating the process on the other hand while I thought about a way to reassure Lummie's kin that we were capable. They knew

Cam, but they had no idea about me and whether I could stand my ground if push came to shove. I sure hoped Cam could convince them, because I so wanted my re-match with the entity. *Hold a grudge much?* The little voice in my head interrupted my beautician's zen and I stopped blending for a moment. *Hell, yes*, I thought to myself. That entity was abusing innocents. Cam should use that as an argument for Lummie's kin. If they were decent people, they would respond to this. I finished my blending and checked my work, holding the two hands up next to each other. Except for the nails, the two hands looked fairly matched. Grabbing the nail polish, I completed my new look and decided to call it an early night once my nails dried.

# # #

"What do you mean I have to go there?" I was on the phone again with Cam. I had just finished delivering newspapers and was about to shower.

Cam exhaled roughly. "Parmelia and Bodean want to cement a mutual assistance agreement with some aid in their neck of the woods."

"Sounds like a test to me."

"Call it whatever you want. You need to come down here."

Thinking quickly, I saw an opportunity for Lucas and for some income. "What do you think of Lucas and his crew coming down to film whatever it is we're getting into? Would they have a problem with that?"

There was more blowing on Cam's end. "I don't know. I'll see what they say about it. Is it important?"

"I spoke to Lucas yesterday. Did you get his message? I think he's under a lot of pressure from the higher ups to get more footage for the show. Obviously, we're not ready to do more on the Changewater house and frankly, I need some positive cash flow."

"I haven't checked my messages. I'll do that after this call. But filming down here might be a good compromise, if everyone here is agreeable." Voices sounded in the background followed by a door slamming. "Let me take a survey and I'll call you back as soon as we come to a consensus."

I ended the call and immediately dialed the

newspaper people to let them know they'd have to cover my route next week. I had officially become a problem employee and I knew it. First, there was time off for medical issues and now I'd be gone a week. It was no surprise when they announced my services were no longer needed and that I'd lost my route. Chewing the cuticles on my good hand, I decided I better start packing. No matter the outcome of Cam's discussion, I'd still be going down there. My stomach was roiling as I dove under the bed to find the old suitcase I used when I moved here. It might be good to have it on hand, since I might be moving again when I could no longer afford the rent. I threw a week's worth of clothes into the suitcase and then laid out some clothes to wear today. I was about to finally take that shower when the phone rang again.

Cam launched in without preamble. "They're huge fans of the show and they can't wait to meet Lucas. I think our stock just went up just from being associated with him."

"You're kidding!" I let out the breath I didn't know I was holding. "That's great news. Let me call Lucas and let him know. I'll start driving down with Zackie right after we have some breakfast."

260

Cam provided directions and warned that there would be dirt roads towards the end of the trip and to tell Lucas to plan his convoy accordingly. My vehicle was used to searches in wilderness areas, so I had no qualms about negotiating the more rustic environments. I rang off and called Lucas. Surprisingly, he answered on the first ring.

"You're awake. I thought I'd be leaving a message." His voices sounded husky and extremely sexy at this early hour and a frisson trailed from my earlobe down my neck.

"Hold on a sec. Let me get into the hall, so I don't wake Hannah." Of course. He'd stayed the night in her room. I listened to him breathe while he had made his way to some place where he could talk without disturbing the other patients. "Okay. What's up?"

I explained the new game plan. Lucas was ecstatic, but then immediately sobered when he realized that he would be away from Hannah. "Do you have a rough feel for how long this project will take to complete?"

"Honestly, I don't even know what they have planned for us. I have no idea how long it might take." I started butter melting in a pan and grabbed the eggs and cheese from the refrigerator. "Maybe you can just get things running and then leave it to the crew?"

"That's a possibility... I'll have to feel this out once I'm on site." Lucas yawned expansively. "Excuse me.... Where did you say we were going?"

Balancing the phone against my shoulder, I filled a bowl with dog food and placed it on the floor near Zackie. "The closest major city is Asheville. We'll be going into a sparsely populated area in the Blue Ridge Mountains."

"That's what? A six or seven hour drive from here?"

"I guess." I cracked some eggs into a bowl and whisked them with a fork before pouring them into the pan.

"Okay. That's not so bad. I can turn this into a day trip if I can get away with just editing the footage with some voice-overs." Lucas's good mood was restored and the smile returned to warm his voice. Irresistible...

My fantasy was interrupted by the thought of him falling asleep behind the wheel. If he slept at all last night, it was sitting up in a chair or curled in an uncomfortable contortion around Hannah and her IVs on the small bed.

"Just don't force yourself beyond your limits, okay? Hannah has been pretty stable and you've got to get some real, quality sleep at some point."

"Yes, mom. I'll sleep soon. I promise."

"Yeah, yeah... the checks in the mail." I crumbled some cheese on to the mostly cooked egg, folded it and then went back to fretting about him. "Lucas, how about if I drive us down? You can sleep in the passenger seat." Kill me now. I could think of nothing more uncomfortable than being trapped for many hours alone in a car with Lucas. The only thing that could possibly be more excruciating was explaining the need to carpool to Hannah. Still, it would be worth it if I could lay my worries for him to rest. "I could pick you up at the hospital and Hannah could have some Zackie time before we leave."

"That is an awesome idea." Lucas sounded genuinely relieved that he would not have to suck it up and find some untapped source of stamina to deal with this trip. "Can we meet here in about an hour? I need to shower and pack and organize the crew."

"Me too, except for organizing the crew. Zackie is pretty organized and requires very little in the way of management." I was starting to babble, so I told him I'd see him in an hour and ended the call.

In the grand tradition of SAR, I ended up taking nothing out of the trunk and only adding to the contents. In went the dog food and my small suitcase. With a little creative organizing, I fashioned sufficient space for whatever Lucas needed to bring. If he was planning on a day trip, it wouldn't be much. I was at the hospital in a little under an hour and rather than linger in the parking lot, I decided to get the conversation with Hannah over with.

Hannah pinned me to the wall with her eyes when I walked into the room. "So, you're going on a trip with my husband?"

"Yes. I'm driving him down because you know and I know that he's exhausted. I don't want him behind the wheel on a long drive."

Zackie crawled into the bed and Hannah automatically wrapped her arms around the dog. Zackie access did nothing to sweeten her mood, but the pain-induced tautness in her body let go and her muscles relaxed. "Well played. I really want to argue with you. More than anything right now, I want to have a knockdown, drag-out fight where I scratch your eyes out and accuse you of manipulating the situation. But the truth is, he needs a break." Her eyes slanted sideways and her lips compressed. "But you are manipulating the situation."

Sighing deeply, I collapsed into a chair next to the bed. "You might be right, but I'm not doing it intentionally. Besides, I told you before – I will not make a move on him."

"While Hannah is alive." Hannah's eyes were downcast and she whispered this mostly to herself. Looking back at me, in a stronger voice, she said, "Not intentionally." She mimicked my words and narrowed her eyes at me. "You might not be able to help yourself. You're a mess when you're around him, you know."

"Who's a mess?" Lucas walked into the room and I blushed furiously. How much had he heard? *Activate diversion sequence*, I thought desperately.

"Zackie's a mess. At least, she was a mess after training in the woods. She's all cleaned up now, so don't worry about Hannah getting exposed to anything." Zackie picked her head up at the mention of her name and stared at me. The communication was obvious: *Do not involve me in your fiasco.*

Lucas glanced at the dog squished tightly to Hannah's side. "She looks all right. Are we taking her with us?" Claiming his position on Hannah's other side, he sat down gently on the bed.

"Yes. We're going to need her for whatever they have planned down there." Thinking quickly for a way to extricate myself from being in the middle of a Hannah and Lucas conversation, I hit on the need for food. "I'm going to the gift store and grab some food for the trip. I'll be right back." I sidled out the door and made for the elevators.

I figured I could burn ten or fifteen minutes doing this and maybe he'd be ready to go by the time I returned. As it turned out, the gift store was devoid of unhealthy road trip snacks, so I made a quick trip to the grocery store across the street from the hospital. Just as well. Things were more expensive in the gift store and this would not be a good use of my dwindling funds. I was mostly pinning my hopes on some Southern hospitality for the trip. If I could rely on our hosts for food and shelter, this would go a long way towards preserving my savings. I would happily clean out barn stalls or whatever in exchange for these necessities.

Returning to Hannah's room after depositing the salty, crunchy spoils in the car, I stared hopefully at Lucas and Zackie. "Ready to go?" They both looked content to stay where they were, but dutifully roused themselves at my urging.

Lucas stretched and the joints popped as he groaned himself back into action. "Call me or have the nurse call me if you need anything at all. Call me if you just get bored and want to talk." He kissed her pale lips and he held her face cupped in his hands a moment longer. The strain of the impending separation showed as he surveyed her for any hidden signs of weakening. Satisfied by something he saw, he straightened and caressed her cheek, prolonging their contact. The dark smudges under his eyes stood out starkly and his face was drawn with fatigue as he finally turned from the bed. With a quick nod to me, Lucas walked out the door.

I also gave Hannah a final once over. Honestly, she looked like she was going to die. I just hoped she could hold out until we got back. Her eyes were too large and too dark in her emaciated face and her skin was practically translucent. Veins that were blue-black from her treatment traced the patterns of her circulation and were the only reminder that she still lived. "We'll get back as soon as we can, okay?" She nodded and then rolled away from me to sleep away some of the lonely hours.

# # #

By the time we reached I-81, Lucas was deeply asleep. Zackie had made herself comfortable in the back seat and she too was gently snoring. The snacks I bought were temporarily safe from her inquisitive nose while she slumbered. Lucas had hung on as long as he could, making polite conversation to keep me company while I drove, but eventually it was impossible to fight off the sleep he desperately needed. I could hear his regular breathing and smell the coconut shampoo he used. As I watched him sleep, the sun streamed in from the window and lighted on his hair. I almost reached out to smooth a stray lock from his brow. For both our sakes, I hoped he would sleep for many, many hours.

I hated long distance driving. There was nothing more boring. My brain bounced from topic to topic, I listened to some history podcasts and I shifted positions every so often to keep my ribs happy. Glancing at my hands on the steering wheel, the makeup was still looking good and there was no need for a touch up, so no excuse to pull over yet. Finally, after about three hours of monotony, I took an exit to get some gas and take a badly needed bio-break. Both Zackie and Lucas showed no interest in rousing, so I let them sleep while I took care of the necessities and stretched my legs. Getting back into the car, I sighed and broke open a bag of chips to make myself feel better. Somewhere around the six hour mark, Lucas was showing signs of life.

Lucas rubbed his face and then stretched as best he could in his seat. "Where are we?"

"I'm seeing signs for Roanoke. We're in Virginia."

Checking his watch, he yelped. "We're only in Roanoke? It's been at least six hours! We should be much closer by now." He dug out his phone and started poking at the screen. "What the hell? It's a nine and half hour drive to Asheville. Why did you tell me it was six or seven?" His wan complexion was replaced by a fiery red. He was pissed.

I kept my voice level. "I didn't tell you it was six or seven hours. You told me that and I just agreed with you.

To be honest, I didn't map out the trip. I'm just going by Cam's directions."

Lucas rubbed his face roughly and muttered some expletives into his hands and then looked up at me abruptly. "How am I supposed to get back to Hannah tonight?" His voice was really loud in the confines of the car and Zackie sat up to see what was going on.

For a split second, I considered winding this up into a cursing, screaming argument. It would be easier on me if I were angry with him. Anger and fighting were in my comfort zone, but ultimately, it wouldn't be good for Lucas. He had enough stress on him as a caretaker. For me to add the stress of useless conflict was beyond what my conscience could tolerate. In the end, I decided on a limited apology, even though I knew this was not my fault. "I'm really sorry, Lucas. I didn't know, okay?"

He was fiddling with his phone and wasn't really listening to me, so I could have saved my breath. "Crap! She called and I missed it." He immediately hit speed dial, pounding his fist on his thigh in frustration. "Honey? Hi… I'm sorry I missed your call. I was asleep… Yeah, I do feel more rested now. Are you okay? Do you need anything?" I zoned out as the conversation continued. It was entirely possible that even though I wanted to avoid conflict for his sake, Lucas might still be royally pissed at me. But maybe this was still good for him. He needed to be pissed at something, after all. His wife was dying and he couldn't be mad at her, since it wasn't like she was dying on purpose. Being angry at the universe did little good. If I've learned nothing else, the universe was indifferent to human suffering. He had no real outlet for his anger, so if he wanted to be mad at me for a while, I guess I could tolerate it. It kept us at a distance and I didn't really have to participate, so my conscience would be clear.

Eventually, he told her that he loved her and then ended the call. "How is she?"

"The same. I guess that's good." Lucas exhaled slowly and then turned towards me in his seat. "Look, I'm sorry I yelled at you." He looked at me for some sign of being forgiven and reached a hand out to brush my cheek. "You have some chips…" My cheek burned where he touched me. So much for getting some distance from him through anger…

I rubbed my cheek and stuttered a response. "That's all right. Not a problem." Thinking carefully, I struggled to put together a sentence that kept my promise to Hannah and did not imply that she was dying, but still acknowledged that their time together was precious. "I understand how badly you want to spend time with Hannah." It sounded gimpy, even to my ears, but it was the best I could do. We sat in silence for a few minutes. It was not a comfortable silence, so I opted for a quick change in topic before I found myself smelling his hair again.

"So, what did you make of the flying objects in the Changewater house?" This was the first thing that came to mind, but clearly, my subconscious was deliberately choosing contentious topics. We might just yet get to that argument, but I had to admit that I was curious to hear what he thought about the incident. He was a self-declared, diehard skeptic, yet here he was, confronted with something that was not easy to explain.

Lucas blinked at the sudden change in topic, but then I guess he decided to just go with it and his expression turned thoughtful. "I don't know what caused it. I know you would like to attribute the phenomenon to ghosts, but I don't live in that world. My mind doesn't work that way." He shrugged his shoulders. "I have an observation of inanimate objects flying through the air. I am willing to concede that these objects moved with force and they did not simply fall. How do I construct a testable hypothesis out of this observation?"

I smiled to myself. He's turning on the scientist. "For the sake of argument, let's say one hypothesis is that a ghost is responsible for launching those objects."

"All right.... if we must. The next step for me is stating a formalized hypothesis. We'd want the statement to contain both 'if' and 'then' pieces. The 'if' piece contains the testable, proposed relationship and the 'then' portion makes a prediction of expected results from an experiment."

"Okay. 'If a ghost is responsible for throwing objects, then returning to the scene will cause more objects to be thrown.' How's that?"

"That's kind of a sucky hypothesis. A better hypothesis would give us something to measure, but let's just go ahead with it." Lucas grabbed the open bag of chips and ate a handful before continuing. "Has that been your experience? Absolute repeatability of action with the identical set up?"

I thought back to the weeping bride. She was not just a constantly replaying movie of a woman on her wedding day. To relive the moment, she would show up when she wanted to and, based on what happened when I called to her, maybe sometimes upon invitation. I could go to the church again and call to her, but it was completely up to her if she wanted to make an appearance. "No. They have free will. They do what they want."

Lucas quirked an eyebrow and seemed a little surprised at my answer. "Okay, so what I think your answer is telling me is that you think that if we just return to the Changewater house and do everything in the same way, the identical thing will not happen?"

I kept my eyes on the road and tried not to imagine the possibilities of what could happen during a return visit. "Truthfully? I think something worse will happen." I shrugged a shoulder and pursed my lips. "Okay, so that was a suckie hypothesis. It turns out, I didn't even believe it. How would you phrase the formalized hypothesis for a ghost-driven movement of objects?"

"I can't. That's kind of my point." He waved a handful of chips in my direction as he finally started making his point. "Repeatability is only one element that is necessary if you want to use the scientific method to study something. For something to be repeatable, it really helps if its properties are constrained by the physical laws of the universe." Lucas took a moment to munch some chips and then continued. "Assuming they exist, ghosts may or may not be part of the natural world. If they have no basis in the physical universe, then they are not subject to the laws of that universe. If I can't make predictions based on known physical laws, laws that govern the actions of everything else, I can't study their existence or lack of existence with the tools of science."

"So, the bottom line is if ghosts are not part of the natural world, you cannot construct a testable hypothesis."

"Correct."

I chewed on my lip as I thought about this. I had no idea if ghosts were made up of atoms and molecules. All I knew was that something could become solid enough to exert a force on a stationary object to make it move, but maybe I didn't even know that. Maybe I was thinking about this all wrong. Magnets could be used to propel other magnets if you aligned the poles with the same charge and they did this without creating a solid contact. So, maybe solid had nothing to do with it. Also, something danced up and down my nervous system to animate the hand on those occasions it moved of its own volition. I furrowed my brow to try to figure this out, but I had even less of an idea of how to conceptualize a mechanism for that. Eventually, I just shook my head to clear it. If ghosts were not part of the physical universe, then all this brain strain wasn't getting at the heart of the matter because it all invoked the natural laws of physics. If they were part of the physical universe, then this was still well beyond the understanding of a humble history major.

"What if you worked under the assumption that ghosts were subject to natural law and you used your scientific training to try to study them?" I was more than willing to pass the buck to Lucas. I was curious and I wanted to understand, but I lacked the tools.

"Well, remember I'm a molecular pharmacologist. I am qualified to talk about the scientific method and how to ask questions that can be tested, but I don't really have the scientific background to properly design experiments to study this particular phenomenon. You'd probably need a physicist or a materials scientist to do this right."

"And they're kind of busy answering questions about the universe and solving problems for the living, right?" I slanted my eyes towards him.

"Yes. That and they don't want to ruin their careers." Lucas gave a half smile and lifted a shoulder. "I made a fool of myself to get Hannah treatment and I'd do it again." There was probably no way back to the hallowed halls of science after the ghost hunting show. What he did for Hannah was heroic and my heart squeezed hard when I looked at him. The tragedy was that he had sacrificed himself and it would not save her, proving once again that the universe was indifferent to human suffering.

I forced my eyes back to the road and tried to make my expression neutral. "Let's take the next exit and get some real food."

CHAPTER 15

By the time we reached the tiny town of Sylva, North Carolina, it was full dark and the last part of the journey was the most hazardous. The crew vehicles had been instructed to set up camp in Sylva, but none had yet arrived. Carefully negotiating the rutted dirt roads to make our way up the mountain to find Lummie's tribe, we eventually arrived at an ancient log cabin that had been enlarged by the addition of a more modern-looking add-on. A steady light shone through the windows and I crossed my fingers that there would also be running water. Lucas said goodnight to Hannah just as I killed the engine and then pocketed the phone in his jacket. It was a wonder that he still had bars in this remote location, let alone power after all the calls during the drive.

Emerging stiffly from the vehicle, I opened the rear door for Zackie, who jumped out, stretched out her hind legs and hips like a yogi and then shook vigorously. We were all that happy to be free of the confines of the car and were unknotting muscles and stretching out the kinks when

Cam appeared at the cabin door. His eyes darted to the exposed hand, so I deliberately raised it and waved at him. He cocked his head slightly in response, acknowledging that the makeup job was good enough for a first pass inspection. Lucas certainly paid it no attention during the entire drive, so I felt confident that I could get away without gloves in polite company, provided I did a makeup check and touch up every so often during the day.

Cam nodded to Zackie as she pushed past him and into the cabin. He then took in Lucas's presence with one raised eyebrow. "You people took your time getting here."

Lucas's voice was muffled as he stuck his head in the trunk and grabbed the bags. "This is a long, long way from Jersey. I'm not really sure I ought to be here." I mentally added 'while Hannah is alive' to his statement. Taking my bag from Lucas, I shuffled doggedly behind the two men as they entered the cabin. My eyes were gritty, my brain was buzzing and I was more than ready for some quality sleep as I crossed the threshold.

Zackie lay near a pot belly stove planted near the back center of the old cabin. She looked at home and it was obvious that she was reclaiming her accustomed place. The interior walls of the cabin were horizontal stripes of alternating light and dark as some ancient white material intercalated between the rude logs to plug the cracks and insulate the interior from drafts. Nearly hidden in the shadows of the back corner were stairs to a loft and two people holding bed sheets, poised to climb the stairs. They stood so perfectly still that at first I could not be sure they were animate. The young man and woman were tall and lanky and looked to be fraternal twins. Their skin was a white so pale that light appeared to reflect from their faces as they emerged from the shadows. This paleness was offset by rich, ebony hair that fell to their shoulders in soft waves. They might have been attractive had it not been for the shock of their ice blue eyes. Cold and inhuman, I found myself avoiding their thousand mile stare.

"Zackie," the man nodded, simultaneously acknowledging her and paying respect. His body leaned ever so slightly away from the dog. The woman peeked at Zackie from behind the man and also gave a small nod. Her eyes were large and wary and she held tightly to the man's hand. For her part, Zackie yawned cavernously at them, displaying a set of razor sharp teeth and her enormously long canines. Taking a quick step away to gain some distance from Zackie, the two next turned their attention my way, regarding me with open suspicion.

The woman cleared her throat and stepped forward. "My goodness, where are my manners?" The words were soft and had the gentle twang of Appalachia, but they were spoken by reflex and lacked true warmth. She took Bodean's set of sheets and together with her own folded bedding, she set them down on a scrubbed, unfinished table next to the pot belly stove. "My name is Parmelia Sinclair and this here is my cousin Bodean Sinclair." Bodean extended his hand to me and before I could respond, the dead hand shot forward and grabbed it.

Bodean's eyes went wide and impossibly, he turned a whiter shade of pale, yanking his hand back as if the contact burned. "Whoa, girl! That ain't right!" Parmelia ducked back behind Bodean and watched me with frightened eyes.

Lucas looked back and forth between the cousins and me, trying to make sense of what just happened. "What's wrong?"

I took a step back to reduce whatever threat I might represent and improvised. "Um, I guess I have a strong grip for a girl?" Cam was smirking and Zackie showed a toothy grin. Neither was going to be any help to defuse this situation, so I decided a distraction might be the best way forward. "Pleased to meet you both. I'm Fia Saunders and this is my friend, Lucas Tremaine." As I hoped, their attention was immediately taken by the presence of a celebrity.

"Mr. Tremaine, it is a true pleasure to meet you. We are huge fans of your show." Parmelia gushed as she stepped in front of Bodean, who massaged his hand and shot me small looks of shock and dismay, but mainly turned his attention to Lucas.

"Please call me Lucas." Turning on the charm, he shook both their hands and this simple act seemed to put them more at ease. "I want to thank you both for inviting us down here. I'm really looking forward to investigating the anomaly you witnessed. Can you tell us anything about what you experienced?"

Bodean and Parmelia shuffled their feet, glancing at Cam and me without quite meeting our eyes. They exchanged a look and Bodean cleared his throat. "Well, you see, the main problem is that we don't really understand what it is we're dealing with."

Parmelia interrupted and her hands shook as she tried to hide them behind her back. "We got too much on our plate right now." She tucked her hands under her arms to hold them still and began to gently rock her upper body. "We think y'all might be better suited to deal with this thing."

Bodean put a comforting arm around her. "We tried--" he began, but an infinitesimal shake of the head from Cam stopped him from elaborating. Lucas did not need to hear the particulars of what we do. Bodean closed his eyes briefly and exhaled through his nose before he began again. "We heard about it from thru-hikers on the A.T. who came to rent goats from us."

I was swaying on my feet with fatigue and my monkey brain took control. "This might be a stupid question and totally off topic, but why do Appalachian Trail hikers need goats?"

Parmelia shrugged and blushed. "They're pack goats. They can carry up to fifty pounds, so if you want some relief from carrying your pack..." She scrupulously avoided my eyes as she spoke and my tired mind latched on to the fact that there was some weirdness regarding the goats.

I probably should have let it go, but apparently I get

a little obsessive when I'm exhausted. "So, how does this work with the goats?" I looked directly at Bodean and extended the dead hand as if I were gesturing. He followed its every move as if it were a venomous snake. "What are you not telling us about the goats?"

Bodean cleared his throat again. "Well, our goats are pretty good about carrying stuff for us and we thought we could make some extra money if we could rent them out to hikers. By the time the hikers get here, they're hitting the highest mountains on the Trail. It seemed like a good business opportunity...." His voice trailed off and he shrugged.

I took a step forward. "And?"

Parmelia looked up and flapped her hands nervously at me. "And we charge thirty dollars a day for each goat, all right?" I raised my eyebrows and encouraged her to tell us the part she was holding back. Her voice rose shrilly as she continued. "And then we charge them for the rescue."

Lucas frowned. "Why would they need rescue?"

Bodean took up the explanation at this point. "Look, we didn't know when we started, okay? Our goats worked fine for us and we didn't know that they need to adopt you into their herd before they'll cooperate right." He pulled uneasily at the neckline of his t-shirt and shifted his weight. "When we found out that the hikers would get stranded out there with a bunch of stubborn goats, we thought we'd send them out with a GPS and tell them it was so we could find them to pick up the goats when they left the Trail. When they call us to say that the goats refuse to move and they are stuck, we get their location and then offer to get them mobile again for an additional fee."

Parmelia sighed and looked down. "We thought it was a smart business plan, since we made a whole lot more off the rescue than the rental."

I looked at Cam and silently shook my head in disbelief. The little voice chimed in to say *'And that's who you're dealing with, folks.'* Lucas had his hand over his mouth as if he were thinking, but the slight movement in his shoulders revealed that he found this all very amusing. Under other circumstance, I would have thought this was funny too, but I was starting to have some serious trust issues with Parmelia and Bodean. If we were going to have to rely on them to deal with our Entity and their Anomaly, this whole collaboration might be a bad, dangerous idea.

Cam rubbed his face tiredly with his hands and then looked up, gritting his teeth slightly. "If I may bring us back to the original topic of this Anomaly, what exactly did you learn from the thru-hikers?"

Parmelia wrapped her arms around her middle, her body hunching slightly like her stomach hurt. Her voice was low as she answered. "There's this old farmhouse not too far off-Trail and pretty close to us. Some people bought it recently and converted it into an inn for hikers to get a break from sleeping on the Trail." She ran a hand through her thick mane to force it from her eyes and went back to hunching. "The hikers were there the night the innkeepers' little girl got hurt."

Bodean nodded and took up the tale. "The little girl is three and can't really say what happened to her, but her parents said she was having bad dreams since the day they moved into that place. She'd come to their bedroom at night, crying and wanting to crawl into bed with them. She'd never been that way before and they just chucked it up to being in a strange place and that she'd get used to things eventually."

Parmelia crooked her mouth and her eyes drifted to the side. "Well, instead of the little girl getting better about things, things started getting worse for her parents. To save money, they were doing all the renovation work themselves. But during the renovations, tools would disappear, they'd hear sounds coming from empty parts of the house and see something dark moving out of the corner of their eyes."

Bodean nodded and stuck his hands in the pockets of his jeans. "To be fair, the house hadn't been left derelict that long, so things weren't in terrible shape. They got the kitchen done and a couple of rooms ready for hikers and then started taking in guests right away, figuring the rooms were still more civilized at less than half done than sleeping out in the open. They thought they could put up with the weird, minor nuisances in the house, but as soon as they started accepting guests, things began to escalate."

Wringing her hands, Parmelia's face pinched as she told the next part. "They started getting bookings pretty much right away and, like Bodean says, that's when the trouble really started. As soon as the sun went down, something started stomping through the house, yelling, making pictures fly off the walls and throwing things. The little girl woke up screaming hysterically every night and a lot of the hikers left before the sun rose, deciding to trade a soft bed for the lesser comforts of the great outdoors. A man without a face began terrorizing the people in the house, slamming doors open in the dead of night, yanking people out of bed and throwing them to the floor. That's what they think happened to the little girl. It broke her arm."

Lucas's eyes went wide and he grabbed a small pad and a pen from his pocket. "Really? A full-body apparition? That's something... You've really got something there. The viewers are going to love this story." He scribbled furiously to capture the conversation.

"What do you mean about his face? He had no head?" Cam frowned deeply and began to unconsciously rub his broken arm.

Shaking his head, Bodean made a circle around his own face. "He has a head, but where the face should be, it's just a black hole. The thru-hikers are already trading stories about this on the Trail. They say that if you meet up with this spirit, you kind of start losing your own mind. Your thoughts get all jumbled and you get disoriented – and these are people who have a pretty good sense of direction."

While everyone else focused on the ghost, I felt a surge of protectiveness for the little girl. *That was me twenty years ago*, I thought. "The family is still in the house?"

Parmelia shrugged her shoulders and shook her head with sigh. "They got nowhere else to go. They sunk all their money into that place."

"So, you and Bodean went to the house after you heard the story from the thru-hikers?" Lucas poised his pen above the pad and waited for Parmelia to answer.

"Not exactly…" Parmelia once again wrapped her arms around her belly and began rocking.

"What do you mean 'not exactly?'" Cam demanded. "It seems you had a clear duty here to help the family."

Bodean's eyes shifted as if he were looking for an escape route. He ultimately settled on staring at the ground. "We eventually got called into that mess because some folks around these parts still remember Lummie. Anything that goes bump in the night was her purview and I suppose, as her kin, we inherited that responsibility." Bodean glanced at Parmelia, who nodded her head miserably in resignation that this was the way things were. Sighing, he continued. "After how Lummie was treated, we try to keep a low profile in the community. We don't just go diving in anytime there's a bump in the night. That's not what our family does anymore."

Zackie made a huffing sound, clearly unimpressed with what Bodean and Parmelia thought was their responsibility. The cousins winced at the rebuke. Cam narrowed his eyes at the pair. "So, that's why you called us in? To deflect the responsibility from you two?"

Lucas stared back and forth between the cousins and Cam. Finally, he looked at me. "Who is Lummie?"

"I'll tell you about her later," I murmured, unwilling to let Parmelia and Bodean off the hook by changing the topic. Looking directly at the cousins, I jutted my chin towards Cam. "Answer him."

Parmelia, her eyes downcast, whispered her response. "Yes… yes… that was the plan."

I grabbed my bag, the sheets from the table and headed for the loft where I presumed I would find somewhere to sleep. "I'm going to bed. Tomorrow, we're all going over to that house." Pausing on the steps, I stared hard at Bodean and Parmelia. "All of us."

# # #

I woke up feeling tired, cranky, and completely lacking in the patience necessary to infinitely blend the foundation colors to just the right hue. Putting on the fancy gloves after dressing, I headed downstairs intent on finding food and saw Cam sitting at the table near the pot belly stove. He was eating scrambled eggs and bacon with gusto and my stomach growled at the sight. His mouth full, he gestured towards the stove and handed me a plate from the table setting next to him. My stomach growled again loudly as I piled eggs and bacon on to the plate and then grabbed some buttered toast for good measure. Cam was filling a cup with coffee for me as I sat next to him. Nodding my thanks, I tucked in and fed the beast in my belly. When I finally looked up, Cam handed me a napkin and I absently wiped away the evidence of the meal. I could see Lucas outside through the open door as he paced and spoke on his phone. Must be Hannah, I thought. Zackie was lying comfortably near an empty bowl, her back to the pot belly stove. All accounted for except for Parmelia and Bodean.

I took a sip of coffee and then looked to Cam for answers. "Where are the wonder twins?"

"Tending to the goats. They left after they prepared the breakfast for us. They'll be back."

"They don't live here?"

"No, this was Lummie's house. The Sinclairs do the upkeep for the property, but no one in their family wants to live here. They find the history a bit off-putting. I think they rent the house out to summer tourists, mainly folks who like to day-hike, but don't have the stamina for a real run at the A.T."

I nodded and decided not to give into my feelings of irritation for the cousins. They did feed me, after all. Right now, it was far more important to be tactical than emotional. I fired off a question to better understand our current resources. "What are their abilities? I don't want to walk blind into this situation with the Anomaly."

"Bodean can bind spirits. They cannot disappear, move about, or influence anything in the environment when he binds them. Parmelia, well... her talent is a little harder to describe. I think the best I can do is say that she can sense the threat level of beings, both human and non-human." Grinning, he added, "She's terrified of you."

I frowned and gave in to my irritation. "Me? What

did I do? I haven't done jack to them… yet."

"Exactly. It's the capability for violence that she hones in on. How much destruction a being may be capable of under a particular set of circumstances." Cam sipped his coffee and winked at me, clearly trying to get my goat. "I think she pegged you just right."

Rolling my eyes, I muttered, "Commencing eye roll sequence…"

Lucas walked into the room grinning. He looked significantly better after getting some more sleep. The dark circles under eyes had faded and he had regained some color in his cheeks. My eyes ate him up until I caught myself looking. Embarrassed, I coughed into my elbow and looked away.

"I'm calling the fashion police." Lucas picked up my normal hand and examined the glove. "Didn't these go out of style in the eighties?"

I yanked my hand back, blushing furiously. Why was he always touching me? I immediately started grumbling to cover my reaction. "What are you? Some kind of backwoods fashionista?"

"He must know all about the glamorous fashion world and then some." Parmelia stood at the door and examined Lucas appraisingly. Bodean stared at the gloves. Dressed in jeans and t-shirts, they smelled pleasantly of hay and unpleasantly of barnyard. Parmelia turned her attention to Lucas'sapparel. "You're not wearing the great coat with all the silver buttons for the house visit?" She sounded vaguely disappointed at his lack of costume.

Lucas, still grinning, shrugged his shoulders. "We're going for a different look this season."

Cam took the opportunity to aim a friendly jab at Lucas. "I, for one, will miss the Goth look." Picking up his coffee mug, he raised it in a toast. "The Goth is dead. Long live the Goth." Lucas landed a light punch at Cam's good arm, I suppose a guy's way of appreciating another guy's joke.

Cam's good humor was getting on my nerves. I was concerned about having to deal with the Anomaly and definitely not in the mood for jocularity. We were still nursing broken bones and now we had to face another one of the dangerous dead. Damn right, I was nervous and irritable. I glanced pointedly at my watch. "We're burning daylight. How far is this house anyway?"

Bodean and Parmelia provided directions and we decided that I would drive Lucas and Zackie, while Cam would hitch a ride with the cousins. Lucas called his film crew and told them where to meet us. During the short drive over, I filled Lucas in on what I knew about Lummie. He appeared to be intrigued by the idea of a sin-eater and took copious notes on the subject.

When we arrived at the house, the production crew had already set up and was taking background footage for the episode. Lucas went to speak to them and Zackie walked about the grounds sniffing at things. There was a scattering of metal sculptures on the lawn. One made of copper particularly caught my eye as it reflected the morning light. It looked like an advancing ten foot sinuous dragon with red eyes and a flared, scaly mane that ruffled out around the head and then created a ridge down its back. It appeared to be barely held back by a chain that went around its neck that was staked to the ground.

Tearing my eyes away from the dragon, I examined the house to understand its layout and to see if I could pick up on anything. The building was a large Queen Anne farmhouse that looked like it was built in the early nineteen hundreds. It was altogether ordinary. Worn, white clapboard siding covered the exterior of the home, but a graceful wrap-around front porch compensated for the shabbiness of the outer walls. Scattered along the three floors of the structure were tall, narrow windows that looked out at the surrounding forests in all directions. Peeking in one of the ground floor windows, I could see an artist's easel with a blank canvas. Two chimneys were visible at the roofline, but only one of them appeared to be in service to fight the chill of the early morning. The farmhouse gave the impression of old-time coziness and would have been a welcome sight to trail-weary hikers. There was no atmosphere of foreboding, but I wasn't about to let my guard down.

Parmelia, Cam and Bodean were huddled in a group near the front porch, talking to a dark haired man and a blonde woman dressed in jeans and flannel shirts. Both wore their hair unfashionably long and pulled back in pony tails. The woman had a small child with a white arm cast on her hip, so I surmised these were the innkeepers. Walking closer to join the conversation, I got a definite crunchy granola vibe from them.

The man folded his arms across his chest and shook his head. "Dude, y'all are here at exactly the wrong time.

296

We won't get any action until sundown."

"We tried to tell them that last night, but they were hell bent on coming this morning." Bodean shot me a told-you-so look as he spoke. "They being Cam Ramsay over here and Fia Saunders over there." He pointed his chin at each of us in turn. "Lucas Tremaine – you know Lucas? From the ghost show? - he's come here to do some interviewing of y'all about your ghost." Bodean puffed up a little when he referred to Lucas by his first name in front of the innkeepers.

Not to be outdone, Parmelia chimed in, wringing her hands nervously as she spoke. "Lucas is staying with us in Lummie's old cabin. His camera guys are down in Sylva. That was good for us. We couldn't put up so many people." That girl was on a constant state of high alert. Even in the midst of a humble brag, her eyes darted toward the house, towards me, into the woods, always scanning for danger. She was like the canary in the coal mine and I was starting to find this concept useful.

The mother adjusted the little girl on hip and looked at the film crew. "The camera guys were real polite. They showed up early and knocked on our door to ask permission to start filming the house and yard." As if this made her recall her own manners, she turned her gaze back to me and Cam. "It's nice to meet you, Fia. You too, Cam. I'm Janie McLean and this is my husband, Neil. This little one is Gretchen."

The little girl started squirming at the mention of her name, so her mother put her down. As soon as she had her feet on the ground, she pulled down on her yellow sweater to show us the duckie on her chest. Like her mother, she was fair and the sun glinted off the golden locks almost making a halo around her head. She toddled over to Cam and pointed at his cast. Obviously, they had something in common and she wanted to discuss it.

"Well, hello Gretchen." Cam knelt down to get closer to eye level. "Yes, I have a cast too. Mine is blue. See?" Cam offered his blue wrapped cast for the little girl to examine and she touched it tentatively with her fingers. "Can you tell me how you hurt your arm?" Gretchen shook her head shyly and tried to hide her cast with her hand before ducking behind her mother's legs. Cam looked to me for help, but I just shrugged. I had no idea how to make kids cooperate.

I looked to the parents. "Was she able to tell you anything?" Janie looked a lot like her daughter as she shook her head. Neil mumbled a tight 'no,' his fists clenching at his sides. I called Lucas over to join us and he jogged over with Zackie at his heels. I waited until they joined us and then asked, "Can you tell us what happened the night she got hurt?"

Janie looked at Neil and he nodded for her tell the story. "We had two guests that night, college boys taking a semester off to hike the A.T. They had been on the Trail for a few weeks and they looked like they had lost a lot of weight. I wanted to hand each of them a stick of butter to just snack on." Janie reached down to smooth Gretchen's hair as she spoke. "We fed them a big dinner and they were starting to fall into a food coma, so we urged them to get on upstairs to bed and get some rest."

"We were in the kitchen washing the dishes when the footsteps started up. We could hear someone walking with real heavy steps in the back rooms." Neil jutted his chin toward the rear corner of the house. "We hadn't had time to renovate this area yet, so we just kept it closed up. The guests were wandering around in stocking feet, happy to be free of their hiking boots, so we knew it couldn't be them."

I stared at the rear corner of the house. "Was this

299

something you heard before?"

Janie nodded. "We first heard the footsteps during the renovation work on other parts of the house. We heard it a bunch more times when we started taking guests. It was always in those back rooms."

"We were set to ignore it as usual when we heard the door to the back rooms flung open hard and smashed against the wall." Neil slapped his hands together imitating the suddenness and sharpness of the sound. Gretchen's head snapped toward the unexpected sound and she stared with big eyes. Neil made soothing sounds to her in apology before picking her up. "That never happened before. We just stood at the sink staring at each other, wondering what now. We heard it stomping down the hall and then the pictures started crashing off the walls on the stairway."

Janie swallowed hard and took up the story. "At this point, we started fearing for Gretchen because it was heading upstairs. We feed her early and put her to bed before we feed the guests and she would have been sound asleep. We both started running up the stairs when we heard Gretchen wailing. Then she screamed and we heard a crash."

Neil hugged the little girl and buried her head in the crook of his neck. "When we got to the landing, we saw one of the boys sprawled on the floor out cold outside Gretchen's room and we ran past him to get to her. She was on the floor crying hysterically and her arm was twisted under her. We heard another crash from the guest room and then a lot of swearing. The other boy said later that he was ripped out of bed and thrown to the floor. We figured that's what happened to Gretchen to break her arm." He rubbed her back and kissed the crown of her head.

Janie reached out to put a hand on the little girl. "Everything quieted down after that. The boy in the hall had been thrown against the wall and hit his head. We wanted to get him to the hospital with Gretchen when the ambulance came, but he said he was okay and both boys were hell bent on just getting away from the house. They said they'd sleep in the woods, thanks all the same."

Neil shook his head in disbelief. "After that night, we got pretty much a repeat performance every time we took in guests. Folks would get regularly yanked from their beds and few of them wanted to stay after that."

Cam's brow wrinkled with worry as he stared at the house and then at the family. "Did it ever come after

Gretchen again? How did you protect her?"

Neil and Janie exchanged another look and Janie shrugged. "We moved her bed to our room and we made sure one of us was with her at all times. But it was always the guests that were targeted after that first night. Gretchen would even sleep through all the noise." Janie squinted her eyes as she thought. "Come to think of it, she stopped having bad dreams after that night."

Lucas was scribbling a mile a minute taking down the story. "Can you show us through the house, so we can see where things happened?"

Janie and Neil led the way up the porch and through the door. Neil held the door open for us. "You won't find anything this time of day. Everything's always real peaceful during the day." Both he and Janie were relaxed and decidedly not fearful or apprehensive as they brought us into the house. Cam asked permission for Zackie to come into the house and neither homeowner was averse to a dog in the house, in fact, they were planning to get a dog as soon as Gretchen was a little older.

A front parlor was located to the right as we entered and I again saw the canvas propped on an easel. As we were led down the hall to the back of the house, I walked with Janie and asked her if she was an artist.

"Both Neil and I are artists. You can see some of his work outside on the lawns. He works with metal. I like to paint with oils. Neither of us sells enough to support a family, so that's why we ended up trying to convert this old house into an inn."

Lucas was walking on her other side and he tilted his head as he heard this. "I tend to think that artists are somewhere to the left in their political beliefs. This area seems pretty conservative, so how does that work for you?"

Neil barked a short laugh, looked over his shoulder and winked. "The far right and the far left both hate the government. We all get along here."

As we came to the back of the house, there were a number of empty picture hooks on the wall. At the end of the hall at about the height of a doorknob, the plaster had been smashed in. The door in question appeared quiescent at the moment and I didn't sense anything to worry about, but I shot a look at Parmelia to see how she was interpreting the threat level. Parmelia was about as far away from me as she could manage and still be part of the house tour. She had her arms crossed over her chest and appeared to be concentrating, but she wasn't overtly nervous or panicked. As she caught me looking her way, I raised my eyebrows in silent question. She gave a curt shake of her head that there was nothing she was sensing.

Lucas put his hand on the doorknob and looked to Neil and Janie. "Okay if we go in the room?" They shrugged and said it was all right, but advised us that we wouldn't find anything right now that would be of any interest. The room was small and empty of everything except a few stacked cardboard boxes and built-in bookshelves that lined two of the walls. It had a single, bare window where the sun poured in to highlight peeling wallpaper that might have once been a textured cream design, but it was now yellowed with age. The wallpaper had long ago passed from being decorative to being functional and was now holding water damaged walls together. Janie mentioned that this was a common problem with old farmhouses. They had already spent a small fortune repairing the gutters, roof and downspouts. Zackie did a quick inspection of the room and then headed out the door towards the stairs and began climbing. Taking our cue from her, we also mounted the stairs and made our way to the second floor.

The upstairs had a simple arrangement of two guest rooms facing each other across the hall. Gretchen's room followed on the right side, while a bathroom lay on the left. At the end of the hallway was the master bedroom where, currently, the entire family slept. As we made our progress down the hall, Janie opened the doors to each room to give us a look. The guest rooms were small, but cozy with quilt-covered beds and cheerful yellow curtains. Entering Gretchen's room, I expected more of the same, but Parmelia's eyes went wide and she wrapped her arms tightly around her middle.

"I need to get out!" Parmelia elbowed past the crowd to reach the hallway where she blew out a shaky breath and went to sit at the top of the stairs. I shot a look to Cam and shrugged my shoulders slightly. I felt nothing. Cam shook his head at me indicating that he too felt no presence. Zackie's reaction was most telling of all. She did a lap through the room, exited and walked to the end of the hall, where she sniffed at the closed doors and then turned back to the stairs. Pushing Parmelia out of her way, Zackie walked down the stairs and then sat at the door looking distinctly bored as she waited to be let out.

Bodean went to Parmelia and helped her to stand.

"Let's go outside and get you some air." The rest of us followed the cousins as they slowly made their way down the stairs and out of the house.

Standing on the porch, Neil looked at each of us, his brow knit with worry. "Did something just happen? I didn't see or hear anything." He put Gretchen down, but held her hand as Janie grasped his other hand.

Parmelia put a shaky hand to her brow. "Nothing happened. What I was feeling was old, but it was pretty bad."

Lucas pulled out one of the patio chairs, helped Bodean to lower Parmelia into the seat and kneeled in front of her. "Are you okay? Can we get you anything? Water maybe?" Parmelia declined and said she was starting to feel better. Pulling up another chair, he sat next to her and gave her a few minutes to recover. Motioning to his camera crew, he let them set up before asking questions. "Can you tell us what you felt or any impressions you might have gotten?"

Parmelia was starting to enjoy the attention and looked a little less like a frightened field mouse. "All I can tell you is that something bad happened in that room. I can't tell you what. It doesn't work that way for me."

Lucas nodded. "What did you feel?"

"I felt terror most of all." Parmelia swept her hair behind an ear as she thought. "But I felt rage and disgust."

Lucas gazed at Neil and Janie. "Do you know anything about the history of the house?"

The McLeans looked at each other and Neil answered. "The house was owned by the Clark family for about a hundred years until the last descendent died in the 1990s. The property was put on the market and various people owned it for a while, but no one stayed for more than a few years. We didn't think anything of it, since there was almost always some reasonable explanation for leaving."

Janie nodded. "People gossip, so I found out about the property from the neighbors. One family had a sick child and they needed to move closer to the specialist hospital in another state. There was also a veterinarian who was going to set up a practice in the house, but he had a gambling problem and couldn't pay the mortgage anymore. There were maybe two or three other owners before them and I don't know what their stories were. But you get the idea. We had no reason to think there was anything wrong with the house."

Lucas quirked an eyebrow. "So, no history of anything unfortunate happening in the house that you know of?" Janie and Neil shook their heads. Looking at the camera, Lucas summed up his interpretation of events. "Parmelia either got a false positive reading or some incident that didn't make the newspapers happened in that room. If it were something well-known, the local rumor mill would have clued Janie in by now."

Parmelia looked slightly offended, but Cam nodded in agreement. Cam waited until Lucas cued the cameras to shut down and then said, "I don't think there is anything else we can do here at the moment. As the McLeans have said, nothing will happen until the sun sets, so I make a motion that we reconvene here at dusk. Fia and I need to go to the county's Register of Deeds office to get the details on the former occupants."

Lucas stood up. "Works for me. The crew and I will take some footage inside the house with the McLean's permission."

CHAPTER 16

The deed search pretty much reflected what Janie had told us. We were able to flesh it out a bit more with the names and dates of all the owners since the Clark family. Cam provided the names to Lucas and asked if he could put resources behind finding the former occupants in order to ask them if they had any untoward experiences in the house. Cam whipped out his laptop and went about determining if any of the occupants had criminal records, just in case that could provide evidence in favor of attributing the incident in Gretchen's room to any particular family. No criminal records were uncovered, but we did discover that Daniel Clark, the last of the Clark family, had been a deputy sheriff for the county.

The clerk was an elderly lady and she was every bit as forthcoming with information as Janie had indicated about the local populace. "I remember Daniel. He was a fine man, a truly fine man. It was such a pity how he got the Alzheimer's and had to leave his home in the end. He loved that old house and I know he would never have left if he hadn't lost his mind like that. Such a pity, such a terrible pity." She would have gone on a good deal longer, but we asked her if Daniel ever said anything about his house being haunted. "No, never a word about that. His family had lived there forever and I guess they all just went peacefully. No one ever had any tales about ghosts or anything when Daniel lived there."

As we left the office, Cam murmured, "That narrows down the time in which this Anomaly arose. It must be Daniel or one of the other families that owned the property after him. It would be highly irregular for someone who passed at peace to return to complain about the current conditions."

I paused for a moment as we went down the steps of the building. "Do you think someone in one of the other families might have died in that house or while they were living there?"

"Possibly. It's worth looking into. Let's go back to Lummie's cabin and I'll check the databases for any death certificates for these folk."

We got back into my car and found Zackie snoozing in the backseat. We had left the windows open and figured that it was cool enough that no one would accuse us of leaving a dog in a hot car. I snickered to myself and thought how silly all our pretenses were, since she could enter the wormhole and leave any time she wanted.

Back at the cabin, Cam did his internet research while I hunted for food. I found the leftover bacon and toast and then located some tomatoes. We would have apple cider and BLTs minus the lettuce for lunch. I bit into my sandwich and mouthed my question over the wad of food. "Did you find anything?" Cam rolled his eyes and cupped his hand to one ear. I swallowed and tried again.

"None of the other property owners suffered any deaths in their families during their years of occupancy." Having answered my question, he bit into his sandwich and chewed thoughtfully.

In deference to Cam's need for good manners, I first asked my question and then took another bite. "Could one of the families have brought an attached spirit with them?"

Cam swallowed and took a drink of cider before answering. "It would have stayed attached and left with them, I would think."

"I guess that leaves us with Daniel Clark." I reached

for a napkin and dabbed at the mayonnaise clinging to my lips. Cam nodded his approval at burgeoning table manners. "Why would he hide his face?"

Cam shrugged. "Maybe he was ashamed of something he did in his life?"

I tilted my head, putting two and two together. "Maybe something to do with Gretchen's room?"

Cam squinted as he thought about it. "Possibly. If that is the case, we'll need to confront him with it. He'll need to know that we know, so he can stop trying to hide his identity and own up to his deeds. I need to spend some time researching Daniel Clark's life before we return tonight. Maybe I can figure out what he might have done."

While Cam returned to his laptop, I cleared the table and then stripped off the fancy gloves as I prepared to wash the dishes. In fairness, Cam was best suited to do the necessary searches to find information on Daniel Clark, but so help me, he was going to do the next batch of dishes with his good hand. While I was mulling over principles of justice regarding household chores, I ran out of dish detergent. The sink was retrofitted into older woodwork that might have been only cabinets with a countertop in days gone by. The most likely place to find more detergent was inside the cabinets, so I opened a door and started rummaging.

The dead hand took the opportunity to clear the stash of sponges, cleansers and dish towels out of the way to expose the bottom of the cabinet. Before I could protest the sudden autonomy of the hand, it forced its fingers into a crack along the boards and lifted a small plank of wood away from the others to reveal a hidden recess. At this point, the hand stopped its activity and left it to me to remove whatever items might be hidden there.

I called over my shoulder as I sat on the floor and reached into the recess. "Cam! Something weird just happened."

"What, again? Can it wait? I'm a little busy here."

I pulled out a heavily dusted rectangular item. It was wrapped in a cloth. "No, you better come here. The hand found something."

The chair scraped as he stood up, muttering imprecations on being interrupted. "The hand did what, now?"

"It opened up a secret compartment under the sink."
I carefully unwrapped the cloth as Cam appeared over my
shoulder. At the same time, Zackie ambled up to me and
stuck her face in my hands to explore the item. Her tail
began to wag as I removed the protected contents from the
old cloth. "It's a book." The book was slightly moldy in
places, but it seemed to be fairly intact, so I gingerly
opened it and gently thumbed through the pages. "Cam, it's
a journal and look at the first page...It's dated August 15,
1900." Squinting at the faint writing, I began to read. "'I
am Lummie Sinclair and I will record in these pages what I
cannot share with anyone.'" My lips went numb and I
stared at Cam with wide eyes.

Cam reached for the book and I gave it over. "It's
Lummie's journal all right. I can't believe it. She didn't
seem the sort to commit her memories for posterity." His
eyes misted a bit as he spoke. Zackie's tail continued to
thump against the cabinets. "She was one of a kind. Always
ready to help, but she was such a curmudgeon. I never met
anyone so surly." I suppressed a smile at his words.
Maybe this was a common trait among people like us. Cam
handled the journal with great care and turned to the last
entry. "Lummie last wrote in this book in 1968. That was a
few years before I met her." As he returned to the book's

beginning, something fluttered out from between the pages.

I picked up a sepia photograph of an old, bent man with gray hair standing next to a car that looked to be from the 1950's. The thing that caught my eye was the background of the picture. The farmhouse was in better shape then, sporting a fresh coat of paint and a roof that looked like it could weather any storm. The addition on the back corner of the house had yet to be built, but the wraparound porch was a dead giveaway and there was no mistaking that this was the same house that the McLeans now lived in. I checked the back of the photo to see if there was anything written that would identify the man, the place or the year. No luck.

I held the photograph up to Cam. "Look…. It's the farmhouse from this morning."

Cam took the picture from me to give it a closer look, also checking the back for any information. "It is the same house." Scrutinizing the photograph, he declared, "This man is too old to be Daniel Clark." He walked over to his laptop and I stood up and followed. "But I do see a family resemblance." Angling the screen toward me, I saw a newspaper story from 1938 with a grainy picture of a dark haired man. The caption said he was Sheriff's Deputy

Daniel Clark. Comparing the photograph with the newspaper picture, Cam was right. Both men had the same deep-set eyes, high cheek bones and square jaw, although the features of the older man had softened with the years.

I nodded my agreement with Cam's assessment. "You keep investigating Daniel Clark's history. I'll read the journal entries from the 1950s and see if there's anything that can identify the man in the photo." Even though the suspense was killing me, I quickly cleaned up the mess under the sink and finished the dishes before sitting across from Cam and beginning my task.

Slipping on the fancy gloves in case Lucas or the cousins suddenly made an appearance, I rifled through the journal entries until I found the decade of interest. A quick scan of her writing as I leafed through the pages told me that Lummie did not have a large number of social engagements, other than her sin-eating activities. I saw some references to what I thought might be Zackie, but Lummie referred to her as Maple because of her coat color. My guess was that every handler through the ages must have given her an equally inane name.

The decade opened with thoughts of the new year and a depressing forecast of what the year would hold.

More ritual funerary meals were anticipated and she named those who she thought were on their way out. She recognized that more social rejection would be aimed her way because of the sin-eating, but she was in turn philosophical about it and then resentful. Lots of conflict in that woman, I thought. Throughout it all, there was a stubborn will to do what she saw as her vocation, but she was bitter about the cost. As I moved through the entries, there was mention of celebrating her seventieth birthday. At this point, I discarded any hopes I may have harbored about the wisdom of age mellowing the burden of being a handmaiden to a psychopomp. Apparently, it sucked from day one and didn't get any better, at least for Lummie. I saw many of the same themes from my list of complaints emerge in her writing and I could only hope that the difference in the eras and the cultures that we lived in might have a differential impact in how our lives turned out. Sometimes I think I am foolishly hopeful.

Lummie's birthday entry was surprisingly upbeat compared to everything else up until that point. She mentioned getting a letter from Timothy and that he said Daniel was doing well. She was so proud of Daniel. Flipping forward, I searched out other birthday entries and it was nearly the same every year. She would receive a letter from Timothy that lifted her spirits and shining words were written about Daniel. Flipping backwards, I saw the same pattern until 1905. Before this year, the birthday entries were short and seemingly inconsequential. I made a mental note to go back and review events between 1900 and 1905 after I finished my assigned decade. I wished I had the time to do a slow reading of Lummie's journal, but nightfall was approaching and we needed answers.

Continuing to read through the 1950s, I eventually found the page where I thought the photograph had been tucked. Timothy had died and Lummie was inconsolable. She pulled herself together and attended his funeral, performing the rites as only she could. Lummie's only solace was that she was able to witness Maple/Zackie bringing Timothy over the threshold to the afterlife and she knew for certain that he was at peace. There was no mention of any conversations with Daniel or any contact whatsoever and I found that distressing, but mostly sad that they had not consoled each other. The decade finished out with no other major events and if anything, Lummie was more depressed than before Timothy's death. It was no wonder that Bodean and Parmelia were so dead set against following in Lummie's footsteps.

I started reading again from the beginning and marked off the end of 1905 with my finger in the pages. The entries were scant and irregular during most of 1900. Lummie seemed to be using the journal to expunge her anger toward her kin and neighbors, who used her services and then ostracized her once they had what they wanted. This sublimated anger would not have been how I would have handled the situation, but hey, whatever gets you through the night. The pattern changed towards the beginning of the next year when she made the acquaintance of Timothy Clark. Lummie met Timothy in his capacity as local law enforcement. He was chasing a thief who had robbed a neighbor and the thief, not being local, ran blindly towards Lummie's cabin in the hopes of hiding out. Lummie brained him with a cast iron skillet when he forced his way into her home. She had my full approval on how she handled that situation. Timothy also apparently approved and he began looking out for her, a woman living on her own on the mountain. He made his home in Sylva and was a city man, less inclined to lend any credence to the superstitions of the mountain folk. Still, he must have felt some societal pressures, since something kept him from making his relationship with Lummie public. My heart rose to learn that Lummie was not alone her entire life and that she loved at least one man during her time on earth. Go, Lummie!

The clandestine love affair went on until 1905 when baby Daniel came. Lummie was almost immediately conflicted by the thought of the little boy growing up isolated and alone. She did not want to give him up, but eventually, even though it broke Lummie's heart, she let Timothy take the baby to his brother Randall to add to his large family. With a little bit of interpolation, I finally came to realize that Randall Clark and family lived in the farmhouse. It wasn't clear what story Timothy gave Randall, but the baby slipped in among the eight other brothers and sisters and the neighbors never batted an eye. I would have like to learn that Timothy and Lummie eventually married and lived happily ever after, but I had already read the entries from the later years and I knew that's not how the story went. Skimming through later entries, I found out that Timothy, in time, moved on and married someone else and had more kids. The fact that he kept in touch with Lummie over the years seemed to be a blessing to her, but I couldn't imagine it being anything but bittersweet.

As I closed the book and sighed, I felt Cam's eyes

on me. "Are you ready to share what you learned from the journal? I'm about done here with what I can find about Daniel Clark."

"Daniel was Lummie's son." Cam's eyes bugged out when I said this. I quickly filled him in on everything else I learned.

Cam looked wistful and slowly shook his head after he had a chance to process the information. "So, Lummie had a lover and a son. I met her when she was an old woman and even under normal circumstances, it's always hard imaging how people spent their youth. I always thought it was just Lummie and Zackie living here from the beginning of time." A frown eventually crept into his visage and he stared at my dead hand. "I wonder what it means that your dead appendage dug out the journal for us?"

I had been so engaged in Lummie's story that I had not given this particular mystery any thought. "Do you think it was Lummie? Lummie controls the hand?" I picked up the hand and stared at it. The fancy glove hid the details of the decomposition, but as always, the hand was a strange, alien thing.

Cam sighed. "I would like to think so. That would at least be a benign presence, but this reticence in acting is not her style at all. She would not be passive. It appears to me that most of the time, that hand is fairly inert." He thought some more and then shrugged. "Maybe things change when you pass over."

It was my turn to sigh. I put the hand down, deciding that I still did not trust it and would not seek answers from it. To divert Cam's attention before he grabbed up pen and paper for the hand, I asked about his research into Daniel's life.

"Like his father, Daniel was law enforcement. He might have even trained with or reported to Timothy early in his career. Over all, Daniel served as a sheriff's deputy in this area for over forty years. The thing that caught my attention was that he was a canine handler. He had a successful career tracking down criminals and he was something of a local hero. I saw at least a dozen news stories on how he foiled bank robbers, found missing children and the bodies of murder victims."

I sat forward and leaned my elbows on the table. "Well, that would explain why Lummie was so proud of him."

Cam raised his eyebrows and pointed to the journal. "Now that I know his true parentage, I tend to think that with Lummie's blood running through him, he had better intuition than most." As I nodded my agreement, Cam stood up and poured some cold coffee into a mug and offered it to me first. I declined, so he started drinking before he continued. "Anyway, so as to his career in law enforcement, I think he would have died with his boots on if it hadn't been for Alzheimer's disease. I found a newspaper story on his retirement ceremony. He wasn't shy about sharing his diagnosis and urged people to donate to charities that supported research into this disease."

I nodded my approval. "It sounds like he was a really decent guy. I take it you didn't find anything to say otherwise?"

Cam shook his head. "Not one thing. This doesn't mean there wasn't anything, but there was nothing that made the newspapers. The only thing that remotely resembled trouble was a short report of local police activities. Within a year of retirement, the police were called to the farmhouse by some nieces and nephews. The disease had advanced and Daniel was suffering with something called 'sundowning.' For some people who have dementia, there is confusion and agitation that worsens in the late afternoon and evening. It can be physically difficult for caretakers to deal with this, especially when the person is otherwise able-bodied. It got bad enough that the family had to call in the police. I think he was moved to a geriatric facility shortly after this incident."

I suddenly straightened as the thought occurred to me. "It's the same with the Anomaly. Nothing much happens during the day, but all hell breaks loose when the sun goes down. Do you think he's still sundowning?"

Cam blinked. "I think you have something there." He put down the mug and his good hand came up to rub his chin as he thought. "Maybe, just maybe, the lack of a face on the Anomaly is also a symptom of the disease. If he has been stripped of his memories, it is possible that this is reflected in his spirit body by not being able to reveal his face. He might not know who he is."

I stood up, excited that we may have cracked the case and I began pacing. "That all seems to fit. It's logical." Whirling to face Cam again, I tilted my head as the thoughts formed. "But if he lacks a face because he lacks his identity, then he's not symbolically hiding his face in shame. So, what terrible thing happened in Gretchen's room? That event might be completely unrelated to our Anomaly."

Cam sat down again and picked up his mug from the table. "We can only ask the question. Maybe the Anomaly, if it is Daniel, may be able and willing to answer it." Cam took another swig of coffee and looked at me squarely. "Let's try to stay open minded about the case. This disease aspect all looks good on paper, but it may not be true. We haven't heard back yet from Lucas about the other occupants of the house. If no one else has experienced paranormal activity, we're going to have to look harder at Neil and Janie. This might be something exclusive to them or maybe caused by something they brought into the house for one of their projects."

I stopped pacing and crumpled into the chair. Cam was right. This might be another case of a perfectly good hypothesis being nailed by reality, so I tried to rein it in and not allow myself to get too excited. But my gut told me we were right. In another hour, the sun would start setting and maybe all would be revealed.

#

When we arrived at the farmhouse, I immediately pulled Lucas aside and asked him about the other people who had lived in the house.

"We weren't able to get in touch with all of the families, but of the three we made contact with, each said that they had some weird things happen in the house. It was all similar to what we've heard. They all talked about noises in the back room at night and household items sometimes disappearing. It never went beyond that, though. No one else experienced the nighttime terrors that the McLeans described."

I nodded at Cam. These were points in our favor. "I don't think any of the other homeowners ran this place as an inn, so maybe having strangers in the house is some kind of trigger."

Cam frowned. "But when people newly move into the house, they would technically be strangers and that should elicit the nighttime activity."

I waved him off, frustrated that we didn't have a clear line of reasoning that neatly connected everything. "You're right, you're right," I muttered. "Anyway, we should tell Lucas what we've found out so far." Turning to Lucas, I advised him to take good notes as Cam recited our findings from the day.

Lucas scribbled in his notebook. "But how did you find the journal?"

I compressed my lips for a moment and then lied. Sort of. It was mostly true. "I was looking under the sink for some dish detergent and I found a loose board." Before Lucas could ask another question, Parmelia and Bodean made their entrance. Both were dressed in their Sunday best, ready for their television debut. Parmelia looked like she had just had her hair done.

Walking over to the cousins, I tried to be pleasant before asking them what was really on my mind. After reading Lummie's journal, I was filled with questions. "You both look nice." They nodded their thanks and I continued, keeping my voice low. "So, how does it work for you? You keep a low profile about what you can do in your community, but you're going to advertise it nationwide on Lucas'sshow?"

Bodean raised an eyebrow and crossed his arms over his chest. "That's right. If we can get Lucas to take us on, we can move away from here. We'll be able to hire security and only have to do our thing for the show. If you earn enough money, you don't have to rely on community for anything and you don't have to take any shit from anyone. That's the goal."

Parmelia poked her head out from her position behind Bodean. "That's right. That's the goal." Her face was as hard as his.

I just nodded. After having read Lummie's journal, I had a little more sympathy for what Parmelia and Bodean might have to put up with. This was a small community and memory was long in small towns. Maybe they had the right idea to want to leave. What I could not wrap my head around was how mercenary these two were. They didn't care about either the living or the dead, only themselves. But then, who was I to judge? I only cared about half the equation until I met Cam. I had my own litany of sins to contend with. Before I walked away, I tried one more time to connect with them. "We found Lummie's journal today. It was hidden under a floor board in the cabin."

Parmelia's expression softened for a second, but then she shook her head. "That's all right. You go ahead and keep it. All that's in the past and we don't want no part of it." Before I could say anything else, the cousins turned and walked towards the back room where the crew was setting up. I watched them go and decided to let it be. I needed to accept that trust would be a rare commodity when working with them, since it was clear that their priority was looking out for number one. The best I could hope for was that they would use their abilities honestly and not make stuff up to create good television.

Cam came up behind me with Zackie at his side. "I couldn't help overhearing. I'm not sure we can trust those two." Zackie made a sound like she was coughing up a hairball and I took that as her two cents worth on the cousins.

"Yeah, that's about what I think too." I was about to say something more when Parmelia cried out, an edge of hysteria to her voice.

"Aw, crap! Here it comes!" A loud impact sounded in the back room that rattled the windows of the entire house. Her hands flew up to shield her ears and she dropped to her knees.

Bodean whirled around, first one direction and then the other. "I can't find it, Parmelia! Show me where." She paid him no mind and seemed to be in sensory overload. All she could manage was a low keening as her arms went up protectively around her head and her face turned an alarming crimson.

Lucas was unaware of her distress as he rushed forward to join the crew. "Cameras ready to roll?" There was a chorus of affirmatives as equipment powered up. Spinning to identify the source of the impact, he caught Neil's eye as he searched. "It sounded like a sonic boom. Are you in the flight path of any military operations?"

Neil looked uneasy and he slowly shook his head. He put his arm around Janie. "No, we got nothing like that here. That was the loudest I ever heard it. All y'all better be careful."

"Where is Gretchen?" Lucas stopped what he was doing and started moving toward the stairs to find her.

Janie clung to Neil, but stretched out a hand to stop him. "It's all right. I asked the neighbors to take her tonight."

My ears were still ringing and the impact of the sound reverberated on my breastbone. I could still sense a low frequency vibration, as if it were winding up to do some more. "Cam, there are four of us here. What if it's drawing power from all of us?"

Cam appeared calm and gave a quick nod to Zackie as he strode forward into the mayhem. "Shields up, if you please." When Zackie responded, Bodean and Parmelia suddenly hunched as if the wind had been knocked out of them and wrapped their arms tightly around each other. I only felt a warm, comforting feeling, but at that moment, I was not on the shit list of the psychopomp. The thrumming went down significantly and the only sound that could be heard was heavy-footed pacing on the hardwood floors of the back room. After Cam and I entered the room, we pressed ourselves against the wall next to the door. I tried to pinpoint where the walker was pacing, but my concentration was broken when the stacked cardboard boxes slammed violently against the far wall, spilling their contents and knocking over some of Lucas'sequipment before they came to rest. A jumble of baby clothes and toys tangled with cables and metal supports, creating an impassable pile of debris on the floor. Some of the crew scrambled to right the fallen equipment, while others worked to continue filming with what remained. The temperature plummeted and the breath of everyone in the room became visible with each exhale. Crew members exclaimed curses as first the electronics died and then all house lights began to dim.

"Get out! Get out!" Parmelia screamed as she struggled to her feet and forced Bodean and anyone near him out of the room. I slipped out the exit with Cam, yanking Lucas by the arm to bring him with us. The temperature radically shifted and a blast of scorching air blew my hair forward into my eyes as we retreated from the room. Parmelia shrieked as the blast caught her. Whatever I might have thought of her, she was the last to leave the room and paid the price. I turned back to find her crumpled unconscious at the threshold with the clothing on her back smoldering from the heat. Lucas was closest and grabbed her under the arms to drag her away from the room.

As we retreated farther up the hall to the staircase, I heard from the room the sound of a deep growl with harmonics that played in and out of the range of my human hearing. I could feel the threat more than hear it and I hunched myself to protect my throat as I ran. The sound raised the hackles on the back of my neck and drove Parmelia out of her stupor. She screamed and started crying. Zackie, I thought. Of everything that had just happened, nothing made my gut churn like the sound of that growl. I thought I would piss my pants and wanted nothing more than to run out the front door and not look back. The dead hand took that moment of weakness to grab the banister and not only stop my retreat, but propel me past Cam and back towards the room.

I saw the look of wild fear in his eyes as I staggered under the sudden change of direction. "Cam! It's making me go back!"

"All right! We're coming with you." Cam gasped out these words as he collared Bodean and dragged him away from Parmelia. Over his shoulder, he shouted instructions to Lucas. "Get everyone out of the house."

Bodean swore and tried to break free, but Cam had a tight grip. "Shitshitshit! Lemme go!"

The dead hand grasped at any purchase it could find and forced me back down the hall where the growling became louder. The sharp odor of disinfectant penetrated my overwhelmed senses and I shook my head, trying to clear it. I knew that smell. Hospital. I reentered the room with Cam and Bodean on my heels. Zackie had the spirit clamped in her jaws and with each growl she shook it off of its feet. It was a man, but he was stripped of all natural color, being visible to my eyes in only shades of gray. The spirit was in agony. I could feel the pain, but the face was a black hole devoid of any humanity and showed me nothing. Despite everything, I reached out towards him, wanting to stop the pain.

Cam's voice rang out. "Zackie, let go. Bodean, bind him." Bodean looked like he wanted to run and Cam gave him a firm shake using the grip on his collar. Zackie released the spirit, but the hackles were still raised from the back of her head all the way down her tail. Her teeth were bared. I had never seen her as anything but gentle and loving with the dead and this side of her shocked me to my core.

The spirit began to flail and fight again and I blocked his blows, striking back and keeping him at bay as Bodean worked. As the spirit began to rise from the floor, the smell of disinfectant became caustic and I slammed him again to keep the momentum on our side. In another moment, Bodean had him pinned and helpless, floating before us.

Sweating and grunting, Bodean doubled down and held the spirit. "It's stronger than anything I've seen before. I don't know if I can hold it for long."

Cam took a breath and nodded. "It's because he's Lummie's son. You know how strong she was." Bodean's eyes went round, but he held his grip and increased his focus on the spirit.

Cam walked up close to the spirit and I cringed, even knowing he was now bound, I worried that he would somehow break free. "Your name is Daniel Clark. You were raised by Randall and Flora Clark. You had eight brothers and sisters." With each word, the spirit became more animated with color and the stench of disinfectant faded. Cam continued relating the story of his life and was somehow sensing what I could not. There was sweat on his brow as he concentrated and he was visibly straining as he drew out the identity from deep within the spirit. As Cam described Daniel's time as a sheriff's deputy, the black hole of his face lightened and eventually color entered even this void. Features formed and he was given a face. I saw the man from the newspaper article before me, complete with uniform and a badge on his chest. This, then, was the core of his identity and his reason for living when he was human. I felt no sense of identity or emotion beyond pain until Cam had completed his efforts and gave the spirit back the life he had lived.

Cam wiped his brow and took a shaky breath. "Let him go, Bodean." Bodean slanted a look at Cam that was laced with fear, but he did as he was told and freed the spirit. Zackie had stood down as the process unfolded and she was sitting peacefully at Cam's side, hackles down and fangs concealed. Seeing this, I finally let my guard down and almost fell to the floor as the adrenalin drained from me. The dead hand was also quiescent. I suppose it got what it wanted.

"Are you ready to move on?" Cam eyed the spirit and I could tell he wanted this to be finished.

I heard a definitive *No!* as I tuned in and my eyes went wide. I dug down and started pulling energy, readying for another battle. Bodean changed his stance to put himself at the ready and started swearing.

Cam put a restraining hand up towards us. "What is not done for you? Why do you not move on?" At this question, I got a flood of information, but all of it was from after the death of Daniel and I saw a bright image in my mind of Gretchen. He told us that he did not remember much of anything until Cam helped him, but he did remember decency.

Daniel had been locked into the last patterns of his life in the house, confused and agitated, but he meant no harm to anyone living here. That was true until the McLeans took in the two hikers. The terror from the little girl penetrated his disordered mind that night. One of the hikers had taken her from her bed and was touching her in a way that was frightening her and making her cry. Before anything worse could happen, Daniel stormed up the stairs and tore the man off the little girl, battering him into the wall outside of the room. The man did not immediately release his grip and the little girl's arm was broken in the struggle. Daniel tried to comfort her, but he sensed another man in the house and assumed he was another threat. From that point on, the idea was fixed in his mind that these people in the house were threats and had to be removed. He would protect that little girl at any cost.

When he heard the tale, Bodean spat the words, "Fucking pervert!" Cam turned his face in disgust and his fists clenched at his sides. I thought that some people just didn't deserve to draw breath. The man had walked out the door as free and easy as you please. He would do it again, preying on some other child, and Daniel could not move on to his peace knowing that this man could harm another innocent. Daniel wanted to go after that man.

Cam stepped back from the spirit. "Do what you must. You have our blessings." And we all knew what this spirit was capable of. I felt a cold wind as the spirit swept passed me and I almost pitied the man.

# # #

Standing outside the farmhouse, I dug through my trunk to find a bottle of coconut water that I chugged until it was empty. Wiping my mouth on my sleeve, I felt better and opened another bottle. I took more leisurely sips as I thought about what happened. Parmelia had some blisters on her back, but the injury was not nearly as bad as I had thought. Janie put some homemade salve for burns on the blistered skin and that seemed to soothe the pain. Despite all the damage to the equipment, Lucas did succeed in getting some film footage and sound recordings. That should hold his producers at bay until we were ready to confront the Entity.

I listened as Cam finished explaining the course of events to Parmelia, Lucas and the McLeans. Bodean was sprawled out on the front steps, exhausted and not up to participating in telling the tale. I handed him my unfinished

338

bottle of coconut water and told him to drink. When Cam got to the part about Gretchen, Neil was livid and would have grabbed his shotgun and hit the trails to look for the man, but Cam told him in no uncertain terms that Daniel was on the case. There would be no escaping Daniel. Janie calmed Neil down further when she declared that nothing they could do to the man would rival Daniel's wrath. She trusted the spirit to mete out justice.

On our drive back to the cabin, I asked Cam the question that had been niggling at me. "How did you know the spirit was Daniel Clark? I thought you had some doubts when we talked about it before. That was a huge risk, approaching him like that. What if you were wrong?"

"I didn't know. I took a chance. We didn't have any better ideas going into this." Cam yawned and fell silent for a beat. "You know, maybe the hand is directed by Lummie. It was brooking no argument when it came to saving the spirit from Zackie. Lummie would have wanted to protect Daniel."

I chewed on my lip and shook my head. "I can't say no, but I don't know. I just don't get any consistent vibe from it that I would associate with Lummie. After reading her journal, I think I have a pretty good sense of her. And yeah, Lummie would have tried to save Daniel." I focused on the road for a bit and then cleared my throat. "There is one thing about the dead hand that I'm now sure about." I paused because for some reason, the hand embarrassed me. To me, it was like talking about venereal disease. Cam nodded for me to finish my thought, so I soldiered on. "Glove, no glove… it doesn't matter. Keeping it under wraps has no effect. I was wearing gloves tonight and it did what it wanted to do. I'm starting to think it's just being polite and staying quiet when I put a glove on it."

Cam frowned. "That is disconcerting." Rubbing his eyes, he yawned again. "Maybe it takes energy to act, so it simply can't be active all the time."

I shrugged. We could speculate until the sun came up and it wouldn't change anything, so I just let the matter drop. Stifling a yawn, I pulled up to the cabin and killed the engine.

Stepping out of the car, I stretched until my ribs complained and then shuffled towards the door. "Looks like we beat Lucas here."

Cam drawled words through another yawn. "No, he's gone back with the crew." I heard the words 'gone' and 'crew' and surmised the rest until he added to the sentence. "They're driving home tonight, so they have a fighting chance to edit the material in time for the next show. I'll pack up his things tomorrow and we can give them to him next time we see him."

I just grunted a reply and headed up the stairs to bed. Part of me was happy not to have to control my hormones during another cramped drive together. Most of me regretted not having this chance. Still, the long drive with Cam and Zackie felt like a comforting prospect after a fast and furious spirit encounter. It surprised me how attached I'd become to the two of them.

CHAPTER 17

The drive home had me thinking about everything that awaited me. The practicalities of finding a new job were mundane, but necessary to my survival. Maybe something would materialize from all the applications I submitted before heading to North Carolina. Mentally sighing, I conceded that it wasn't like anyone had left messages on my cell phone with job offers while I was away, so I shouldn't keep my hopes up.

Thoughts of how we would deal with the Entity were another major topic of discussion. Parmelia and Bodean had promised to meet us in a few days after they had a chance to organize things so that the goats were cared for and the rentals/rescues could go on while they were away. It was not beyond the realm of possibilities that they would blow us off and not show up. Still, we held out hope that they would honor their commitment, if only for the paycheck that Lucas'sshow promised.

As we drove past a state park entrance just a few

miles from home, we were diverted by state troopers away from the main road and towards a detour. Crawling along, I swore every time I had to hit the brakes. Because I knew myself to be a favored daughter of the universe, it made perfect sense that we would face traffic problems this close to home.

Cam stared from his window into the darkness as we approached the park entrance. Blue and red lights from emergency vehicles flashed on a continuous loop and a bright light illuminated an area near the back of the lot. "There's a search going on. I see a bunch of people in high vis orange." He opened his window and leaned out to get a better look. "They've set up staging right there in the parking area and there are searchers working the side of the road up ahead." Cam and I had informed our teams that we would be unavailable when we departed for North Carolina, so it was not surprising that we did not receive the call out for this search.

I slowed to a stop in front of the officer directing traffic towards the detour. "Tell him we're search and rescue and that we can help if they need it." Cam dug out his county SAR ID and asked the cop if we could be of any use. He pointed us towards the parking entrance and told us where to sign in. Pulling into the lot, we drove around a car parked towards the middle that was surrounded by safety cones and flagging tape.

Once we secured a parking space, I popped open the trunk and handed Cam a safety vest with reflective strips to wear over his jacket and found some eye protection for each of us. Digging a little deeper, I found a flashlight and handed that to Cam as well. I put on a high vis orange jacket with reflective strips, grabbed my ready pack and started moving some of the contents to a fanny pack. Being careful around the cast, I helped Cam put on the backpack and locked it down with some strap adjustments. I next placed the GPS in one cargo pocket and the radio in the other and then strapped on my helmet, so I could go hands-free using the headlamp. Strapping on the fanny pack, I adjusted the weight so that it was secure on my hips. Hopefully, this arrangement would allow both of us to carry the weight of necessary items in a way that would cause the least amount of distress to our healing bones. While I checked my headlamp light, I asked, "What are you going to do about Zackie's harness and lead?"

Improvising, Cam grabbed an LED armband for jogging at night and affixed it to Zackie's collar. "That'll do. And by the way, if anyone asks, she is a scent discriminating trailing dog who works off lead." He winked and then examined his arms. "Check me to make sure my cast is adequately disguised by the jacket?" I thought we passed muster and it was unlikely that anyone at incident command would even notice that we had injuries and turn us away as the walking wounded. Even though neither of us was in that bad shape anymore, it would be unconscionable if we became liabilities during the search and distracted workers from the real subject. We both did some experimental maneuvering to make sure we would hold up if we had to walk a few miles over rugged terrain. Satisfied that we were physically able, we presented ourselves at the trailer to sign in as an available resource.

Until we were tasked, we waited with the other searchers in staging. Among the people milling about, I recognized Bill Fry from the search for the autistic boy and approached him to find out any additional information about the current subject.

Bill remembered me and shook my hand. "Her name is Amy Turpin. She normally runs trails here in the early hours of the morning before work, but her company announced a reorganization today and she got some bad news. When she didn't return home at her usual time, her fiancé became worried that the job loss had hit her pretty hard. She's had a history of depression, but had been taking meds and coping all right up until now, at least according to the fiancé. Anyway, he tried her cell and got no answer, so he started calling friends and driving around to the places she frequented. He thought she might have gone running to work off the stress, so he headed here and found her car. It was locked up tight and her cell was on the passenger seat."

Cam looked troubled. "Wouldn't she normally take her cell with her when she went running?"

Bill nodded. "Yeah, the fiancé said she had an arm band that she stuck it in, so she could listen to music while she ran."

"Okay, so she's a possible despondent." I blew out a sigh. "Does anyone know if she owns a gun and maybe took it with her?"

Bill shook his head. "No, no gun that we have to worry about." Bill paused to unwrap a protein bar and took a bite before continuing. "The cops unlocked the car, but didn't find a suicide note. Right now, they're running hasties on the trails to see if they can find her and they sent another team to a high point with a scenic view, in case she took a leap. A bunch of other teams are sign cutting along the road to see if she went in to any of the trails from the road."

Cam glanced at Zackie. "Were they able to establish direction of travel with any dog teams?"

Bill shook his head again. "Not yet. We had a few air scent dogs respond, but no trailing dogs yet. You're trailing, right? They'll probably task you next to see if you can do that." Thrusting his chin at Zackie, Bill asked, "Will it mess up your dog having all the searchers walking around over where Amy might have walked?"

Cam shook his head. "No, we train for contamination. We do exercises like having her follow a specific scent through a high traffic area, like a Walmart entrance. She has to work through all the other old and new scent from the hundreds of customers and follow only the correct scent." Bill's eyes widened and he nodded, clearly impressed by this ability. "But if someone has been in the car touching things, that will likely have contaminate scent articles for the subject. We would need to negative her off of that person, so she can rule out their scent when she starts her trail."

As Bill predicted, we were soon called to the table and assigned a task to establish direction of travel. Cam was eager to start, so rather than take the time to pick up scent from the subject by incubating gauze pads on the car seat, he announced that he would scent her directly from the seat. He asked for the police officer and anyone else who might have been inside the car, so Zackie could negative their scent. The man assigning tasks called out for Officer Creighton and within minutes, a tall woman in uniform approached the table. She had wheat blonde hair and piercing green eyes that missed nothing. When I looked at her, the words 'strong,' 'capable' and 'Amazon' came to mind. Cam explained what was needed and the officer confirmed that she was the only one to access the vehicle and it had been secured since that access.

We all walked to the vehicle together and asked the officer to open the door, since her scent was already on the handle. While I turned on my GPS, Cam reached down to turn on Zackie's jogger lights and then asked the officer to present her hands for Zackie to sniff. Pointing to the driver's seat, Cam then told Zackie to take scent and then gave her the final command to find the subject. Zackie began following the scent and we took off behind her, thanking the officer for her help as we left. As we walked away from the floodlights of staging, we each turned on our light sources and kept a sharp eye on Zackie's red blinking light.

Following Zackie, we went towards the far corner of the parking lot and to the blue trail head. She paused for a moment to spy us over her shoulder and then took to the trail. She kept up a good pace and we did our best to keep our balance as we traversed a field of jiggly rocks on the path. Our lights helped, but they could only illuminate a short distance in front of us, so we were constantly surprised by the treacherous footing. Thankfully, Zackie was mindful not to lose us in the dark and would frequently pause, waiting for us to catch up. It was cool and I sucked in and out the tangy scent of wet earth as I panted with the effort of moving uphill. After only a tenth of a mile on the trail, I was dripping sweat and thinking of peeling off the jacket. Just as I was about to ask for a halt to accomplish this adjustment, Zackie shot into the woods on our right. Finding the deer path she followed, we went in after her, forcing our way through the brush. I scanned the area for the blinking red light on Zackie's collar and froze as I caught the muzzle of a revolver in the light of my headlamp. Cam touched my arm in warning and we both stood stock-still.

"Call your dog off." The man with the gun was dressed in camo and carried a large bowie knife at his belt. He kept the handgun trained on us. "I'm not going to ask you again."

Cam's voice was steady as he called Zackie to him. "Zackie, come." She stood directly in front of the man with her nose in the air, scenting him. At the command to come, she looked back at us and then back at him. She did everything except to jump up and touch him with her front paws to tell us that this was the scent from the driver's seat. Cam nodded to her and tried again. "Zackie, come." This time, she looked at us with her 'screw you' face and sneezed her objection. "Sorry, she's not as well trained as she might be."

The man didn't answer, but the muzzle lowered towards Zackie and I heard a deafening bang at the same time that my eyes registered a brilliant flash of light that was synchronized with the flare from the muzzle. Zackie must have phased out and then back in again faster than I thought was possible and the bullet passed harmlessly through the air where she had been before she reappeared. "What the hell! That was point blank." Twigs snapped as the man took a step forward to shoot her again. In that same moment, Zackie lunged forward to meet him and her teeth clamped down on the wrist of his gun hand, grabbing not the flesh, but a silvery white substance that she pulled and stretched before letting it go. The man collapsed and the substance retracted back into his body.

Zackie trotted back to us and acted like she had finished her assignment. She fully expected us to compliment her on her find. I stared, my eyes wide and my breath coming fast. "What the fuck was that, Cam? Is he dead?"

Cam exhaled loudly and then took a deep breath before he answered. "She could have killed him. She could have yanked his soul right out of his body. When they take him to the hospital, they'll find a perfectly natural explanation. Maybe a cerebral hemorrhage or heart attack."

I rubbed my face and got a grip. Reaching for my GPS, I marked where we were and then grabbed my radio. "We need to call this in. They must have heard the shot." As I contacted command to give a report and our location, Cam rolled the man over and checked for a pulse and breathing. He gave me a thumbs up and I began manufacturing a story for IC. "Yes, a man with a gun. He tried to shoot us, but the shot went wild and then he collapsed. Send a medical team and a rescue team with a stokes basket. Stand by for our coordinates." That done, I handed the radio to Cam, so he could give an update on the subject's condition.

While we waited for the teams to make their way to us, we dug the tarp out of Cam's pack and collected leaves to serve as insulation between the tarp and the ground. We placed these under the man to keep him from losing body heat to the cold ground. Cam then inspected the man with his flashlight before covering him with a mylar blanket. "He's got blood on him and it's not his." Sweeping the light, he focused on the knife. "There's quite a bit on the knife."

I looked at Zackie and then looked back at the man. "Zackie said she was following his scent, so he must have been in the car. Do you think he grabbed Amy and drove her here?"

Cam sighed as he squatted down to look closer at the blood. "I think he killed her. There's an awful lot of blood."

As if on cue, the radio crackled and one of the hasty teams made a request for law enforcement to come to their location. They would never report finding a body over a radio, since anyone could be listening to the frequency. They would use their cell phones and call IC to tell them what they found. I strongly suspected that they found Amy's body.

# # #

Hours later, near dawn, we were still in staging as the police asked their questions and gathered their evidence. We and the hasty team who found the body had been interviewed by the critical incident management team shortly after we returned from the trails. They told us that we could attend a debrief in the next few days if we felt stressed by what we experienced. We were handed cards with contact information in case we needed to talk about things sooner. The critical incident team assured us that our reactions were normal and gave us a list of symptoms to watch for over the short term. I read over the symptoms and found that I'd been identifying with nearly everything on the list for years. Nothing different here. I tucked the card in a shirt pocket and forgot about it.

We were asked to stay put, so the police could get

statements from us. While I made my statement to the police, Cam put Zackie back in the car to let her doze and to keep her out from under foot. While Cam answered their questions, I sat around feeling increasingly restive as I waited for them to finish with us. Fortunately, someone had the decency to bring in food for the searchers during the night, so we at least had slices of cold pizza to soothe ourselves as we waited to be released.

"You were crazy lucky." I looked up to see Officer Creighton standing over me. "Do you mind if grab a slice?"

I pushed the pizza box closer to her and she sat next to me on the ground before taking a slice. "Either I was lucky or the shooter was incredibly unlucky."

Chewing slowly, she looked at me. "No, you were lucky. I've never heard of anything so freaky. Just as he's about to shoot you, he has an aneurysm. That just doesn't happen." She shook her head in disbelief.

"I guess it gives me a story I can tell for the rest of my life. I'm Fia, by the way."

Wiping her hand on her slacks, she extended it toward me for a shake. "Jill." Jill went back to demolishing her pizza and spoke between bites. "I wish everything in life turned out that good."

"Tell me about it." I picked off a pepperoni and popped it in my mouth. "I am spared a gunshot wound, only to face unemployment. The fun never stops."

"What did you used to do?"

I explained to Jill how I cobbled together an existence with an assortment of odd jobs and she nodded approvingly. "It worked okay for me for a while, I guess." Looking around, I spied a carton of water bottles and got up. "I'm getting some water. Do you want some?" She nodded her thanks as I handed her the bottle and sat down again.

Jill took a long pull on the water and then wiped her mouth. "Maybe you should contact this business I know. You've got bloodborne pathogen training for search?" I nodded. "That's good. You'll need that... You're probably not squeamish, right?" I rolled my eyes and shook my head. After everything the dead have shown me, I could definitely say it took a lot to gross me out. "So, this business does crime scene clean up. It pays well, but the hours can be kind of random. You'll probably spend your life in a hazmat suit if you want to do this for a living."

I hesitated for a moment, but then looked her in the eye. "I hate to admit it, but this might be my dream job. Where do I sign up?" Some of my confession was bravado, but I was still surprised to hear myself say this. I might be desperate for a job, but in the very recent past, I would have gone screaming into the hinterlands at the thought of deliberately going into a situation where the dead were likely to be lurking. Props to Cam and Zackie for bringing me this far this fast. From a practical standpoint, when I thought about the work conditions, this job might actually be tailor made for me. If I wore gloves all the time, no one would bat an eye.

Jill took out a pad and a pen from her shirt pocket and wrote down a number. Tearing out the sheet, she handed it to me and said to mention her name when I called. She next handed me a tissue and told me to wipe the sauce off my face before she got up and went back to work.

#

Days later, the full extent of the tale started to emerge as we talked to other searchers and read the newspapers. The shooter was an ex-boyfriend. After finding out that Amy was affianced to someone else, like most deranged ex-boyfriends, he decided that if he could not have her, no one could. He became fixated on no one having her and devised a plan to grab Amy from the parking lot of her work place. It was coincidental that he did this on the same day that the layoffs were announced, convincing the searchers that she was a despondent and completely befuddling the lost person profile. After shoving her in the trunk, he drove her car to the state park and forced her up the blue trail and then into the woods. He tied Amy to a tree and slashed her throat, covering himself in her blood in the process. He was on his way down the trail with the intent of moving her car at the same time Cam, Zackie and I were heading up the trail, unknowingly following his scent. Once he realized that the parking lot was lousy with search and rescue, emergency medical services and law enforcement, he went off trail and thought he could bushwhack his way out and avoid notice. He did not count on scent betraying his location to a search dog. Panicking at being discovered, he must have decided that after having already killed one person, a few more dead people on his conscience would make no real difference to him. If not for Zackie, we would have joined Amy on the other side.

As soon as we were certain that the police had completed their investigation of the crime scene, we made plans to return to the state park to look for Amy. After such a violent death, we were sure that she would be unable to move on and would need our help.

Cam sent an e-mail to one of the guys on the hasty team and explained that he was putting together a canine search report to submit to his SAR chief and needed some information to better understand his dog's behavior during the search. If the guy could give Cam the coordinates of where the body was found, it would be possible to reconstruct the shooter's movements and maybe what Zackie did would make sense. The guy replied minutes later with the coordinates and wished him luck with report writing.

Armed with the exact location, we returned to the state park and hiked up the blue trail to the point where the shooter dragged Amy into the woods. Within seconds of going off-trail, the temperature plummeted around us and a weak sobbing echoed in the woods. Triangulating on the sound and using the GPS to get us closer, we eventually came to the tree where Amy met her end. Crime scene tape still surrounded the area and there was a telling stain on the tree bark. As Zackie approached the tree, a woman dripping blood from her throat emerged from behind it. Clots of blood hung from her lank brown hair and her wrists bore the burns from struggling with the rope. Amy had suffered enough.

"It's all right now, Amy." Cam approached her slowly, as if she were a fawn that might spook and bolt into the forest. "We're here to help."

CHAPTER 18

Hannah lay in a fetal position, clutching her belly and curling herself around Zackie. The last round of treatment had been delivered the previous day and things were not going well for her.

Lucas sat near the bed, bowed with his elbows on his knees and his hands clasped. "The second day is always the worst. She'll rally soon." His voice was low and even he didn't sound convinced. Cam and I nodded dumbly, not sure what to say. Pity welled up in me as I looked at the two of them. There was a real devotion between Lucas and Hannah and if circumstances had been different, they would have had a long and happy marriage. It was odd that I could recognize this truth, while at the same time have such strong feelings for Lucas. I really am an idiot some times.

Lucas' eyes drifted around the confines of the small room. "Still no sign of Bodean and Parmelia?" I'm not sure he was much interested in the answer, but it was a diversion.

Cam shook his head. "No, not yet. They said they were having a hard time finding a temporary goatherd."

I chimed in, babbling because it was uncomfortable to stand by impotently while people suffered. "A likely story. I read just yesterday that goat herding was a booming growth industry and many young people were entering the profession." Even if the part about goat herding wasn't true, the part about this excuse being prevarication was most likely true.

"Speaking of professions, did you follow up on the tip from Officer Creighton?" Cam shifted uneasily in his chair as he did his part to distract Lucas.

I nodded. "Yeah, I called them yesterday and they want to hire me. It was probably the SAR experience that caught their eye, the willingness to do recoveries to bring the bodies back."

Lucas lifted his eyebrows in question, so we filled him in on the last search. We gave him the same sanitized version of the story that we gave law enforcement and then told him about the possible job opportunity for me. Lucas'seyebrows stayed up, but now he looked dismayed.

"You almost got shot?!"

Cam made a motion with his hand for Lucas to stay calm. "'Almost' being the operative word here. It wasn't even close." Lucas continued to stare wide-eyed at him, so Cam leaned forward and held his eyes while the point was made again. "We were never really in any danger." Which was true. Zackie was the one who might have been in danger, if a life threatening situation meant anything to an immortal.

Lucas nodded and sat back, evidently too tired to argue with Cam's version of things. His eyes moved back to Hannah and he reached out a hand to touch her cheek. Hannah murmured something to him and he immediately stood and headed for the door. "She wants some ice chips. I'll be right back."

Hannah's voice was weak, but she made sure we heard her. "I don't want him here when I die."

Cam looked at me, his face etched with worry. "Hannah, are you sure about this? It might not be the best thing for Lucas or for you."

I nodded. "Listen to him, Hannah. Think this through. It might seem like it's the easier thing to do right now, but later, he's going to suffer with a huge amount of guilt for not being there with you."

Hannah sobbed softly. "I know... I know... But if he's here, I won't be able to do this, to let go. I don't want to die in front of him. That's the last thing he'll remember about me. And he'll carry that memory with him for the rest of his life. I don't want to do that to him."

I blew out a breath. I understood where she was coming from. Nurses have plenty of stories about people who kept vigil with a dying loved one and the minute they leave for even the shortest period of time, the dying take that opportunity to let go. Those left behind are wracked with guilt for not being there at the final moment, but the truth was, the dying needed that space of separation to make the transition. I honestly didn't know whose needs took precedence.

Cam got up and walked to the window. "I don't know how to help here, Hannah." He sighed and looked down. "We can't very well drag him away. He'd fight us tooth and claw."

"Who's fighting?" Lucas entered the room carrying a Styrofoam cup. Taking his seat near the bed, he removed some ice chips and put them to Hannah's lips.

Hannah swallowed the melted ice and answered Lucas'squestion. "I'm fighting. I'll take on the lot of you."

Lucas smiled fondly at her. "That's my girl." Looking at us, he grinned triumphantly. "I told you she'd rally."

Cam and I exchanged a tortured look. Hannah had placed us squarely between the proverbial rock and a hard place. If we didn't help her, we were denying a dying woman her last wish. If we helped her, Lucas would be tormented by the belief that he abandoned her at the end. Maybe we could sway Hannah's decision if we could convince her that Zackie would help her to cross over. We could try to assure Lucas that she wasn't suffering and give him a play-by-play of the action to let him know when she'd made it over, but I wasn't sure he would buy it. Sometimes, there was a high cost to being purely rational. Speaking as an expert, certain situations in life require the irrational and there are just times when you need to let the crazy out.

We waited until Hannah was able to sleep and then silently made our way out, leaving Lucas to watch her while she slept. Gazing at him over my shoulder as we went through the door, I thought that maybe there was hope for him. On the one hand, he showed every evidence of a man storing up time with a wife that he would soon lose. This was the rational Lucas. On the other hand, he espoused the belief to anyone who would listen that Hannah would make a full recovery. This was the wish fulfillment Lucas. There was a definite left brain – right brain conflict playing out and it gave me hope that he would believe at least some of what we told him when Hannah's time came. I shared my thoughts with Cam as we rode the elevator down.

Cam rubbed his brow and closed his eyes briefly. "We should at least try to convince her. Whether or not we convince him of anything is anyone's guess."

I shrugged. "At the very least, she has Zackie. That has to make things easier." Cam nodded absently as he exited the elevator and we made our way to the parking lot.

Unlocking his truck, Cam found Zackie waiting patiently in the truck bed. "Speak of the devil." Turning back towards me, Cam checked his watch. "Would you be interested in having dinner at my place? I have some leftovers that are becoming surprisingly ripe." Cam had been generous about sharing meals since we returned and I appreciated that he went to the effort of buying extra napkins for me. I also appreciated how his actions spared my bank account.

I grinned. "Happy to help you dispose of your kitchen waste. I'll meet you there."

When we arrived at Cam's house, a red pickup truck was already gracing the driveway. Parmelia and Bodean emerged from this vehicle to greet us.

Cam smiled broadly. "Very glad you've come. I hope you weren't waiting long." Zackie climbed out of Cam's truck and then sat in the driveway, watching the cousins with no great interest.

Bodean dipped his head in response. "Fair's fair. We couldn't have cleaned up that mess at the McLean's without you, so we figured coming up here was a necessary inconvenience." I didn't say it out loud, but I wondered what changed. They certainly took their sweet time getting here. Cam and I had just about moved on to trying to develop a plan C to deal with the Changewater situation. Instead of voicing my opinion on the matter, I extended the dead hand to Bodean to shake. "Unh-uh. I'm not doing that again, girl."

Turning to Parmelia, I offered her the same greeting. She narrowed her eyes at me and turned away to get her bags. "Not funny."

Cam unlocked the front door and called over his shoulder. "We were just about to have dinner. Are you two hungry?" He was met with a chorus of agreement, so while he showed Parmelia the futon in the office and pointed out a comfy couch in the living room for Bodean, I set the table and started some food nuking in the microwave. Seeing the nature of the leftovers, I put an extra stack of napkins near my plate. Meanwhile, Zackie followed them around as they settled in and I caught her watching the cousins as if they had larceny in their hearts.

When we sat down to eat the leftover spaghetti and meatballs, it was a quiet affair. We made small talk, asking them about their trip, how the McLeans fared and if they heard anything more about Daniel. They asked after Lucas and we told them of his struggle with Hannah's cancer. Surprisingly, it was the topic of Daniel that brought the most news. I had fully expected him to disappear from the record, never to be heard from again.

Parmelia sipped her coffee and stared at her hands as she related the tale. "The McLeans were doing a little trail magic - "

My monkey brain latched on to this new term and I interrupted. "What do you mean by trail magic?" As everyone looked at me, I automatically started wiping my face with some of the extra napkins, feeling self-conscious that I'd probably made a mess.

Bodean, determinedly ignoring my efforts at hygiene, lifted a shoulder and explained. "It's not entirely altruistic. What they do is set up a cooler with some fruit and cold drinks and a few camp chairs. They wait around and offer the goodies to thru-hikers as they pass by the trail near their house. These people might not have seen a cold drink in weeks and fresh fruit is like the food of the gods to them."

Cam tilted his head and furrowed his brow. "So, why isn't this altruistic? Do they do some sort of price gouging?"

Bodean shook his head. "Naw, nothing like that. What they offer is free. It's just that it's a way for them to advertise their inn. A hiker might be drawn in by the sudden appearance of creature comforts and decide to stay the night with them. At the very least, hikers talk and spread the word about the inn."

Parmelia interrupted this off-topic discussion and brought us back to her story. "Anyway, while they were doing trail magic, they met this thru-hiker who had a weird story that sounded to them a lot like something a cop would do." She took another sip from her coffee and braced her elbows on the table as she cradled her mug, staring at the design painted on its side. "You know how there are all these caricatures of the different types of hikers on the Trail?" I shook my head when she glanced my way. I told her that it was my impression that you only had your thru-hikers and your section hikers. "Not exactly." Her gaze went back to examining the mug. "There are maybe a dozen different types. For instance, you got your romantic, prancing through a meadow in bare feet and quoting Thoreau. Then you got your survivalist out there eating what he can catch, building his own shelter and more than ready for the zombie apocalypse. And then there's the stoner. You'll smell him coming because of the patchouli and pot." She cracked a small grin. "So, a bunch of stoners were in a shelter and they're ready to party. As soon as one of them was able to light up a joint, it would go out. The joints just wouldn't stay lit. The weed was dry, the paper was dry, and it would start smoldering when they touched the fire to it, but then something would make it go out. They kept trying until they heard a deep voice say, 'Y'all stop that now.' One of them got yanked out of his sleeping bag and something they couldn't see started stomping around the shelter. Eventually, it left for the woods and the stoners put all their weed and paraphernalia away, just in case it came back."

Cam chuckled and slapped the table with his palm and Parmelia jerked a little at the sudden noise. "That sounds exactly like something Daniel would do." I had to agree.

After a beat, Bodean cleared his throat and sat up straighter. "Okay, so tell us about this thing you got here."

Squaring my shoulders, I took a deep breath and started explaining to them how Joel was remodeling the house for a disabled veteran and the little girl he saw. Cam told them about John Castner, who we found in the pit, and the hanged men buried at the crossroads, Peter Parke and Joseph Carter. When we described the fight with the Entity in the field, the cousins began to exchange worried looks. Cam then told them about Zackie's rescue of the little girl,

Maria Matilda, and how brutally the Entity retaliated against Mary, the mother. Holding up his broken arm, Cam described the chaos and the violence that ensued. Bodean and Parmelia looked at us with wide eyes and appeared paler than usual after the story was done.

Parmelia, her brow puckered and her shoulders hunched up around her ears, was the first to speak. "So, what is it... you got four spirits left trapped by this Entity?"

Cam shook his head. "Actually, it's five. John Parke was the homeowner and was also killed in the house. We have not yet encountered him, but there's no doubt that he's there as well."

Bodean rubbed his face and looked balefully at us. "You two are like magnets for this stuff. You know that, right?" He took a quick look around the kitchen before settling his eyes on Cam. "You got any scotch? I'm gonna need something after a story like that."

Cam got up and found some tumblers and a bottle, pouring a finger for each of us. "Cheers," he offered as he raised his glass. It burned my throat and I cautiously swallowed small amounts, careful not to embarrass myself by coughing or sputtering. Once the heat hit my belly, it was strangely fortifying.

After a few sips, Bodean raised his drink and watched the light play on the amber liquid. "I think there is something in the field as well. Your Entity had a strong reaction to you being there."

I leaned forward, joining my fingers around the tumbler. "I hadn't thought of that. I had thought the Entity was reacting to us interfering with the hanged men."

"You interfered with the man in the pit too, trying to get him to move on. No action on the field after that little foray, so it can't have been for messing with the hanged men." Bodean drank and wiped his lips on the back of his hand.

Cam frowned, tapping his lip as he thought. "It can't be another body buried there. We didn't detect a spirit presence either time when we crossed the field." He paused and after a moment picked up his train of thought again. "It must be an object and it must be something significant to fight so hard over that piece of ground. If we knew what it was, it may help us defeat it."

I sat up straighter, suddenly gripped by an epiphany. "Whatever it is, I'll bet we could find it if we did a grid search. We could bring both our teams in for a joint training and have enough people to grid that field."

Cam shook his head and his brow creased with worry. "And what if the Entity came after the SAR people? I don't know if we could protect them."

Squinting, I struggled to put the pieces of a strategy together. "So, just the two of us were able to beat it back the first time. It only won the second time in the house because it was able go all poltergeist on us." Nodding to myself, I continued. "I don't think an open field offers any tactical advantage to the Entity. We should be able to keep the searchers protected while they grid if we put Parmelia and Bodean to good use."

Parmelia exhaled and began rapidly chanting a mantra under her breath. "Aw, crap, crap, crap..."

Cam ignored her. "I have to say, I'm dubious. Still, I'm trying to keep an open mind. What are you thinking?"

"Pretty simple. First, we'll need to create a diversion to draw the Entity away from the field." I pointed to Parmelia. "She'll be the look out. We'll know when and from where the Entity is coming." Pointing to Bodean, I continued. "He should be able to bind the Entity. I don't think it's stronger than Daniel and Bodean was able to hold him."

Parmelia stopped muttering to herself and raised a question in tremulous voice. "Sorry if this is ignorant, but this part of dealing with spirits is not in my wheelhouse. If Bodean can bind the Entity, why don't we just settle things with it right there?"

"We have no leverage." Cam shook his head slowly. "We can't bind it forever and we can't force it to move on to the next life. We need something to improve the odds that we can persuade it to move on. Whatever is in the field might give us something to work with. Maybe it's something obvious, like the murder weapon."

Bodean cocked an eyebrow. "So, Parmelia and I are working this one. You need to let Lucas know, so he can film it." Cam and I exchanged a quick, knowing glance, but we nodded. "And you guys are what, plan B? You'll be on standby to dispense violence on its ass if it steps out of line?"

I smiled sweetly and fingered the scar on my temple. "I'm very much hoping to be called into action."

# # #

After dinner, Cam and I retreated to his office to plan the grid search with some online tools. We were forced to narrow down the amount of field to be searched once we determined that the entire field covered slightly over fifty acres. An air scent dog could cover one hundred acre areas during searches, but humans lacked the running and scenting skills, so we needed an easier problem for the twenty or so ground pounders who would come to the training.

Reconstructing our trek across the field using Google Earth, we were able to figure out the general vicinity where we were attacked. We then expanded the search area by a bit more to be conservative in our approach and increase the odds that we didn't miss the object. I thought the final plan was a good balance between effort expended and probability of success.

Cam chewed on his lip. "I don't know. I'm still not feeling great about this. We have a plan A with Parmelia and Bodean sighting and binding the Entity. We have a plan B, where you and I do something to its ass if Bodean can't hold it. But what if it gets past us?"

I rubbed my eyes and sat back thinking. "I don't want to put searchers in danger either, but I can't think of another approach to get some traction on this problem."

Bodean was leaning on the doorframe with his arms crossed over his chest. "Why don't you put Zackie to work? She held Daniel while all of us ran with our tail tucked between our legs. Have her guard the searchers."

Lying on the futon that would be Parmelia's bed, Zackie made a grumbling sound. I thought it was the canine version of 'whatever, dude.' She really was less concerned with the living, but she'd do it if we asked her.

"Three lines of defense. That's good." Cam nodded and seemed satisfied. "I'll send e-mails to our respective training officers and suggest a grid search." Looking over his shoulder, I thought Cam was being a little artistic with the truth, suggesting that this grid search would help out a local historical society, that it was possible there were artifacts in the field that were coming to the surface. And while the searchers trained, a film crew might be on location getting footage for Lucas'sghost show. They wouldn't interfere with the training and would give a suggestion to the viewing audience to donate to their local search and rescue teams, so would that be all right?

While Cam crafted the e-mail, I contacted Joel and explained our plan, asking him if he could get the landowner's permission to train on the field. Joel was uneasy about letting people near the house, but I convinced him that we'd stay in the field and not venture anywhere near the house. Since there was a full-stop on the remodeling work and time was slipping away, he grudgingly agreed to reach out to the landowner for permission.

#

On the day of the training, Lucas and his crew showed up to film the spectacle. Lucas marched over to us, looking tired and irritated. "She threw me out, would you believe it?"

Cam's eyes widened with surprise. "Hannah's feeling well enough for an argument?"

Stunned for a moment, Lucas stopped in his tracks. "Huh, I guess she is." He grinned broadly, happy to talk about Hannah. "We had a great day yesterday. She even got out of bed for a few minutes and we wheeled her to the lounge, so she could get a change of scenery."

Maybe he was right and the treatment would save her. I was absolutely sincere when I told him that this was great news. No one should have to die just so I can get what I want. To distract myself from Lucas, I walked over to join the searchers and we surveyed the field. I sensed nothing ominous, but just to be sure, I glanced over to Parmelia and made eye contact. She shook her head and I felt reassured that the field was clear.

To figure out how to work the grid, we threw a quarter down in the field. Since we didn't know what we were looking for, if the searchers were calibrated on something the size of a quarter, we stood a good chance of finding the object. A number of searchers formed a close circle around the quarter and then each stepped back until the searcher just lost sight of the quarter. On average, the eagle-eyed searchers could still see the quarter at ten feet in the grass, so the sweep width was set to this value. Cam asked that the teams perform an evidence search with overlapping sweep widths that would extend from a road on the one side about fifteen hundred feet to a copse of woods on the other side.

The searchers assembled themselves at the base line and waited until the training officer for the day called out the instructions for the grid. After a short pause, I heard, "20-guide right-15!" Twenty searchers separated themselves by fifteen feet and looked to the road on the right to give them a bearing to follow. Next, the training officer called out, "Searchers ready?" The line called back that they were ready and the training officer responded with "Step off!" The people in the line walked forward, swinging their heads to and fro to check for any objects in their lanes. The searcher in the lane furthest from the road placed flags as she progressed over the field to mark her leftmost boundary. When the searchers reached the road at the top of the field, the training officer called a halt. The line then reformed in the same order with the same spacing past the flags that they would now use to guide them. They would repeat this process until the area of the field Cam and I had isolated as high probability had been searched.

While the searchers made progress on their task, Cam and I took the cousins to the man in the pit, out of sight from the searchers. Zackie stayed at the edge of the field, looking like a herding dog keeping watch over the humans. Part of the film crew also stayed with the searches so they could capture the find if it was made. Lucas, meanwhile, took a camera and a few of his people to record what happened at the pit. He looked a little disappointed, since all he could see was a subtle dip on the side of the road. To the four sibyls, a pit with a broken body at the bottom was clearly visible.

John Castner moaned and begged us to protect his wife and child, that they were in grave danger. We did not engage him, since we did not want to draw the Entity out. We stood ready to go through the motions of freeing him if Parmelia sensed the presence of the Entity nearby. That should sufficiently piss it off to come to us and leave the searchers in peace. In our estimation, the man in the pit would refuse to move on, but the Entity, jealously guarding its captives, would need to be sure of its hold over the spirit in the pit. At least, that was the theory.

From the field, someone yelled out, "Hold the line!" Someone had found something and this told the searchers to hold their ground until it could be determined if the found object was relevant.

As Cam held his broken arm steady and jogged towards the field to claim the object, I turned to query Parmelia. She was making a gagging noise. Covering her mouth with her hand, she gasped out some words. "Coming to the field." Bodean leaped down into the pit and began helping John Castner to rise.

"Where did he go?" Lucas was panning the camera around, unable to locate Bodean. The other crew members were doing the same. To their perception, Bodean had suddenly disappeared.

I felt my adrenalin pumping and I began channeling this energy into my hands. I screamed at Lucas to back up, to stay clear. Whirling and throwing my senses outward to try to find the Entity, I called to Parmelia. "Where?"

"Coming here! It's coming here!" She dropped to her knees and put her arms protectively around her head.

Bodean called from the pit. "Ready!" Just as he said this, I found myself knocked clear of the edge of the pit and sprawled on my face in the dirt.

Struggling to my feet, I yelled to Bodean. "Do you have it? Is it secure?"

"Got it, but it's…it's enveloping me!"

Standing at the edge of the pit, I raised my hands, but then hesitated. If I slammed it, would I hurt Bodean? When I heard him struggling for breath, the decision was made for me. I let loose. The darkness surrounding his body recoiled and he gasped in a breath, but bent double under the force of the blow. I had to give him credit. Through suffocation and being hammered by the energy I hurled at the Entity, Bodean did not let go. The dark mass writhed and curled, trying to escape him. Failing to free itself through contortion, it went back to suffocating him. I sent another jolt to make it free him and I heard Bodean suck in another breath, but his color was bad and he was bleeding from his ears now. Standing was difficult for him and he swayed unsteadily on his feet. Before the Entity threw another wave of darkness over him, he managed to yell to me. "Nuke it again! I can take it."

Parmelia crawled over to me and grabbed my leg. "Don't! Don't do it! He won't survive the next one."

"Bodean, you have to let it go!" I was pleading with him to save his own life. "I'll nail it when it tries to run. Just let it go!"

The Entity lifted and seemed to solidify as Bodean crumpled to the ground. I battered it again and again as it tried to lift from the pit. Things were starting to go gray around the edges of my vision. Blood gushed from my nose and soaked my shirt, but I kept trying. When I dropped to one knee, firing only weakly, the Entity hobbled passed me. It was weakened, but it was on the move. "Shit!"

Parmelia cupped her hands around her mouth and hollered as loud as she could, her body straining with the effort. "Cam! Zackie! It's coming your way." She then turned to the pit and extended her hand to Bodean to pull him up.

I got to my feet, but my limbs weren't working right. I tried to run to help Cam and fell hard. I could hear Bodean struggling up from the pit and Parmelia grunting as she pulled with all her strength. John Castner was wailing from the depths and I could do nothing for him. I looked up in time to see Zackie running uncertainly back and forth between Cam and the portal. She was bawling, clearly tortured by indecision. Cam finally told her to go and with his agreement freeing her, she leaped into the portal and was gone. There goes our last hope, I thought. Either the sky was growing dark or my eyes were failing again. I heard Cam in my mind say that it should leave or he would destroy it. And then I passed out.

# # #

Parmelia and Cam were hovering over me when I came to. Bodean was sitting next to me on the ground, drinking coconut water and swearing. Parmelia handed me my own bottle and told me to drink. I drank. And then I drank a whole lot more. I finished that bottle and chugged a second one before my thirst was slaked. Still, I needed to start a third bottle before I was able to ask questions.

"What happened? Why are we still alive?"

Cam looked critically at me. "Oh good. So you're not brain damaged."

"I also have no physical disabilities." To prove it, I flipped him the bird. I was still very weak and it cost me to do that, but the look on his face made it worth it. "Now, tell me what happened."

Bodean looked at me and uttered one final profanity. "Cluster fuck. That's what happened." His words were slurred and he looked like he was having trouble focusing his eyes.

Cam sat down heavily on the ground and looked old to me for the only time since I've known him. "What he means is that there was a confluence of events that resulted in catastrophic failure of our carefully made plans." Ticking off each incident on his fingers, Cam enumerated the series of events that led us to our current situation. "I was removed from the scene by the discovery of the artifact in the field, thus destroying implementation of plan B when plan A failed. Plan B needed both of us to work and I abandoned you." I was about to contradict him when he shushed me and continued. "Plan C failed when Zackie departed. She really had no choice in the matter. Hannah was dying."

I immediately sat up and looked for Lucas. My head started spinning and I thought for a moment that I would vomit up all the coconut water. Cam forced my head between my knees and told me to breathe before he continued. "Lucas was called to the hospital a few minutes ago. I'm quite sure he didn't make it in time, so she got her wish. I do think Zackie was with her, so we can at least be grateful for that."

I sat up again, but more slowly. "But Lucas said she was doing well, that they had a really good day together yesterday."

Cam shrugged. "I think she willed herself well enough for long enough to give him one last good memory and then sent him packing when she knew death was imminent." He sighed deeply. "Anyway, the thing that saved our hides was the object. I threatened to destroy it and the Entity backed off. It's quite fragile, so it would have been easy to do."

I lay down again and felt immediately better. "What was the object and how did you know the threat would work?"

"It's a cross, but it's badly corroded from being in the ground for so long. As to how I knew the threat would work, I didn't. I took a chance."

I looked at him from under my lashes. "You seem to do that a lot and somehow, it works."

Cam lifted a shoulder non-committally. "You and Bodean had also weakened it. I don't think it could have won another fight."

Smiling faintly, I intoned the sacred words. "Yeah, you should see the other guy." I was feeling really tired, but there was one last thing I worried about. "What about the searchers? How are we going to explain this to them?"

Cam lifted the corner of his mouth in a partial grin. "They never saw anything that went on at the pit. The only thing they noticed was Zackie running around and the sky growing dark. A dog running amuck is nothing interesting to them. They see it all the time when a high drive dog needs to burn some energy. As for the sky, they thought it might be an eclipse or some other celestial event."

"Oh, okay. That's good then." My eyes shut and I fell into a peaceful sleep for a few blessed minutes. Eventually, Parmelia patted my arm and told me it was time for us to go. I got up with her help, while Cam worked on getting Bodean off the ground. Somehow, we managed to get to Cam's truck and my car. The walking wounded claimed the shotgun seats and Parmelia and Cam drove the vehicles to his house. Bodean made it to the couch and passed out. I thought this was such an excellent idea that I went to Parmelia's futon and crashed. I awoke several hours later to find myself precariously balanced on the edge of the mattress. Zackie had joined me at some point and was slowly and insistently forcing me from the bed as she spread out to claim it. I ceded the sleeping space and went to drink some more coconut water.

Cam called Lucas as the sun began to set. He was alone with his grief and still numb with shock, but Lucas being Lucas, he had already organized the funeral and made the calls to family and friends. Cam brought him to the house to feed him and offer what comfort we could. Lucas wasn't ready to talk and just ate mechanically, Parmelia piling more food on his plate when his attention was elsewhere. He had lost some weight over the grueling months of balancing hospital visits with a 24/7 work schedule. Lucas's phone buzzed even now and he just took it out and stared at it blankly, letting it ring. I gently removed the phone from his hand and turned it off, leaving it face down on the table. Cam replaced the device with a tumbler of scotch and then handed out more to the rest of us.

Raising his glass, Cam made a quiet toast. "To Hannah." We all took a drink in her memory and then Lucas tilted his head back and determinedly drained his glass. Shrugging, Cam refilled it and let him drink. We made quiet conversation as Lucas drowned his sorrows. Eventually, I went to our vehicles and pulled out sleeping bags and sleeping pads from our SAR supplies and brought them into the house for Lucas and me to use that night. Cam nodded his approval, since Lucas was becoming increasingly inebriated and I could not be trusted to stay awake behind the wheel.

#

By morning, I was feeling more myself. Bodean had heavy bruising around his throat, but was otherwise returning to his normal vigor. Of all of us, Lucas was in the worst shape, sitting at the breakfast table in a terrible state of hangover, but uncomplaining. The three of us sat around the table, while Cam cooked breakfast in the kitchen. Parmelia was still sleeping, drained from her part in yesterday's fiasco, so we kept our voices low.

Not knowing what to do for Lucas, I got up to get him a bottle of coconut water. "Here, drink this. I don't know if it will do you any good…"

"Thanks." His voice was rusty, but I was happy that he was talking. He needed a shave and his eyes were an appalling shade of bloodshot. I marveled that he was still incredibly attractive with a raging hangover and bed-head and my eyes lingered a bit too long. Resisting the urge to smooth his hair, I folded my hands on my lap and turned my head to look away, but ended up staring into the eyes of Bodean. He simply raised an eyebrow, but said nothing. I was saved from further embarrassment by the arrival of breakfast and Lucas's rapid departure from the table.

As we devoured the French toast, Cam reminded us that we still had a job to complete. "We may be damaged, but so is the Entity. We need to strike again soon and finish this."

Bodean swirled a piece of the eggy bread in syrup and drawled out his question. "So, we damn near kill ourselves getting that artifact yesterday. How's it gonna help us to finish this?"

"The object was a corroded silver cross. It was roughly of the size and shape that a nineteenth century clergyman could have owned. While the rest of you were comatose last night, I looked up some information on the Reverend Jacob Castner."

I struggled for a moment to recall our discussion about the Changewater murders. It seemed so long ago... "Wait, he was the one who officiated at the funerals and drove up the bloodlust for revenge, right?"

"The very same." Cam downed the last of his coffee and dabbed his lips with a napkin.

Bodean put down his fork and folded his arms

across his chest. "Again, how does this help us?"

I brightened and leaned forward. "Can we just destroy the cross and this will rid us of the Entity?"

Cam rolled his eyes at me. "Don't you think I would have done that while we stood in the field if this were the case?"

I expertly rolled my eyes right back at him. "Then why did it all stop when you threatened to destroy the cross?"

"The spirit backed down not because its existence is linked with this object, but only because the cross is still sacred to it." Cam paused and lifted a shoulder. "And maybe because it does not want to draw divine attention to itself. It has a lot to answer for."

Bodean sighed dramatically. "Focus people! Back to the point. What did you learn and how can we use it to finish this business? I got a bunch of goats waiting for me at home and a herder who doesn't know his ass from a hoof."

I cocked my head at him. "So, you really did have problems finding a goatherd?"

Bodean glared at me. "What did I just say about focusing?" I ducked my head and turned back to Cam, who was drumming his fingers on the table.

"As I was saying, we may now have the identity of the Entity. This may help because the Entity's personal symbolism of appearing as a dark, unknowable mass strikes me as a deliberate attempt to hide his identity. Once he can no longer act in anonymity, we may be able to persuade him that the jig is up and he needs to move on." Cam caught my dubious look. "Don't look at me like that. This has worked before with spirits who were trying to hide their guilt for something they had done."

I shook my head, still not a believer. "Let me work through this. I need a rationale." Rubbing my lip while I assembled the facts in my mind, I tried to apply some logic to the illogical to understand why things were in their current state. "Reverend Castner was a troublemaker and caused the deaths of two innocent men because of his rabble-rousing. In death, he held hostage all parties who were unjustly affected by the murders. And he didn't want his identity to be known." I scrunched my face and concentrated for a long moment. "He's holding them hostage because they are witnesses to his misdeeds. There was never justice for the murder victims because of him. And the hanged men, well, that was kind of a homicide instigated by him. He does not want them to move on because he is afraid that he will finally be made accountable if they bear witness against him." I looked hopefully at Cam and Bodean.

Cam shrugged. "Could be. If you think hard enough, you might come up with something else that makes sense."

Lucas cleared his throat from the doorway. "Let's just call it your working hypothesis. It doesn't have to be true, but it's a starting point." His hair was wet from showering and he looked slightly less stricken. Maybe the coconut water helped him after all. I held up the plate of remaining French toast to him, but he shook his head and swallowed. Okay, so better, but not perfect.

Parmelia stumbled past him and took a seat next to Bodean. Cam poured her a cup of coffee as she reached for the plate that was lately offered to Lucas. "I heard what y'all have been saying. Kind of rude to wake someone up like that, but I agree with Cam. We gotta finish this. If Fia has the right of it, outing him might just give us enough influence to send him over. Tell him that Zackie knows who he is and he can't stop her from going between this world and the next."

We agreed that we should not wait to act and decided to take the remainder of the day to recharge. We'd return to the house in the afternoon and settle things. Cam admonished us all to keep thinking of a plan B, since there was no guarantee that this was going to work.

I got up from the table and drifted towards the door to the living room. "Because that worked so well the first time?" I had to admit, Cam really was getting quite skilled at rolling his eyes. Walking over to the bedding on the floor, I began rolling up the sleeping bag. Lucas grabbed the pad and also rolled it, tying it off with a bungee cord to keep it compressed. I glanced up at his face and he was looking at me intently.

"What?"

"Why did she tell me to go when she knew she was dying?"

"What makes you think I know?" I deliberately avoided his eyes as I said this.

"You know. She talked to you. She told me she

trusted you."

At this, I looked up at him and couldn't hide my surprise. "Why would she trust me? We barely knew each other."

"She said you were honest." He paused and asked again. "Why did she tell me to go?"

"She didn't want you to see her die." I blurted it out because I didn't know how to say it more delicately. "Hannah didn't want your last memory of her to be her death. She had that one last good day with you and she wants you to remember that."

He nodded and sat on the floor. A single tear trickled down his face, but his voice was steady. "I really loved her."

"I know." I touched his shoulder. "And she knew that. You did everything you could to help her to live, to keep her with you." Before I could react, he pulled me into his arms. I rested my head on his shoulder and closed my eyes tightly. He needed basic human comfort and this was going to kill me. When at last he let me go, I backed up as far as I could without him noticing how badly I needed distance from him. "I'm sorry for your loss," I whispered.

Standing up, I went to the office to tie up the other sleeping bag and pad.

# # #

Lucas decided to come with us for what we hoped would be the final confrontation. "It's a distraction." He made some adjustments on the handheld camera as we sat in Cam's truck waiting for the cousins to park. "I also owe it to my crew to keep them employed. We need the footage." I wondered how long it would take until he quit the show.

Cam stepped out of the cab as the cousins killed their engine. Opening the tailgate, he let Zackie out and she stretched and shook herself like it was another day at the beach. "Right. I want everyone at the pit. If this goes well, the house will be safe enough to enter later."

We did as he requested and headed to the pit. Lucas kept a few paces back to better get the participants in frame. As expected, John Castner lay at the bottom, quietly bleeding. Bodean peered over the edge at him. "That's one hell of a relative you got there, John."

Cam took the cross out from his pocket and asked each of us to call the Entity. Parmelia sucked in her breath. "It's coming fast. Get ready." I channeled what energy I had managed to scavenge during the day into my hands and waited.

The air shimmered around us and an inky black smoke began to coalesce. I felt a moment of smug satisfaction that it was not nearly as opaque as in previous encounters.

Cam held up the cross. In a normal, almost conversational voice, he made the accusation. "Reverend Jacob Castner, I hold your cross and I say that it is you who caused the death of the two innocent men who died by hanging. I hold you responsible for tormenting these spirits and keeping them here." The smoke writhed and fought as the shape solidified into the silhouette of a human. Bodean shifted his stance, binding the figure as it clawed at him to free itself. Cam continued. "It's no use, Jacob. We all know who you are. The psychopomp knows who you are. You need to release these spirits and release yourself from this earthbound state. The psychopomp will help you to cross over." Zackie approached the shadow man. "The scales must be balanced. Are you ready to face the consequences of your actions?" The spirit seemed to shrink in upon itself and it looked like its head nodded. "Bodean, release him to Zackie."

As the change of guard was being made, Parmelia gave a strangled cry. "Stop him, Bodean! Bind 'em!"

The spirit twisted and writhed into a smoky column that lunged toward an unsuspecting Lucas. The Entity was going after the member of our group with the least ability to sense it and defend himself. Zackie snarled at this treachery and sank her fangs into the black mass. A sound like metal being shredded pierced the air and my hands shot up to protect my ears. The stench of feces and putrefaction permeated the air and my gut clenched in revulsion. Stretching itself despite the agony of the bite, the Entity extended an oily tentacle toward Lucas. The world came into a tight focus, everything was too bright and all I saw was his face.

"Lucas!" I cried his name and raised my hands to defend him, knowing I was too slow. From behind Lucas, Hannah lunged forward to stand protectively between him and the reaching appendage. Momentum carried the smoky arm into Hannah's spirit body and her eyes glittered as she grasped the probing black limb with both hands to prevent it from retracting. The tentacle thrashed and struggled to be free, but she held fast as the sound of screeching metal intensified. Finally, Hannah released it, smiling grimly as she stepped back behind Lucas. The Entity shrieked in anguish as tumorous masses grew on its form, consuming its dead flesh and contorting its shape into a necrotic, spastic heap. Spitting out what was left of the diseased soul, Zackie backed away and allowed the scales to be balanced.

Parmelia was shaking, flapping her hands uselessly as she walked in a circle. "Holy crapping crap! Never in my life… I have never seen…" Bodean put his arm around her and she held on to him as she worked through a delayed reaction. I took in a deep breath of fresh air and let it out slowly as I recognized the significance of what I had seen. The Entity had been neutralized. Lucas was unharmed. Hannah had not allowed Zackie to help her cross over. I should have been reveling in our victory, but my heart thudded painfully in my chest and my face was wooden, unable to crack a smile or swear away the trauma. Since my motives were suspect, I could not tell if this creeping sadness was truly for her alone.

I caught Cam's eye. "What's happened to the Entity? Does it exist anymore?"

Cam gave me a glassy stare and his fingers fumbled as he tried to place the cross in his pocket. Dropping it, he stooped to pick up the artifact and stared stupidly at it for a moment. His gaze then shifted to Lucas and he began shaking his head repeatedly. Lucas was filming what was transpiring and was none the wiser about what almost happened to him. "This one has nine lives," Cam mumbled.

"Cam, the Entity?"

"Oh, right…" He rubbed his face and exhaled. "It still has consciousness, but it is severely debilitated and will no longer be a threat to anyone." Shrugging his shoulders, he continued. "Zackie might decide at some point in the distant future to offer it another chance to cross over. I don't know. It's damaged in a lot of ways besides what Hannah did to it, but maybe it can be rehabilitated on the other side."

After we took a few private minutes to process what had just happened, Cam cleared his throat and his voice sounded raw. "We're not done yet. We still have to free the other spirits." We all nodded and tried to get our heads back in the game. The events had drained us and it was a struggle to stand upright, let alone concentrate on next steps.

Bodean nodded and shut his eyes briefly. "What's our game plan?"

Cam glanced at Zackie and then replied. "Let's do them in the order they were murdered. I think that makes sense for sending them off."

We started with the man in the pit. Cam and Bodean helped John Castner to his feet and out of the pit. We formed an exhausted honor guard and escorted him to the house.

"Maria?" Cam called. "You must come to see John." Maria appeared, sobbing quietly and opened her arms to embrace her husband.

Rocking as he held his wife close, John kept repeating, "I'm sorry... I'm so sorry, Maria."

Wiping the tears from his face, she murmured, "Hush, John. It's not your fault." She glanced back at Zackie and then tenderly cupped his face in her hands. "Are you ready to see little Mary? I know I sure am."

Zackie brought them through the portal, their arms around each other and the scent of baking bread wafting back at us. I wiped a stray tear from my lashes and then motioned to the others. "Come on. There's one more in the house."

We found John Parke sitting in the bed where he was murdered, holding the pieces of his fractured skull in his hands. Bodean knelt in front of him. "Sir, y'all ready to leave this place?"

He stared at each of us and then asked, "They've gone ahead, haven't they?" We nodded and he let out a sigh of relief. "Oh, that's good. Thank the Lord they're finally safe."

When Zackie appeared out of the darkness, he stood up in polite deference and thanked her before following her through the portal. The scent of wood burning in a hearth drifted towards us and a glowing warmth spread as the portal closed behind them. The atmosphere in the house had turned airy and light and I thought even Joel would be able to sense the difference. Everything would be all right now. The new family would be able to move in and feel secure in this new home.

With the last of our energy, we trudged through the field and made our way to Peter Parke and Joseph Carter. The hanged men stood by their graves, waiting expectantly, one arm companionably on the shoulder of the other man.

One of the men stepped forward. "It's over? It's really over?"

Cam nodded. "You're freed from this place."

With a great whoop, the men slapped each other on the back and embraced. When Zackie appeared for them, they each raised a hand in farewell to us, as if they were leaving on a grand journey. Their joy was contagious and I smiled as they went through the portal, accompanied by the sound of a fiddler playing a lively reel.

CHAPTER 19

Bodean and Parmelia stayed for the funeral. I wore my best black gloves and cobbled together a decent enough outfit from the dark clothing I wore at the restaurant. Looking in the mirror, I thought I was dressed well enough to show respect.

The affair was simple and tasteful. Lucas said only a few words, but they were from the heart and many people needed to find their handkerchiefs after he spoke. I only saw her once briefly during the ceremony. Hannah appeared from behind Lucas and put her face to the flowers that were arranged near the casket. I couldn't tell if she was happy or just relieved to have the dying over with. After the interment, the team broke up. We hugged awkwardly and then said our goodbyes. Parmelia and Bodean returned to their goats and Lucas said he would spend time with family before returning to work.

I turned towards Cam as he drove us to his house. "So, what now?"

"He'll be back."

I swallowed and nodded, started to say something, but then changed directions. "What do I do now?"

Cam raised an eyebrow at me. "Do now? You have a new job to start and do I have to remind you that you have only just begun to learn the tools of the trade if you want to assist the psychopomp? That was only the first semester. There's still a lot of work ahead, you know."

I smiled just as Zackie emphasized his words with a muzzle punch to the back of my head. It's always comforting to know your place in the universe.

ACKNOWLEDGMENTS

This book would not have come to be without the kind help of many people. The author would like to thank: Katherine Furman for reading an early version of the manuscript and providing useful feedback; Bill Cafferty for scrubbing the first three chapters and Sandy Williams for catching the last(?) typo; Sara Ehrlich, Dr. Rich Kliman, Elke Favis, Kathy Ann Stagg, Lee Kliman, and Germana Callow for serving as beta readers; Sara Ehrlich for providing useful information on what it takes to be a therapy dog (any errors related to this are my own); the Writers Group of Belvidere and First Friday Writers Group for providing critical feedback during decisive moments in the book's development; the Phillipsburg Free Public Library for serving all of my local history reference needs; Dr. Nadine Cohen, Laura Furman and Arturo Chaparro for moral support; and the Search and Rescue Teams of Warren County for helping me to train for my SAR Tech II certification while I wrote this book. Lastly, I would like to thank my husband, Rich Kliman, for steadfast support and never once blinking when I told him that I wanted to leave a steady job to write the Zackie stories.

Reyna Favis

AUTHOR'S NOTES

Plott Hound History

The story of the Plott Hound's origins is true and has been adapted from Bob Plott's history of the breed (reference below). Only a little dramatic license was taken when describing how the Plott brothers acquired the breeding stock before emigrating to the Colonies.

Bob Plott. (2007). *The Story of the Plott Hound: Strike & Stay* (Second edi). The History Press.

Psychosis

Information regarding Folie a deux and childhood psychosis were derived from the following references.

Joshi, P. T., & Towbin, K. E. (2002). Psychosis in Childhood and Its Management. In K. L. Davis, D. Charney, J. T. Coyle, & C. Nemeroff (Eds.), *Neuropsychopharmacology:The Fifth Generation of Progress* (pp. 613–624).

Newman, W. J., & Harbit, M. a. (2010). Folie a deux and the courts. *The Journal of the American Academy of Psychiatry and the Law, 38*(3), 369–375.

Sclerosis, M. (2010). Helping Children and Youth with Psychosis Information for Parents and Caregivers. Children's Hospital of Eastern Ontario. Retrieved from http://www.cheo.on.ca

408

Moravian and Delaware Indian History

The grave of John Lewis Luckenbach can be found in the Moravian Burial Ground in Hope, New Jersey. Information on the burial ground and the Moravian community in Hope can be found in the references cited below. I suggest visiting the graveyard to get the full effect of history and to reacquaint horror fans with the scenery depicted in *Friday the 13th*. Jason and his victims really did run amuck in both the Moravian Burial Ground and the Blairstown Diner.

Some license was taken with the historical dates associated with the Moravian missionary efforts with the Lenape in order to maintain the accuracy of the information found on the headstones in the cemetery and for the sake of the story. While the Moravian community in Hope did suffer a smallpox epidemic in 1799 (one of several factors that led to the failure of the community and the return of the Moravians to Bethlehem, PA), this outbreak did not coincide with missionary efforts by the Moravians. In fact, the Lenape had been forced by treaty to give up their ancestral lands in 1758, which led to a diaspora and a resettlement of the Delaware People in Oklahoma and Canada.

Rosenfeld, Lucy D. and Harrison, M. (2006). History Walks in New Jersey (pp. 76–79). New Brunswick, New Jersey and London: Rivergate Books.

Sarapin, J. K. (1994). Old Burial Grounds of New Jersey: A Guide (pp. 92–94). New Brunswick, New Jersey: Rutgers University Press.

Changewater Murders

The Changewater murders described in *Soul Search* were extensively documented at the time of the killings and although two men were executed for the crimes, their guilt was not widely accepted by the community. In deference to the victims, the descriptions of the people and the circumstances surrounding their demise were kept true to the historical record described in the references below. In deference to the descendents of possible suspects, I did not endeavor to play detective. Too much time has passed and too much evidence has been lost to make any definitive assessments regarding culpability. Since the historic Reverend Jacob Castner did much in the way of railroading two innocent men to be executed for the crimes, it did not disturb my conscience to make him the villain in the story.

Meeker, S. and R. (1998a). *The Changewater Murders: A True Historical Account.* Budd Lake: Legacy, of America.

Meeker, S. and R. (1998b). The Changewater Murders: Case Closed. Budd Lake: Legacy, of America.

Baseball Trivia

Eddie Gaedel's famous at-bat is a piece of baseball lore that is so well-known that even a non-participant like me has heard the story. The details of the story were derived from the reference below.

Cellania, M. (2011). The Strangest At-Bat in History. Retrieved from http://www.neatorama.com/2011/08/19/the-strangest-at-bat-in-history/

Hikers on the Appalachian Trail

Additional characters that can be found hiking on the AT are best described in the citation that follows.

Wallace, M. (2015). The 10 Hikers You Meet on the Appalachian Trail. Retrieved from http://appalachiantrials.com/the-10-hikers-you-meet-on-the-appalachian-trail/

Search and Rescue

While many of the locations described are real, no actual case histories of searches are used in *Soul Search*. The descriptions of the searches are drawn from my imagination and conglomerations of personal experiences, as well as stories related to me by SAR friends. As part of the search community, I am committed to protecting the privacy of the missing and their families.

Zackie (true name Zackie-O), Merlin and Simber are real search dogs and are included in the story with the permission of the handlers. All of these canines serve the Search and Rescue Teams of Warren County. Their appearances and personalities were depicted as accurately as I could manage. Their handlers in the story are completely fictitious.

SOUL SCENT

The second Zackie novel from

Reyna Favis

Please turn the page for a

special advance preview

CHAPTER 1

A lot can happen in a day. You could be born in a day and you could fall in love in a day. If Maggie Pierceson had waited just one more day, maybe she would not have taken her own life. Her remains lay face down on a thick layer of decaying leaves. Next to the body was a Sharpie, dropped after she had finished scrawling a final message to loved ones on her arm. Her hands were bagged to facilitate testing for gunpowder residue and the fingers curled inward as if grasping for something.

I flexed my own fingers in the stiff, leather gloves, unconsciously imitating the rigor mortis contracting Maggie's digits. I felt cold and this small action did little to alleviate the discomfort in my fingers. I had been warm enough while I tramped around the deep woods all night, but being forced to stand and wait had allowed the drying sweat to chill me. At irregular intervals, my leg muscles contracted uncomfortably in little spasms and I had a crick in my neck from carrying the backpack. The worst thing about the aftermath of an all-night search was having to struggle to put two simple thoughts together. I stood among a crowd of other searchers who were gathered outside of the crime scene tape. We were a sea of high visibility orange, ready to surge forward once law enforcement had finished processing the scene. It would fall to search and rescue to bring the body out of the woods and the mood among the searchers was somber. Because the subject was found, the search was considered a success, but it was still heartbreaking to everyone who had worked all night to find Maggie to see that we were too late.

The police had found the expended round embedded in the trunk of a tree near the body, but the gun itself was still missing. The force of the recoil would have sent it flying from her hand after the shot was fired and the officers were working to narrow the search field by mapping the trajectory. After being called out to so many searches for the missing, there were many familiar faces among the officers who scoured through the fallen leaves for the missing gun.

I sidled closer to Cam and waited with my question as he was gripped by a jaw-cracking yawn. Cam was my mentor and partner in crime. He taught me everything I know about surviving the unseen world. The rising sun highlighted the dark shadows beneath his eyes and he hunched his tall frame against the early morning chill. Warm in her glossy, red coat, Zackie lay at his feet, mimicking the appearance of a well-trained search dog. In reality, she was neither well-trained, nor a true dog, but to the uninitiated, she appeared to be a Plott Hound, sleekly muscled and ready for the hunt.

"Did you or Zackie see her yet?" I kept my voice

low, so only Cam and Zackie could hear. Still, I made sure my words were vague. With so many people around, there was no way that I could openly ask Cam if Maggie's spirit had made an appearance.

At the sound of her name, Zackie's ears twitched and she briefly pointed her muzzle at me, but then her gaze drifted away. She displayed her level of concern for the proceedings by yawning in sympathy with Cam, her mouth gaping and her long canines exposed. Zackie's only real interest was the dead. It was her duty as a psychopomp to escort the dead to the next life and she made no secret of the fact that the living bored her. After witnessing how our kind played out the same little dramas century after century, humans had long ceased to be amusing to her. Because Cam and I were devoted to helping her cause, Zackie would sometimes make exceptions for us, but mostly, she made it pretty clear that we were on our own and we were not to involve her in our shenanigans. Cam

shook his head. "No, neither of us has seen anything, Fia."
His crisp British accent was slurred with fatigue. Cam
rubbed his face in an effort to wake up and then ran a hand
absently through his mop of gray curls. Staring at the
body, he frowned. "You know, it's unusual for a woman to
choose suicide by gun. Most of the time, women overdose.
I wonder what brought her to this."

My brow furrowed and stray locks of sweaty,
auburn hair crept into my eyes, irritating me as I tried to
think. I shoved the bangs under my baseball cap and then
also turned my gaze to the body, trying to understand. "Do
you think she was making some sort of statement by her
choice of death?"

"Don't know. Using a handgun is a particularly
violent way to go. Maybe she felt that she had to suffer."

"Dying isn't penance enough?" I shook my head,
unable to process what may have motivated Maggie to end

things like this. Pain, depression and being ostracized by society are things I understood, but wanting to take your own life because of these factors had never once occurred to me. Perhaps this was because at the lowest points in my life, I thought I had firsthand knowledge of what waited on the other side and the idea of becoming one of the earthbound dead was thoroughly revolting to me. Aside from appearing as bottomless pits of pathetic need, these revenants also revealed the most horrifying aspect of life after death - being damned to constantly relive the brutality of the perimortem state. I wanted no part of either of these conditions and so I had endured the humiliation of being thought mad by the rest of the world because I could see the suffering dead. I had tried living separately from society, but came close to falling apart during my solitary struggle. If it had not been for Cam and Zackie, I would never have learned that the dead can move on from the earthbound state. The true afterlife was still a mystery to me, but in my mind, anything beat clinging to a half life on earth.

A low murmur erupted among the searchers and I came back from my navel gazing to learn that the police officers had found the gun. After another few minutes of taking photographs of the gun *in situ* and carefully packaging the weapon in an evidence container, law enforcement signaled the searchers that the body could at last be removed.

Among the searchers entering the crime scene area, I noticed Peyton. I touched her arm in silent commiseration as she walked past me. She and K9 Simber had found the body a few hours before dawn. The light glinted off her glasses as Peyton nodded her head in acknowledgment and I saw a few small twigs caught in her flaming red hair. Simber must have taken her through the scenic route to find Maggie. Dropping her eyes and sighing slightly, Peyton ran her fingers lightly over Simber's ears and the silver gray fur of her flanks. Peyton was strongly built and her hands were larger than most men I knew, but each fingernail was painted a delicate pink and flaunted a perfect French manicure. Sensing her distress, Simber leaned into Peyton, and then began making the signature gargling, mewling sound for which Huskies were famous. Simber was a Husky-German Shepherd mix, but her vocalizations tended to favor the Husky in her and under other circumstances, these spellbinding ululations made for high entertainment. The final task facing the searchers precluded any feelings of amusement, so there were no smiles at Simber's antics.

In the end, the carryout was accomplished with a minimum of fuss. After Maggie was packaged into the stokes basket, the searchers alternated between carrying the litter and clearing the way of brush. A carryout was exhausting work and by the time we reached the trail, my arms were aching and trembling with the effort. After covering a mile through wilderness, the waiting crossover utility vehicle was a glorious sight. We secured the stokes

basket to the back of the vehicle and left it to the driver to

take the litter the rest of the way to the parking area where

an ambulance would transport Maggie's remains to the

morgue.

Cam groaned as he held a bent arm over his head

and tugged on the elbow to stretch out his triceps. "I'm

done for. Time to go home and get some sleep."

I nodded and waved to him as I turned to walk

away. "Love to, but I have to go and break down the trailer

first." Because the missing person was in my team's

backyard, we were responsible for running the show for

this search. Cam's team had been called in for additional

support, but all they had to do was show up and search. My

team ran incident command and there were laptops and

printers to take down, a generator to be shut down and a

radio antenna to be dismantled, among other things.

Everything needed to be squared away and made ready for

9

the next search before the trailer could be towed to Peyton's property to await the next callout.

The rest of the team was hard at work by the time I arrived at the trailer. Between all of us, we had the trailer re-packed and ready for the next callout in under twenty minutes. As the last thing, I put the wheel chucks inside the door for ready access and then shut it as Peyton reached for her key. Satisfied that everything was locked and loaded, we began walking to our vehicles, bidding each other a belated goodnight. I had taken no more than three steps when a loud bang and crash could be heard coming from inside the trailer.

Stopping in her tracks, Peyton reversed direction and grabbed her key again. "What the... Did the wall anchors fail?" She yanked the door open to verify and I looked over her shoulder to see if there was any damage. Everything was in place, just as we left it. I scratched my head. "Huh. I almost thought we accidentally locked someone inside."

"Okay, whatever. It all looks all right. I'm locking this up again and driving home." Peyton locked the door one more time and then stepped quickly away before anything more could happen to delay her departure.

Back at home, I stripped off my search gear, starting with the gloves that protected my hands from the briars and other nasty, sharp things in the woods. I looked at my bad hand, flexing the fingers slightly and getting creeped out yet again by the discolored, putrescent skin and blackened nails. The hand belonged to a corpse and had no business being attached to me, but this was my souvenir from reaching into Zackie's domain. It was no place for the living and I had found that out the hard way. Sighing, I admitted to myself that there were times I was an idiot and in need of a refresher course in self-preservation.

I piled the rest of my clothes into a heap of dirty laundry in the middle of the floor and then located the heavy neoprene diver's glove, pulling it over my bad hand before hitting the shower. I hated the idea of that hand touching me, so I went through this ritual of protection every time I showered. Even though it was late in the season, I did a careful inspection for ticks and came up empty. Good for me. Breakfast was a sad affair, since I desperately needed to go shopping. I assembled a small plate of cheese and crackers and vowed to go to the grocery store after I got some sleep. Before consuming anything, I put a light cotton glove on my bad hand, so I didn't have to look at it while I ate. I couldn't bring myself to chow down if that thing touched my food. While I could control the hand and go about doing my normal activities using it, the hand was definitely non-self. There were occasions when it acted independently of me.

As I munched on the poor excuse for breakfast, I

checked my phone for messages. My heart beat a little faster when I discovered a missed call from Lucas. His voicemail implied that he had a job for Cam and me. Lucas's producers must have decided he had spent enough time grieving the death of his wife and that he needed to get back to work. After Hannah died, Lucas's ghost hunting show had gone on hiatus, broadcasting re-runs to hold on to viewers. The audience must have grown hungry for something new and the producers realized that to satisfy their voracious appetite for novelty, they might not care if the new thing was a fresh episode of Lucas's show or another, similar program on a different network. I wondered if the producers would be coldblooded enough to suggest that Lucas try to raise the ghost of his own wife for ratings.

I put the phone down and chewed contemplatively on a stale cracker. The order of the day would be sleep, shop and then call Lucas back. Because I knew that hearing his voice would bring on a hormonal tsunami, I did not trust myself to have any kind of conversation with him while I was sleep-deprived. Lucas continued to be off limits to me and I didn't want to make either of us uncomfortable by accidentally saying something unwise. He was newly bereaved and I would not take advantage of his emotionally vulnerable state. In addition to my commitment act honorably where Lucas was concerned, an additional incentive was that his wife's spirit lingered near him and she would very likely kick my ass if I made any kind of move.

#

Jarred awake by the sound of Glenn Miller's *In the Mood*, I bolted upright and grabbed my phone to make it stop. Ordinarily, I found the tune upbeat and happy, but Peyton was calling and I didn't feel like I had nearly enough sleep to deal with what she wanted. I paused for a beat thinking that I might let her leave a voicemail and go back to sleep. When I considered the consequences of making her wait, answering the call seemed to be the better part of valor. Peyton was not known for her patience and she might call repeatedly until I picked up. If I shut off my phone, I was sure she'd make the trip to my place and pound on the door until she got what she wanted. Peyton Bell was one of these high drive humans. She was ex-military, competed in the local Highland Games, throwing everything from telephone poles to small boulders, and was training to be a master stonemason.

I began the conversation with a whine and a whimper. "What, Peyton? It's too soon to be calling me."

"Fia? Can you get in touch with Cam for me? I need him to bring Zackie here."

"What? Why?"

"I think there's a raccoon trapped in the trailer. I need her to flush it out."

"Can't Simber take care of it?"

Peyton exhaled a long, dramatic sigh. "I've tried that. She's showing no interest and meantime, the crashing and banging won't stop. I need a coonhound. Zackie's a coonhound, right?"

"No, not really. She's a Plott Hound. They're bred to hunt big game – bear and boar, mostly."

"But some people use them to hunt raccoons, right?"

Rolling my eyes, I said the next bit imitating an Applachian twang, so I would say it the way I had first heard it. "It's a damned waste of the breed, Peyton."

"Did I start this conversation with the words, 'If it pleases your majesty?'" She paused to let this sink in and then reiterated her demands. "I have a problem that might end up damaging equipment. Cam has a solution. Get him over here." As an afterthought, she added "please" and then "thank you" before hanging up.

I stared at my phone and blinked my eyes a few times before sending a text to Cam, asking him to call Peyton about a raccoon in the team trailer and providing her contact information. I filed this away in the big pile of things that were not my problem and tried to go back to sleep. It had been maybe twenty minutes and I was close to falling asleep when my phone went off again. This time it was the theme from *The Good, the Bad and the Ugly*. Why hadn't I turned the phone off after sending the text? Did I have such a huge fear of missing out that I would sacrifice sleep for the dubious honor of being included in other people's nonsense?

Fumbling with the phone, I poked the screen to accept the call. "Ugh... what, Cam?" I flopped back in the bed and wrapped one arm over my eyes to block the light, while I held the phone to my ear with the other hand.

"Did it ever occur to you that the banging about might be Maggie?" As usual, there was no greeting from Cam. He just started right in with whatever was on his mind.

Author contact information

If you enjoyed reading *Soul Search*, please, please

write a short review. Your review is incredibly important –

it is the currency that establishes a book's worth to other

readers and also enables indie authors like me to qualify for

desperately needed promotional opportunities. Please make

the next book possible by leaving a review now.

Many thanks for reading and reviewing.

www.reynafavis.com

83416965R00245

Made in the USA
Middletown, DE
11 August 2018